FINDING BABY RUTH

FINDING BABY RUTH

BY SARA HOFFMAN

Sara Hoffman

For my husband, Randy Myers,
and my daughters, Kelsey and Morgan Myers

In memory of my father, Harry H. Hoffman,
and my son, Erik Hoffman Myers

CHAPTER 1

Madam Isabella Luna

A bona fide fortune-teller would have known better than to arrive in Garden City, Kansas, on a summer day so hot the Santa Fe Trail cracked. Madam Isabella Luna came anyway. She claimed the bumps only made the rest of the road seem smoother. As usual, she was a little bit right.

The day Madam Isabella Luna and her entourage arrived, I was taking smoking lessons from my friend and employer, Cora Mae Daisy. We'd been up since dawn, trying out different marble cake recipes in the kitchen of her boardinghouse. When the heat grew intolerable, we'd escaped to the screened-in porch to beat our gums and slouch away the afternoon in ancient leather armchairs.

Cora Mae was teaching me to smoke as a replacement for a candy habit that made my apron strings too short. So far, her lessons had only given me another way to kill time while we sat on the porch and beefed about how nothing ever happened in Garden City. Cora Mae had come from the Kansas City area, where putting on the ritz was apparently an everyday occasion. I'd lived most of my life in Garden City and wouldn't know a ritz if I saw one. But with Cora Mae's help, my vision was improving.

After all, it was 1921, and even in Kansas, a new world was emerging. The Great War had ended three years before, and the toll of deaths and injuries was high. A sense of cynicism permeated our flag ceremonies and honor parades. Our parents and grandparents were first-rate patriots, but they weren't the ones sent overseas to fight in a war so remote it seemed impossible that it could truly make a difference in our lives. We rebelled.

Of course, most of the action those days had taken place in the big cities — New York, Chicago, Boston — but even rubes like us in Kansas got the message loud and clear through newspapers, magazines, books and motion pictures: Our generation was going to make the most of our remaining young adult years. We wanted a little whoopee.

We'd abandoned our horse-drawn wagons for automobiles — here in Kansas, mostly Model Ts — and that alone opened up another world. Automobiles took us places and gave us private opportunities to explore beyond the gaze of our righteous elders. Dirt roads like the Santa Fe Trail were spruced up to improve driving conditions. Auto-motels, diners and service stations sprung up to serve weary travelers.

Lots of people — even women, behind closed doors — smoked cigarettes and drank bootleg liquor, even though

Kansas lawmakers had tried their hardest to abolish them both. We also danced — the cakewalk, the Charleston, the black bottom and the flea hop — to jazz and blues music brought North by colored folks fleeing the South, where they'd been kept as slaves only a generation earlier.

A year before, we women had finally been given the right to vote nationwide. We'd had to prove ourselves by holding down jobs and managing the farms while the men fought the war, but once we got accustomed to having a little cash of our own and a say in our government, we weren't about to go back to the old ways. Electric vacuum cleaners and washing machines, if you could afford them, made housework less monotonous. You could order ready-to-wear clothes through the catalog rather than sew your own. The big city flappers cut their hair, hiked up their skirts and lowered their necklines, and those of us in the countryside did our best to imitate them.

Anybody who was anybody didn't want to be left behind. Truth be told, I wasn't much of an anybody. I was more of a nobody, even in Garden City. I had just turned 26 years old, and I was unmarried, which put me on the edge of old maidenhood. I lived with my sickly older brother, who was a bachelor, and I earned a little money playing the piano around town and helping at Cora Mae's boardinghouse. She's the one who took me by the hand and refused to let go as, even in Kansas, a new world emerged.

That morning at the boardinghouse, I was reading a Saturday Evening Post magazine that carried F. Scott Fitzgerald's story "Bernice Bobs Her Hair." I'd read a few of the author's other stories and liked them. This one, however, hit a little too close to home. Bernice, the main character, is an awkward girl whose cousin tries to teach her how to behave around boys. Near the end, the cruel and uppity cousin tricks Bernice into having her hair bobbed, a moral and fashion error.

I was halfway through the story when Cora Mae looked at me over the top of the daily Garden City Tribune, a cigarette burning in her hand. "Sounds like the Santa Fe Trail has gone blooey. Looks to be another killjoy of a day in Garden City."

I nodded, put down the magazine and looked at her with burning eyes as smoke eked from my lips into hazy, gray shapes.

"Jules, how many times have I told you to blow the smoke away from your eyes?" Cora Mae said. "Nifty. Now listen, I know you don't appreciate my dream illuminations, but this one last night had clear implications."

I settled in for a good listen. Vampires usually stalked Cora Mae's nights, and in last night's dream, she explained, they were joined by a stork with sea-green feathers. Her head swirled as she described the bird circling ever closer to the boardinghouse.

"The stork swoops so close I could have hit it with a broom, although I'd never do that to any animal, in dreamland or elsewhere," said Cora Mae, a confirmed animal lover. "It's carrying a bundle wrapped in a blanket, and just as the vampires start to gather, the bird's beak opens, and a marble cake tumbles out from the blanket. I get a close look at the vanilla swirling through the chocolate just as the cake hits the ground — smack — and wakes me up."

"Heavens," I said. Not because of the dream but because

just across the dirt that was Cora Mae's front yard, a Studebaker had stopped. It was layered with the dust of a Kansas summer, pulling a two-wheeled, wood-sided trailer with "Madam Isabella Luna's Spiritual Consultations" painted on the side in flowing, black script.

"What in the world?" I pried a peppermint from the roll I kept in my skirt pocket as a holdover from my candy habit and, when Cora Mae looked away, popped it in my mouth.

The automobile shivered into a death rattle just as a pack of Cora Mae's dogs cornered the house and surrounded the car, snarling and scratching to get inside. Cora Mae grasped her cigarette in one hand and struggled to stand as her crimson silk robe shimmied against the leather armchair.

"Big Blackie! Wide Whitey! Stop that racket!" she shouted. As always, the dogs ignored her because they were spoiled animals with only a few names among them. Cora Mae was unique among Kansans in that she named her animals. Her distinctiveness was diminished, however, by her lack of creativity. Each animal was simply named for its color, with an occasional reference to size tossed in for false clarity. So far, her brood included three cats — Little Whitey, Tiny Brownie and Goldie — and three dogs — Wide Whitey, Big Brownie and Big Blackie.

Two women cowered inside the car, peering through filthy windows. Cora Mae put the dogs in the house, and the driver slowly emerged.

She was an apparition in white, tall and looming, with creamy leather gloves climbing to her elbows. She seemed to glide rather than walk toward us, and when I saw her complexion, I reached for another peppermint. Her skin was translucent, undisturbed by freckles or moles, which made her black eyes all the more haunting. She looked like one of Cora Mae's vampires.

"Hallo," she said. She sounded like the Italians who lived across the street from me. "I am Sister Margery, assistant to Madam Isabella Luna. Are you owning the boardinghouse?"

Cora Mae turned pale, probably because her dream was coming to life in the dirt of her own front yard. She brushed her fingers across her throat and nodded. "I'm Cora Mae Daisy, and this is my friend Jules Greer."

Sister Margery's dark eyes flickered to the porch, where a sign advertised rooms for rent. I looked at the sign too, as if her strange vision could change the message. She smiled, and my jitters dropped a notch because where fangs belonged, a mess of teeth twisted.

"We are needing to rent two rooms," she said. "We bring letter of endorsement from the great Sir Arthur Conan Doyle. You are familiar with the writer smoking the pipe?"

Cora Mae must have regained her composure, because she clapped her hands, sending ashes from her cigarette flying and reminding me that my own smoldered on the porch, hanging over the edge of a saucer.

"Jesus H. Christ!" she shouted. "Finally something interesting is happening in Garden City."

I wasn't as enthusiastic. As much as I craved excitement, I wasn't interested in the type that turned every eyeball in our direction. As I mentioned, I've lived here for most of my life. I wasn't exactly an insider in Garden City, but I'd known most of the townsfolk for years. I certainly wasn't as willing as Cora Mae to simply throw my reputation to the wind and let it drift in any direction.

Sister Margery looked toward the Studebaker, where the passenger door opened and a woman climbed out. She was so small the car took on the magnitude of an autobus, and she used both hands to shut the door.

Cora Mae grasped my hand with trembling fingers and whispered what I knew she would. "Do you see what that woman has around her neck?"

It was a boa with sea-green feathers that fluttered in the breeze.

We retreated to the porch, where the miniature Madam Isabella Luna sat in my chair, drank my lemonade and puffed on my cigarette like the professional charlatan she probably was. A sequined handbag hung over one wrist, and she pulled from it a crumpled packet of store-bought cigarettes. It was against the law to sell pre-packaged cigarettes in Kansas, so her Lucky Strikes were most likely illegal swag from Oklahoma or Missouri.

I kept an eye on her while Sister Margery explained that Madam Isabella Luna was fragile, very vulnerable to sunlight. Indeed, her body was inundated by the boa as well as a cloche hat, pulled down like a helmet, and a sapphire cape — all of which made me suspect she was really just a snake charmer.

Cora Mae and Sister Margery discussed the conditions of their stay, although Cora Mae was so obviously thrilled to have them she probably could have been talked into letting them stay for free. She was like that — always bartering with people to repair the front door or put new shingles on the roof in exchange for rent. It didn't always add up dollars-and-cents-wise.

"We are assuming meals are included," Sister Margery said.

"Breakfast, lunch and dinner, and, if you like, a midnight snack. I'm quite the cook." Cora Mae reached for Tiny Brownie, who had wandered onto the porch. "Tell me, though, will you do séances?"

"Spiritual readings and fortune-telling, so we will be keeping out the sunlight by draping the windows," Sister Margery said. "Madam Isabella and I are both having the spiritual gift. We bring guides from the other world."

I looked at Cora Mae as I spoke. "You know, folks around here will be saying that spiritual readings belong in a church."

Madam Isabella Luna fluttered one hand at me. The other clutched an empty cigarette holder nearly as long as her forearm.

"Ish kabibble." She spoke for the first time since they'd arrived, and her voice was unnaturally high-pitched, unless she really was a midget. "A little whoopee would do this place good. Besides, in towns this small, we don't have to advertise our services. Everybody knows everybody's everything."

GARDEN CITY TRIBUNE - WEDNESDAY, JUNE 8, 1921

GLADYS WISENHEIMER'S
Garden of Tidbits

Yack-Yack Club owner Mick McKenzie was visited recently by his brother, Mr. Randolph McKenzie. The visiting Mr. McKenzie spoke to fellows at the Garden City American Legion Club about fighting the Nonpartisan League. During the war, Randolph's neck was broken, and he has to wear a brace to hold his head up.

CHAPTER 2

Everybody's Everything

Cora Mae was flittering about, searching for extra bed linens and towels for the fortune-tellers' rooms. I couldn't understand why they needed more than what was already there, but I thought twice about saying anything to Cora Mae.

The look on her face was one of sheer jubilation. The last time we had this much excitement was at Christmas, when the Grundy's daughter, Fanny, came home from college with her hair bobbed and a boa not unlike the one Madam Isabella Luna wrapped around her neck. Word had it at Grundy's Market that Mrs. Grundy might have liked to tighten the boa a few extra turns when Fanny came home looking like a flapper. It didn't help that our local daily, the Tribune, published a write-up about it in "Gladys Wisenheimer's Garden of Tidbits."

If you lived in Garden City, it was an annual rite of passage to have at least one tidbit written about you in Gladys' Garden. She'd print just about anything people told her — who won at bridge, who got his finger chopped off at the sawmill, who lost his big toenail because his boots were too tight. The stories were usually just accurate enough to create a slight sense of titillation but not so inaccurate that people would show up at the Tribune office with their shotguns, seeking a correction. Her columns were one of the best-read sections of the newspaper, right up there with the weather and obituaries.

I followed Cora Mae into the kitchen, where she was rifling through drawers.

"Do you think Gladys will write up Madam Isabella's visit for her column?" I asked.

Cora Mae looked back at me, and a bobby pin popped from her hair onto the linoleum floor. Cora Mae perpetually wears pin curls in her hair and one of her many jewel-toned silk bathrobes cinched tight around her midsection. Since she'd moved to Garden City three years before, she'd let her hair go natural only a few times. It was straight as an arrow.

She bent over, retrieved the hairpin and nestled it back in her hair. "I certainly hope it gets more ink than that. It's worth a whole story with photographs. Now, where did I put that oversized sheet?"

Like Gladys, Cora Mae relished beating her gums about other people. Unlike Gladys, Cora Mae enjoyed getting people to do the same about her. She adored getting the tongues flickering about whatever eccentricity she'd been up to, or was suspected of being up to, and once the embers got burning, she'd blow as hard as she could to fuel the flames. It made my life difficult to say the least, because in Garden City we believed in guilt by association, and I'd already been the subject of enough gossip to last a lifetime.

Ever since I'd passed age 21 — when most girls married — I'd been walking straight down the path of old maidenhood. I wouldn't have minded a march down the center aisle. I'd have been satisfied with a handsome fellow who'd tell me that my brown hair undulated rather than just waved, that my green eyes were really emerald, and that my nose was anything but button-like. Beautiful women didn't have button noses.

Regardless, in a town as small as Garden City, a woman's odds of meeting even an ugly man relied largely on the chin flappers, who were cranking up even then as I glanced out the kitchen window toward the Grundy's house. Mr. Grundy owned Grundy's Market downtown, where everybody's everything was an everyday topic.

Mrs. Grundy saw herself as the flag bearer of all that was moral in Garden City, and, as she frequently reminded us, it was a heavy burden to carry. Cora Mae called her a fire extinguisher who needed to mind her own potatoes.

Truth be told, the woman probably hadn't moved from her front window since Madam Isabella Luna arrived, and sure enough, there was a flutter of the curtain now.

"I'd be willing to bet that Gladys will get some tidbit from Mrs. Grundy," I said. "She's been watching the house ever since those two pulled up in their Studebaker."

Cora Mae folded a towel over her arm. "Maybe you should

run over there. First you can ask to borrow an oversized sheet, then make sure she knows how to spell Studebaker. We'd hate to have to make the Tribune publish a correction."

Cora Mae was quite the truth-seeker when it came to the Tribune. Three years before, when she'd bought the old Pinkerton mansion for her boardinghouse, they'd published a full-page story with photographs. It was an imposing home, three times the size of most Garden City houses, with gables, dormer windows and a wrap-around porch, a section of which had screens. A winding stairway started near the front door and led to four bedrooms that Cora Mae outfitted with wall-to-wall rugs and overstuffed furniture. The kitchen was also a sight to behold, with a navy blue and white checked linoleum floor and cabinetry painted white. There was a modern icebox, a sink with knobs for hot and cold water, and a gas-powered oven and range.

But what the Tribune writer was really interested in was the indoor toilet, one of the few in Garden City. Cora Mae had converted what had been a servant's quarters into a water closet with a sink, flushing toilet and porcelain bathtub with claw feet undoubtedly designed to resemble those of a lion but that Cora Mae insisted were a dog's.

That was the first correction she demanded of the Tribune. The second was when they called it a water closet. It was a "crapper," Cora Mae insisted, named after the British plumber Thomas Crapper, who invented the flush toilet. The Tribune refused the correction, deeming "crapper" a smut word, and after a month-long battle that eventually involved even the publisher, the Tribune won.

FINDING BABY RUTH

Now I followed Cora Mae into the crapper. "Did I put that extra-large sheet in the crapper closet?" she said, more to the air than to me. "I know it's around here somewhere."

"Why do they need more sheets?" I asked. "I put clean linens on the beds a few days ago."

Cora Mae reached above the toilet to straighten a framed sign she'd hung there. Folks often dropped by the boardinghouse for unsolicited social visits and then got sudden, urgent calls from nature. After a few unpleasant experiences — somebody once tried flushing away old underwear — Cora Mae posted instructions over the toilet with a reminder to flush, but only bodily wastes.

"Have you already forgotten?" Cora Mae said. "Madam Isabella is vulnerable to sunlight. We have to cover the windows."

I rolled my eyes, but she ignored me, adding, "You may need to run to Grundy's after Madam Isabella picks her dinner menu."

"I think Grundy's may come to us," I said. "I've already seen a few cars braking as they passed."

"Really?" Cora Mae smiled as she pulled a bleached-white sheet from the back of the crapper closet then disappeared into the house. I went back to the porch to watch the inevitable parade.

People typically slowed down when they passed Cora Mae's boardinghouse, and not just because it was near the high school, where the speed limit was posted at 12 miles per hour not to exceed 15 miles per hour. People knew there was usually something going on at Cora Mae's that was worth repeating.

I suppose even in big cities like Topeka, people flapped their gums about their neighbors. In Garden City, you couldn't walk down the street without hearing your name dropped like so much horse manure. It's not that we didn't have plenty of streets to cross or issues to discuss. Garden City had 5 miles of paved streets and 30 miles of paved sidewalks, not to mention a courthouse, three banks, six diners, a moving picture theater and the Yack-Yack Club. The next summer, the world's largest, free, outdoor, municipal, concrete swimming pool was supposed to open right down the street from Cora Mae's boardinghouse.

Despite the variety of discussable topics, however, we always seemed to return to who in Garden City was promenading around town in the ugliest store-bought dress ever made, who was marrying, or, on rare occasions, who was divorcing — getting their declaration of independence. It's why people loved Gladys Wisenheimer's column. People gossiped to make themselves feel superior, but to me it seemed wrong, especially when it was mean-spirited. Still, no matter how much I tried to take the high road, I usually found myself leaning close when somebody started with the tongue-wagging. I suppose I wanted to hear about somebody whose life was drearier than mine.

A few months before, for example, the natter mill had really got churning when the Tribune published a poll about religion in Garden City. Nobody was surprised that the Methodists far outranked everybody — Garden City had two Methodist churches for whites and one for Negroes — but it was surprising that twice as many people claimed

FINDING BABY RUTH

to be Methodists as actually belonged to the church. More scandalous by far, however, was that two people in town claimed to be "Spiritualists."

For weeks it was all the talk at Grundy's Market. Who among our 5,000 good citizens was a Spiritualist? Did they sacrifice animals? Were the children safe? Was it just a publicity stunt by the Tribune reporter, who refused to reveal names? And why on earth didn't those Methodists sign on the dotted line to join the church?

The Tribune story launched record high attendance at all 15 of the town's churches, just in case there was another poll. Such dogmatic diligence didn't clarify the Methodist mystery, but it did help narrow the list of suspected Spiritualists to the few dozen people who were not accounted for at Wednesday or Sunday services. Near the top of the list, I'm pretty certain you'd have found Cora Mae, my brother, Art, and me.

Art and I had been prime fodder for the Garden City rumor mill since the turn of the century. We were born on the family farm near Rosebush, an even smaller town 20 miles northwest of here. In 1900, after four years of hail-damaged crops, my father sold the farm, bought a house in Garden City and found work as a hired hand on several outlying farms.

Art and I were youngsters, but because our parents hadn't joined a local church — the hub of everything social — none of us were granted insider status in Garden City. It didn't matter that our parents remained loyal to the Wayside Church of the Lord, halfway between Rosebush and Garden City. Nor did it count that on the third Sunday of every month we made the two-hour roundtrip by horse and buggy so that my mother and I could play the piano for the congregation. We simply attended the wrong church too infrequently.

To make matters worse, when a particularly virulent strain of the measles swept through southwest Kansas in 1914, we were suspected of introducing it to Garden City. The timing was bad, it's true. Folks in Rosebush were dropping like flies that winter, and our little church was particularly hard-struck. We didn't realize how bad it was until we showed up on the third Sunday of January, and the assistant pastor's second-eldest son was the only one healthy enough to deliver the sermon. His lungs were clearly unaffected, because he orated vociferously for three hours while folks in the pews hacked and shivered.

Two weeks later, my parents died on the same day, their eyes pink with inflammation, their skin covered with the telltale red bumps. Art was so sick he didn't know they'd gone. I was the only one who didn't get sick, although I nearly collapsed afterward from the effort of trying to save them. Art recovered but with complications that would haunt him forever.

Garden City wasn't exactly isolated in those days. The 1914 outbreak that ensued could have been carried by the passengers on trains that rattled through town every few hours from as far away as Kansas City, Denver and Omaha, making stops at every bend in the road in between. It might have been introduced by one of the farmers who came to town from every direction, or maybe it was passed on by an out-of-town performer at the opera house. I just knew that on my first visit to Grundy's Market after my parents died, every eyeball in the place was riveted in my direction.

After that, Art and I quit worrying about becoming insiders, even though we would live most of our lives in Garden City. We stopped going to church altogether, which in Garden City ranked right up there with bobbed hair and whiskey drinking in terms of having a toehold in hell. The two of us just didn't have the time to drive our horse and buggy halfway to Rosebush every third Sunday or to make the proper overtures to join a local congregation. We could barely afford to pay the mortgage on our parent's one-bedroom bungalow on Fourth Street. Art worked as a hired hand for my father's former employers and added three farms during harvest. I supplemented what I earned playing the piano at weddings by also playing for funerals, birthday parties and, once monthly, at the Yack-Yack Club, a social outlet that raised the eyebrows of the nonsocial in our midst.

As I watched the parade of cars accumulating in front of the boardinghouse, I realized that Cora Mae was very likely one of the two Spiritualists mentioned in the Tribune. I'd made it my mission to unscramble the identity of the other one. It had to be somebody even lower on the Garden City totem pole than me.

GARDEN CITY TRIBUNE – WEDNESDAY, JUNE 8, 1921

TRAFFIC RULES:
DRIVERS, PLEASE TAKE NOTICE

A great many of you are getting very careless about driving. Get wise to the traffic rules at once! The following rules must be observed by drivers of automobiles, motorcycles, autobuses and trucks:

1. Keep to the right.
2. The speed limit on Main Street is 12 miles per hour not to exceed 15 miles per hour.
3. The speed limit is the same for the blocks by the high school.
4. Cars must not stop in the street or intersection to transact business. Keep close to the curb.
5. DO NOT speed to fires. The firemen do not need you. Keep out of their way.

CHAPTER 3

Twelve to 15 Miles Per Hour

I was contemplating practicing my smoking again when Mrs. Grundy moved from behind the curtain into her yard, where she looked over her rosebushes at Madam Isabella Luna's Studebaker.

Even old women in their 50s like Mrs. Grundy were shedding their corsets and snipping their hair. But Mrs. Grundy was a Rock-Of-Ages type, stuck in the 1890s with her "moral gowns," which clergyman of the time had designed to cover women's essentials and more. The dresses had loose-

      ♠

fitting sleeves that ended at the wrists, collars that rose to the collarbone and hems that dragged on the ground. Mrs. Grundy stumbled over the trim on her skirt as she furtively hung clothes on her laundry line.

A few minutes later, the Fondale brothers drove up to the boardinghouse, traveling well in excess of the 12 to 15 miles per hour speed limit. The mysteriously wealthy Pinky and Hooch Fondale drove the only green Essex Roadster in Kansas.

Most folks drove Ford Model Ts because they were cheap, adaptable to field work, and could be repaired with little more than chewing gum and a pencil. Henry Ford had been a farmer, which explained the pure utility of the vehicle as well as its availability in only one colorless color: black. Mr. Ford had also opposed the Great War, giving Pinky and Hooch a righteous reason never to buy his automobiles. Besides, Babe Ruth drove a green Essex, and that was good enough reason for Pinky to do the same. He idolized the baseball player.

I'd grown up with the Fondales. They'd caused me grief right up until I was in the third grade, when they all dropped out of school. After that the pestering continued from a greater distance. Four brothers had gone to Europe during the war, but only Pinky and Hooch came home. For years their family had been known for planting nothing more than abandoned vehicles and rusted appliances on their farm yet always having enough money to buy fancy cars and clothing. Nobody knew where they got their cash, but everybody had a theory. Mine was bootlegging.

Hooch had been a bit of a gingerbread even before the Great War. He'd walked into a cloud of mustard gas in France, leaving him with a wheezy way of talking, a graveyard cough and a shortsighted view of the world through his damaged eyes. By the end of the war, he'd completely folded in on himself, his superstitious tendencies moving to the top of his list of odd habits. It wasn't unusual to see a rabbit's foot peeking out from his overalls' pocket.

Pinky had spent the war inhaling the fresh air of Camp Funston, in eastern Kansas, where he'd been stationed with the Army. He must have come home with a twinge of guilt because he always let Hooch drive their automobiles while he called out directions from the passenger seat.

They made one pass by the house then circled back and let their car idle in the middle of the dirt street. Their road-hogging would have caused trouble regardless of who came along, but it was guaranteed to create a full-fledged skirmish with the man in the approaching Locomobile.

At least once a week, the Tribune published stories explaining the rules of driving, so most folks knew to pull to the side of the road when they saw Dr. T.W. Livermore's Locomobile coming. First, it was retrofitted as an invalid's coach, an emergency vehicle. Second, people were afraid of Dr. Livermore. He was one of the least expensive doctors in town, but his low fees came at a different kind of price. Only Doc Trundle, the veterinarian, charged less, but he'd been known to stop in the middle of checking your ears to set a horse's broken leg. With Dr. Livermore, however, whether you had a sore thumb or a burst appendix, it would be attributed largely to your moral failings.

Poor vision was the result of reading too many dime-store

novels and not enough classical literature. Hereditary diseases such as epilepsy came from not working hard enough. Female problems could be attributed to not being married or, for the married woman, not having enough babies. Dr. Livermore's treatments included long-winded lectures based on a book he'd studied 30 years earlier, in medical school: "Man's Strength and Woman's Beauty."

Dr. Livermore was even more of a fire extinguisher than Mrs. Grundy. He'd been known to crash parties to confiscate moonshine and chaperone the behaviors of men and women alike until they complied with his definition of good old-fashioned values. He was a fastidious man — his only assent to the untidy being a cigarette habit that consumed him. He inhaled without exhaling and was known to burn several cigarettes simultaneously. Patients left his office with their clothes smelling and, on occasion, splattered with tiny burns.

Despite his countless flaws, Dr. Livermore had a profile not terribly unlike that of Rudy Valentino, the film star who was currently every woman's heartthrob. Both men had classic Roman noses, full lips and hair that they parted on the side and slicked back against their heads with enough Brilliantine to glisten in the right light. Both had muscular builds — Dr. Livermore not quite so much as Rudy, whose body was described by the film magazines as "that of a Greek god." Perhaps most similar — in a disturbing way — were their eyes, which were dark and hooded. The magazines called Rudy's eyes "slumberous, seductive and suave." Truth be told, Dr. Livermore's could only be categorized as "sneaky, sly and scheming."

Still, his status as a doctor, along with his good looks, earned him a measure of undue respect in town. Thus it was that Garden City folks reacted with a certain degree of horror that day in front of the boardinghouse when the Fondale brothers' Essex crept toward the doctor's Locomobile until the two automobiles' bumpers audibly made contact. Dr. Livermore leaned out his driver's window and shouted. Pinky leaned out the passenger window and laughed. For a good five minutes, they beat their gums at each other. I couldn't hear their precise words, but I saw the Fondale brothers laughing so hard Hooch started coughing.

The noise drew the attention of four Benedetto boys walking home from the high school. They stopped to see what was happening, and the smallest one was immediately dispatched to fetch the rest of the family.

The Benedettos were the Italian family who lived across the street from me, a few doors down from the Grundy's. Our houses had been built at the same time and were identical, each with a parlor, kitchen, attic, cellar and a single bedroom. Whenever I felt blue because I had to sleep on the folding bed in the parlor while Art took the only bedroom, I looked across to the Benedettos,' where the grandma, the father and mother, and a dozen or more children lived on top of each other. They were always shouting, they smelled garlicky, and their complexions were a few shades darker than normal for Garden City. The mother always had one child in her arms and another in her belly. Only the children spoke English, and the few times I'd been inside their house, I'd seen two nicely framed pictures of the pope but not even a snapshot of President Harding.

Nevertheless, the Benedettos had helped me on several occasions, so I never joined those in town who questioned their loyalty to our nation.

Not much time passed before the family arrived in full, walking in a cluster from the direction of their house. As they neared the boardinghouse, the grind of metal against wood announced the arrival of their grandmother in her invalid's chair, which one of the older boys wrestled across the rutted road. Dark-eyed children jostled for position around the fortune-tellers' automobile, cupping their dirty hands on its windows. In the grandmother's lap sat the latest addition to the family, a little girl not quite old enough to walk. She was dressed in a faded baptismal dress, and she had hair so yellow it shimmered in the sunlight. In the midst of all those unruly dark-haired brothers and sisters, she was like a solitary sunflower growing on the side of a country road in Kansas.

On the street, the automobile standoff had quieted and the men shut down their engines completely when the tall and looming Sister Margery drifted out the front door to stand on the top porch step. It grew so quiet I could hear the cries of Tiny Brownie, the cat, seeming to come from the folds of the tall woman's skirt.

"I am Sister Margery. I am assisting Madam Isabella Luna." She spoke regally to the crowd. "I am needing four of your strongest men to help unload my wagon."

Everybody eyed everybody else silently for a few seconds until the four oldest Benedetto brothers — wiry thin and wearing matching shirts their mother must have sewn from the same bolt of cloth — elbowed their way toward the bottom of the steps, where Sister Margery greeted them. The youngest one held back — probably because he had the same vampire visions that I had — until Sister Margery smiled crookedly and flashed coins in the sun. The boys coiled around her then, listening and taking the coins she offered before racing toward the Studebaker. Everyone watched while they removed canvas tarps from the trailer. Underneath was a hodgepodge of wooden crates and baskets stashed around what appeared to be a drop-leaf oak table.

Sister Margery held open the front door with her creamy-pale gloved hand while the boys filed past carrying sheaves of dark fabric, crates of feathers and boxes of candles in a dozen shades of white. From my place not far away on the porch, I could smell their sweat along with the spicy, waxy odor of their cargo.

Among the last of the items to be unloaded was the drop-leaf table, which didn't fit through the door until the boys flipped it sideways. Even then, one side scraped painfully against the doorjamb, and one of the boys cursed loudly. Dr. Livermore muttered his disapproval of such language, but the boys' grandmother smiled proudly from her wheelchair, reminding me that she didn't speak English.

Sister Margery swiveled to face the crowd. "Watch the corners, boys. The table is protected by those already passed over."

Finally the trailer was empty, and the youngest of the four Benedetto boys struggled across the dirt yard carrying an oak box with glass on two sides. With each step he took, a mournful bell tinkled from its interior.

"The spirit bell is signifying the arrival of our loved ones from the other world," Sister Margery said. She bowed her head, studied the crowd from the tops of her eyes then slowly turned toward the house. "Madam Isabella Luna will begin consultations after sunset tonight," she called over her shoulder.

On the street, the crowd began to disperse until Mrs. Grundy, who'd come over for a closer look, shook her fist in the air. "All dolled up like a trollop, making light of the Lord's word."

Sister Margery paused, turned back, lifted her head. "The expired elderly man is wanting to see you again, Mrs. Grundy. Are you willing?"

The crowd rumbled, and even I was taken aback that the fortune-teller knew Mrs. Grundy's name. I pulled a peppermint from my pocket.

Mrs. Grundy shrieked, dropped to a knee in the dirt and arranged her black skirt into a concealing pool. Dr. Livermore hurried to her side, carrying his dark leather bag in one hand and a cigarette in the other. He knelt beside her as a string of recriminations fell from her lips. "Decadence. Sin. Which elderly man?"

Sister Margery's eyes were coal against pale skin. "The one recently passing from the aching stomach."

Mrs. Grundy held tight to Dr. Livermore's arm. "Oh my dear Lord. Could it be Grandpa Grundy?" she asked.

The hairs on the back of my neck rose through the sweat and dirt gathered there. I'd played the piano for Grandpa Grundy's funeral. He'd died from locked bowels, which geographically weren't too far from the stomach.

Dr. Livermore swept a hand through the air, his cigarette leaving a smoky arc. "Don't be fooled by these gypsies, folks. They're degenerates of the worst design."

Sister Margery turned toward him. "Doctor, you must be helping your son."

Dr. Livermore's face grew so pale his eyebrows looked three times darker than usual. His son was one of about two dozen Garden City residents who'd died during the 1918 influenza pandemic. The doctor had been traveling across the countryside treating other victims, unaware that his only child was stricken. Few people in the rural parts had telephones, so the doctor's wife had sent the sheriff in search of her husband. By the time he returned, his son was dead.

Not long afterward, Dr. Livermore's wife packed her bags and went to live with her mother in Wichita. That's when the doctor dropped his fees until they were just barely higher than the veterinarian's. Folks speculated that he felt unworthy, and I agreed, although his high-hatted lectures told another story.

Back on the street, people were looking at the doctor, the Locomobile, the weeds of Cora Mae's yard — anywhere, it seemed, to avoid the blazing charcoal of Sister Margery's eyes. Silence swirled then shattered in the middle of the street, where Pinky and Hooch sat in the Essex, elbows dangling from the windows. Pinky snorted, spit on the ground and giggled. He punched Hooch on the arm until he snickered too.

Sister Margery pointed at them. "Your brothers have crossed the ocean of dead. They are saying to leave the car in a tower of grains."

Pinky guffawed, but Hooch's sorry red eyes bulged and

strained in our direction as he turned on the car — naturally, the Fondales had an electric starter — and groped around on the seat beside him for something. Mrs. Grundy screamed, and the Benedettos took a few steps back, pulling grandma and baby with them. Everybody knew the Fondales didn't leave home unarmed.

Grandma Benedetto fainted in her invalid's chair, slumping until her head dangled in the lap of the little girl, who tried to push it back into place with two chubby hands. My heart beat double-time as Hooch's arm reappeared. Whatever was in his hand caught a flash of sun as he waved it over his shoulder. He threw the car in reverse and backed up, nearly swiping the Locomobile before taking off down the road.

People were wiping dust from their eyes when Sister Margery looked at me. "Shaking the salt over his shoulder won't do the trick," she mumbled before turning toward the crowd with a final pronouncement. "Visitations starting at sunset each evening excepting, of course, the Sabbath. Fifty cents for 15 minutes."

CHURCH OF THE BRETHREN TO STUDY EVILS OF SPIRITUALISM

The Rev. W.A. Baker of Dodge City will deliver the sermon Sunday at the Garden City Church of the Brethren. His topic: "The Evils of Spiritualism." Parishioners will learn about the immoral and depraved practice of fortune-telling, palmistry and crystal-ball reading, not to mention the disgusting deployment of ectoplasm. The reverend is alarmed by the recent religious poll taken by the Tribune in which two local residents declared themselves Spiritualists and many others identified as Methodists.

CHAPTER 4

A Plague of Champagne

The boardinghouse had taken on an aura. The sugary vanilla smell of the marble cakes we'd made that morning had been replaced by a musky blend of cedar and juniper that grew stronger as I climbed the winding stairway toward the fortune-tellers' rooms.

At the top of the stairs, the smell was so strong I could follow it to the closest room. It was dim inside. Once my eyes adjusted, I could see they'd covered the windows with sheets and pushed the bed and dresser against the wall to make room for the clutter of crates being unpacked by Sister Margery. Cora Mae was standing on the divinely protected drop-leaf table, trying to remove the room's only electric lightbulb, which dangled from the ceiling.

Directing them both, with one leg slung over the arm of a maroon leather chair, was Madam Isabella Luna. Gone were the cloche hat, the flowing cape, the tiny boots and the feather boa. Instead, she wore a Turkish smoking suit of brown satin with gold tassels circling the neck and the bottom of each pant leg. One foot didn't quite reach the floor, but the other bounced over the arm of the chair, making the tassels jiggle.

"Yeah, yeah, yeah, that's better," she said to Cora Mae in her falsetto voice, which seemed to be her only unchanged feature. "My spirits can't agree about supper, so we'll have chicken, fried and broiled; potatoes, fried and mashed; and eggs, deviled and scrambled. For dessert, the cakes on the table. Also whiskey. A glass for each of us."

"How many are in your party?" I said, stepping into the room and sucking hard on my peppermint. "Truth be told, you only rented two rooms."

The women stopped what they were doing to stare at me — Madam Isabella Luna through eyes rimmed with black kohl.

"Didn't my assistant, Sister Margery, tell you?" she said. "There are six of us — me, her and our four spirit guides. One of the rooms is for readings."

"Ab-so-lute-ly," Cora Mae said, shooting me the evil eye. "Only about supper ... I can do it all but the chicken. Fact is, I'm what's called a vegetarian. I don't eat meat."

"Did you say vegetarian? That's a scream." Madam Isabella Luna sat up straight in the chair, both feet now dangling above the floor, the tassels whirling. "I didn't think I'd ever hear that word again."

"You've heard it before?" Cora Mae's eyes darted excitedly between Madam Isabella Luna and me.

"Oh yeah, yeah." The fortune-teller slapped her thigh and laughed. "My folks got caught up in a crazy scheme to build a vegetarian colony in eastern Kansas. The place fell apart, but the creek where they settled is still there. Vegetarian Creek."

Cora Mae beamed. "That's good stuff! You're from Kansas?"

"Did I say that? I'm some kind of dumb Dora," Madam Isabella Luna said. She looked at Sister Margery with her thin, unevenly painted black eyebrows raised.

"Madam Isabella is growing up in New York City, where we are friends with Sir Arthur Conan Doyle, whose letter of endorsement we are carrying," Sister Margery said. She pulled a wrinkled envelope from her skirt pocket, waved it in the air then stuffed it back in again.

I almost laughed. I wasn't certain how New York City folks talked, but the fortune-tellers' accents were so different from one another's that both seemed counterfeit.

Cora Mae clapped. "Jesus H. Christ, welcome to the Bible Belt. Now about supper, we've got potatoes, fried and mashed; eggs, deviled and scrambled; and for dessert, marble cake with my incomparable champagne. What else would the spirits like?"

"Let me think." Madam Isabella Luna picked up a copy of True Story magazine from the nightstand and flipped through its pages. Cora Mae adored the magazine and left old copies lying about for her tenants. I got a kick out of the stories but preferred serious authors, like F. Scott Fitzgerald and Zane Grey.

The fortune-teller must have found something juicy. Without looking up, she fumbled on the table for a monocle, which she crammed between her eyebrow and cheekbone. Her lips — as red as the stripes on Old Glory — formed a circle. "Ho, ho. The spirits want grapes."

"I'm sorry, but I don't have grapes. I do have grape jelly and peanut butter," Cora Mae said.

"Yeah, yeah. Sam-wiches. That'll be hotsy-totsy. Sister Margery can help."

The two women trotted down the stairs, and although I knew I should help, I stayed, watching from the doorway as Madam Isabella Luna silently mouthed words from the magazine. Finally she spoke without looking up. "You got a ciggy?"

"A what?" I asked.

"A gasper, a cigarette."

"Good Lord, no. I'm only learning to smoke — for my figure."

She looked up, and the eye behind the monocle looked like a trout just escaped from the hook. "What's that on your forehead, bunny?"

I have a birthmark a little larger than a postage stamp over my eyebrows. It's a patch of red speckles, only noticeable when I get emotional, and then it glows like a volcano until it erupts, sending sheets of hot crimson down my face. My mother had a similar mark in the same place. When she died, I'd watched the life drain from her face, the colors disappearing until only the birthmark remained, like a tribute to our connection.

Madam Isabella Luna made my birthmark glow. I managed

to keep it from erupting only by focusing on the sounds of pots and pans clattering in the kitchen.

She asked again, though. "That splotch — somebody belt you, or did you get the pox?"

"It's a beauty mark. Why do you ask?" I said.

She shrugged, put down the magazine and burrowed through her sequined handbag, which from the sound of it, carried enough tools to repair a fleet of Mr. Ford's automobiles. She pulled out her cigarette holder, quarried through her bag again then sighed and took the monocle from her eye. "You sure you don't have a hope chest?"

"What on earth does that mean?" I asked.

"A pack of ciggies," she said.

I shook my head, but she ignored me, pointing with her toes toward a three-legged stool by her chair. "Sit here. The spirits are tugging at me to give you a message. I don't know why. Maybe the splotch is special. A ciggy would make it clearer."

I stepped just far enough into the room to see the magazine in her lap, opened to an article titled "The Primitive Lover," with a photograph of a couple dressed in Tarzan costumes feeding each other grapes. The spirits wanted grapes all right, I thought, but what I said was ridiculous. "Maybe you'd like to hear about my dream. A stork with sea-green feathers dropped a marble cake on the boardinghouse."

Madam Isabella Luna laughed in that unexpected low tone. "You're all wet about Spiritualism and almost everything else. I can tell from looking at you."

What was she talking about? I wasn't the breastless twig

that 1920s fashion demanded. I was overly curvaceous because of the candy, but I had a natural curl to my hair that other women envied, and my long, narrow fingers were perfectly suited for the piano. My mother had given me more than ten years of lessons.

"Now what are you talking about?" I asked.

"Your piano won't save you, which is what the spirits want to talk about if you'll just sit down."

Had I mentioned my piano? It was at home in my parlor, an upright, brush-grained dark brown. Cora Mae must have been gossiping about me while I was on the porch. I crossed the room to sit in a straight-backed chair near the fortune-teller, my feet perched on the stool.

Madam Isabella Luna turned her head to the side as if someone behind her had spoken. She nodded then looked at me. "The spirits say to watch out, or you'll live a life of drudgery."

"Sounds to me like the spirits are referring to the dishes I'll have to wash after we fix them two different types of potatoes and eggs for dinner," I said.

Again she turned her head to listen. This time — like the fool I am — I looked too. She turned back with a smile. "They say to give their love to Arthur."

My feet clattered to the floor. "Don't you dare involve my brother in your hocus-pocus nonsense."

Madam Isabella Luna was prying through her handbag again, setting in motion every tassel on her smoking suit. "The spirits say they're thirsty. They want a ciggy and some hair of the dog. When is your friend bringing the champagne?"

"Alcohol and cigarettes are illegal in Kansas, which you surely know, living just down the road from here. I shouldn't be surprised by you — you're a charlatan — but I am surprised that Cora Mae told you so much about us." Good Lord. I sounded like Dr. Livermore quoting from his book.

"Get hep, bunny. I'm a flapper who talks to the dead. Whether or not you believe me, you should listen to the spirits. You've heard about houdinizing? It means to escape, change, wriggle out, like the magician Harry Houdini. The spirits say you only have one chance to houdinize. One chance." Her eyes shifted to my skirt pocket. "Now, how about for a change you throw me a little something sweet?"

I jumped to my feet so fast I knocked over the stool before stomping across the room. At the doorway, I checked that my candy was still in my pocket. When I looked back at Madam Isabella Luna, she had the cigarette holder between her lips, dragging on it as if it were loaded.

"You really are a charlatan!" I shouted. My birthmark was exploding, I could tell. The flushed feeling burst across my face as I scrambled down the stairway. By the last step, I definitely felt the heebie-jeebies crawling up my spine. Only one person was aware that before I'd left home that day, I'd tucked a roll of peppermints into my pocket. And when I'd last seen him, he could barely get out of bed.

The temperature in Cora Mae's kitchen seemed to have jumped by 20 degrees, what with the volcano erupting in my head and the stove and oven going full blast. It was bad enough that Cora Mae had snitched about me to the fortune-teller, but to tittle-tattle about Art was unforgivable.

The room looked like the Black Hole of Calcutta, every flat surface covered with dirty dishes and food scraps. Two dogs licked clean the linoleum floor, and flies clustered on countertops. Tiny Brownie, the cat, licked from a sugar bowl at the sink until Cora Mae picked him up and kissed his nose. It was one of her sickest habits, but I ignored her as I set about helping to fix supper. I gathered dirty plates and cups, and stacked them in the sink. I put water on the stove to heat and pulled the covers off the three cakes I'd helped Cora Mae make that morning, smiling to myself when I saw that one had fallen.

The sun was starting to set by the time we finished preparing supper. Madam Isabella Luna arrived, still wearing her smoking suit. She climbed into the chair at the head of the kitchen table and let Sister Margery push her toward the table. Then Sister Margery and Cora Mae sat, and I announced that I wasn't hungry. Instead, I flittered about serving them.

"I see no places have been set for my guiding spirits," Madam Isabella said. Nobody spoke until she laughed, and then everyone but me laughed too.

In the middle of the table sat platters of potatoes — fried and mashed — and trays of eggs — scrambled and deviled — and bowls of salads — carrots with lima beans, and pickled beets — along with a plate of peanut butter and jelly sandwiches. Madam Isabella Luna took tiny helpings — I knew she wouldn't eat much — but Sister Margery made up for it, heaping spoonfuls of each item onto her plate along with two sandwiches.

Twice during the meal, Sister Margery excused herself by

saying, "I gotta go iron my shoelaces." Then she'd trundle off to the crapper. I noticed each time she came back out that despite the posted warnings, she forgot to flush.

Cora Mae nibbled on a carrot. "Do you mind if we get back to what we were talking about this afternoon? I'm just so curious about your mystic powers."

Here it comes, I thought. Maybe they'll slip and admit they were gossiping about me while I was on the porch watching the neighborhood parade.

Sister Margery opened her mouth to speak, and my stomach turned when I saw mashed potatoes nestled among those crooked teeth. "We were discussing ectoplasm, I believe. It is a way for the dead to be sending a message. A furry substance drips from the Spiritualist's mouth and nose."

Cora Mae's eyes bulged.

"Don't worry, bunny. I don't do ectoplasm," Madam Isabella Luna said. "It's like spitting hairballs."

"What about the letter of endorsement from Conan Doyle that you mentioned?" Cora Mae asked.

Sister Margery pulled the crumpled letter from her pocket and passed it around. I snatched it when it came by me and could tell immediately that it was fraudulent. In addition to being wrinkled and torn, it was stained by who knows what and smelled of stale tobacco.

No sooner had they finished eating than Madam Isabella Luna slipped her cigarette holder between her lips and looked at me with her daubed-on eyebrows raised, one a good quarter of an inch higher than the other. "Got a hope chest yet, honey?"

I shook my head while Cora Mae put a thin silver box on

the table and opened it to reveal five hand-rolled cigarettes all in a row. She tilted the box in my direction, but I waved it away. Madam Isabella Luna took two. She put one in her handbag, loaded the other in her holder and looked at me again with those mismatched eyebrows.

"What about that hair of the dog?" she asked.

I ignored her, closing the window curtains while Cora Mae disappeared into the pantry, emerging with two Mason jars she carried like trophies. I cleared the table as the others sipped moonshine from teacups, tapped their ashes into empty dishes and beefed about Prohibition. The marble cakes hadn't been touched.

"I'm sure you all know that the temperance leader, Carry A. Nation, was a Kansan," I said, removing Madam Isabella Luna's plate of barely touched food. She'd fashioned a deviled egg into a boat with fried potatoes as oars and two little lima beans as sailors, all awash on a sea of mashed potatoes.

"That's right," Cora Mae said. "The self-described bulldog running along at the feet of Jesus, barking at what He doesn't like, and chopping up the speak-easies with her hatchet."

Cora Mae raised her teacup. "Let's toast to Carry A. Nation."

"The spirits made her do it." Madam Isabella Luna laughed, drained her cup and wobbled from the room.

CHAPTER 5

Art's Misfortune

Barking dogs signaled our first customer, and I followed Cora Mae into the vestibule, where she opened the door. The man there was too thin for his church clothes, and Cora Mae grasped his hand as if he might fall over the threshold. He turned toward me with his whole body, tugged a straw boater off his head and gave a crooked smile.

It was my brother, Art, his 31-year-old body twisted like that of a man twice his age. I rushed to take his hand from Cora Mae. "Good Lord, Art. What are you doing here?"

"Having my fortune told, like everybody else in town, I expect." He held two quarters in his palm, the fingers slightly curled, like crab legs.

"Leave him alone, Jules," Cora Mae said. "Can't he have a little fun?"

"He's suffering a bad spell," I said. "Besides, this isn't fun.

It's smoke and mirrors, a gossipfest with two different kinds of potatoes. Come on, Art, I'm taking you home."

Sister Margery arrived, clutching Art's elbow and speaking softly through her crooked teeth. "You are hearing of the great painter, Renoir? From my homeland of France. He had this crooked disease of yours, and still he painted magnificently."

"That's something," Art said, "but when my rheumatism acts up, I can't even paint a fence, right, Jules?"

"You do your best." I said, watching them start up the stairs, Sister Margery clinging to her skirt, Art clinging to the handrail. Wide Whitey, the dog, stood at the top, where the flicker of candles spilled into the hallway. Madam Isabella Luna emerged from her bedroom wearing a flowing black gown with a jade-colored silk scarf layered into a turban. Now she was the fortune-teller rather than the flapper.

As she peered over the banister, I opened my mouth to warn her to be kind to my brother. But she spoke first. "The spirits refuse to meet with him. They send their regrets."

"What on earth?" I shouted. Part of me feared he'd be hurt by her false prophecies, and the other part was angry that he'd been outright rejected. I watched him shrink into himself as he slowly stepped backward down the steps.

Even Sister Margery, who hadn't moved from her place on the stairway, seemed taken aback. "But why?" she asked. "He is the brother of our hostess. His suffering could be relieved by spiritual guidance. Also, he has coins in his hand. "

"That last bit is all that seems to matter," I said. "Art, let's get you home."

But Madam Isabella Luna spoke to Art from her perch.

"The spirits say his future has been decided. It fills them with sorrow knowing they can say nothing to change what's coming."

I stood speechless, staring at my brother, whose eyes were locked on the floor. Finally, I asked, "Art? What's she talking about?"

He gave me a vacant glance and shrugged his bony shoulders. The coins jingled as he returned them to the depths of his pocket. "I'll head home now," he said.

After we saw Art to the door, Cora Mae nudged me toward the kitchen. "Go get the oil burning. We've got to fix Madam Isabella's midnight snack."

I tromped off to the crapper, where I cried as quietly as I could, which meant that before long, Cora Mae was rapping at the door. I'd never been able to snivel silently.

"Come help me in the kitchen," she said.

"Leave me alone!" I shouted. In the mirror over the water basin, I glimpsed my green eyes, now puffy and red, and my birthmark, blazing brightly. I adjusted my hair, which I wore rolled up and pinned in the back. I splashed water on my face, pinched my cheeks for color and straightened the collar on my blouse before returning to the kitchen.

I watched Cora Mae working, wondering what it was that made her so odd. She hadn't told me much about her past other than that she'd run the family farm by herself for a few months after her husband was killed in the Great War. Apparently, the neighbors pitched a fit about a girl living there alone, and a brute came by late one night to prove the point. Cora Mae stopped short of telling me what happened, but she called him "a beast," which didn't sound like somebody you'd invite to Sunday dinner.

She lifted Tiny Brownie from the countertop to the floor as she explained that Madam Isabella Luna and her spirits wanted a snack of doughnuts — sugar-glazed, chocolate-coated and cinnamon-sprinkled. She emptied half a container of lard into a deep, heavy pot on the stove and brought out canisters of cocoa, sugar and flour. I didn't ask what was wrong with the still-uneaten marble cakes that we'd baked that morning, reaching instead for red and white tins of spice, the labels made nearly illegible by crusted food and years of handling.

"Have you noticed how nervous the animals are?" Cora Mae said. "They've been running in and out of the house all evening, jumping on the furniture. I know you think this is bushwa, but Sister Margery says animals are the most sensitive of all living beings to the arrival of spirits."

"The animals want outside because that's where they belong," I said. "Tell me, though, why did you bring Art into this?"

Cora Mae unhinged the cover on a tin and sniffed. "Think this is cinnamon?" She held it toward my nose.

"Nutmeg. Are you going to answer my question?"

"How was I supposed to know the spirits wouldn't talk to him?" She sniffed another container and held it out. "Allspice?"

I sniffed. "Cinnamon. She's broken his heart."

Cora Mae set aside the spices and searched through the kitchen drawers. "Where's that eggbeater? Don't go overboard, Jules. First you say the fortune-tellers are full of bushwa, then you're mad because they won't share their bushwa with your brother. Which is it?"

"I don't know," I said, reaching past her for the eggbeater. "It just burns me to see Art hurt any more than he already is."

"Art will be fine. He has 50 cents to spare and a sister who loves him." Cora Mae cracked eggs into a bowl and turned the handle on the beater until the batter was smooth. She handed me a rolling pin and a doughnut cutter, then said, "In the meantime, I can't decide how to use my last free consultation. I'd like to know that my dead husband is well, wherever he may be. I'd probably get weepy, though, so I think I'll speak with Russet."

"Who's Russet?" I lowered the first of the doughy circles into a wire basket suspended in the bubbling oil. They looked wet and furry, and it occurred to me that ectoplasm was probably similar in appearance.

"You remember Russet, my potato-colored dog? I'll forever live with the guilt of letting him die here alone last summer while I was at the Electric watching a Lillian Gish film. I'm certain poor Russet has something to tell me."

"Well, Madam Isabella told me I needed to change my life. She said I'd only have one chance."

"You're going to houdinize, then?" Cora Mae said.

My mouth flew open. "How do you know the word she used?"

"Houdinize? It's a common vocabulary word."

With a whoosh, the pot of oil on the stove came to a boil, and a bang came from the front door. It was the evening's second customer, Mrs. Grundy, ready for a visit with her deceased father-in-law.

The stream of customers was steady until late into the night. Just as the hall clock struck midnight, Sister Margery appeared in the kitchen.

"Madam Isabella says it's time for speaking with the dead dog." She grabbed a sugar doughnut from a platter. "Bring the sinkers and champagne."

The séance room reeked of incense and stale cigarette smoke when Cora Mae and I walked in. We'd hardly spoken to each other since our kitchen spat about houdinizing.

I pushed aside candles burnt to their wicks to make room on a side table for trays of doughnuts and drink. The room was so dark I could barely make out Madam Isabella Luna sitting in her armchair, her monocle slightly off-kilter.

"Sisters, we have much to celebrate," she said. "A successful first night in Garden City. Even Mrs. Grundy had a pleasant visit with her father-in-law. But first we talk with Cora Mae's friend. Sit, sit."

We sat around the cluttered, sacred table with the spirit bell like a centerpiece. The dogs skulked at our feet. Madam Isabella Luna adjusted her robe before speaking. "Place your hands flat on the table, little fingers linked with those of the person next to you. Hold on a minute; I'm starving."

We watched, our fingers looped together, while she bit into a doughnut. A sliver of chocolate frosting clung to her upper lip. She brushed crumbs from her hands and said, "Yummy. Now, what's the dog's name?"

"Russet," Cora Mae answered.

"Everybody close your eyes and bow your head."

The bell inside the cabinet rang twice, which gave me the

heebie-jeebies. How did they do that? Everyone's eyes were closed but mine. Wide Whitey, the dog, whimpered.

"Russell has arrived." Madam Isabella Luna lifted her chin dramatically. "He wants the other dogs to leave."

Everybody opened their eyes again, and Cora Mae shooed the dogs from the room. Madam Isabella Luna took another bite of doughnut.

"Close, close, heads down. Russell says you shouldn't feel ashamed over his death. The squirrels were at fault. He hopes you enjoyed the ZaSu Pitts film."

Russell? ZaSu Pitts? Cora Mae was a member of the ZaSu fan club, but she was seeing a Lillian Gish film when Russet died. I looked over to see that Cora Mae's eyes were shut so tightly, her mouth was pulled into a smile. Tears seeped down each cheek, and she sniffled.

Madam Isabella Luna spoke again, "Yeah, yeah, yeah. Squirrels made Russell chase them. His heart was weak. Where he is now, he's happy. No squirrels allowed." Then she barked. "'Woof, woof,' he says. 'Bye, bye.'"

And that was that. Sister Margery crossed the smoke-filled room to pull aside the covering and open a window. A breeze swept across the room. Madam Isabella Luna took a deep breath and, as she reached for her cigarette holder, cocked her head to the side again, as if she were listening. She looked at me. "One more message for you, honey. Keep your eyes open. Watch for your boy where the boots line the rail. And don't forget to houdinize."

"Now what are you talking about?" I said. But Sister Margery clasped my little finger and led me into the hallway, where the dogs panted and paced.

"Madam Isabella is offering a free message," she said. "The meaning will be clearing in the future."

GLADYS WISENHEIMER'S
Garden of Tidbits

Doc Trundle says Motor Foot is a new disease suffered by motorists who take long journeys. It is caused by keeping the right foot constantly on the accelerator, and it can make walking difficult. It may very well fulfill the prediction that Americans will forget how to walk.

That might be good news for a certain somebody who shall remain unnamed who recently lost the toenail on his right foot due to wearing boots two sizes too small. He was last seen three days ago, limping away from Mrs. Cora Mae Daisy's boardinghouse, where the fortune-tellers are staying. Rumor has it they will leave today, which is a relief for the moral in our midst.

Speaking of motorists, the Fondale brothers have mysteriously purchased yet another new automobile. This time it's a maroon 12-cylinder Packard, just like Babe Ruth's. Let's hope the Fondales don't get into as much trouble with their car as Babe Ruth has recently with his.

CHAPTER 6

The Ocean of Garden City

I avoided the boardinghouse for the remainder of the fortune-tellers' stay, and it wasn't because I was waiting for the "meaning to be clearing," as Sister Margery had predicted. I'd had my fill of premonitions fueled by chin wagging, and if I had been interested in what was happening, Gladys kept a running account of the fortune-tellers in her column. I wanted to ask Art about his predetermined future. I didn't, though, because I didn't want to give credence to Madam Isabella Luna's rambling.

Anyway, I had my hands full cooking for the crew at the swimming pool. Art and I had volunteered to work that day. He was driving a team of horses, pushing himself too hard and once again trying to prove his worth to all of Garden City. I'd offered to fix dinner for 30 workers.

Mayor Trinkle had come up with the idea to build the world's largest, free, outdoor, municipal, concrete swimming pool, which seemed like a lot of qualifiers to me. Scheduled to open in a year, the pool was being sold to town residents as a cooperative venture. Everybody was supposed to pitch in with money, equipment, food, labor or whatever else they could spare. The Tribune duly reported the names and amounts of everyone who contributed.

I had always been afraid of the water, never having learned to swim. It wasn't likely I'd frequent the pool, but everyone had to participate in the project, and earlier that week, two of Art's employers — farmers east of town — dropped off supplies that I'd spent three days cooking and baking.

I'd also spent three days listening to the wails and chatter of the Benedetto children. Whether icicles hung from the roof, or heat waves rose from the concrete, the Benedetto children constantly clustered outdoors, probably because the house was too small for them all. From sunrise to sunset they shouted in Italian, cursed in English and cried copiously.

Mrs. Benedetto was too exhausted to notice. She'd walk

FINDING BABY RUTH

right past a brawl on her way to the shed, and send an older girl to comfort the little ones when they skinned their knees or bloodied their noses. Once I did the arithmetic and realized the mother couldn't have been too many years older than me. Italians marry their girls off when they turn 15, and the Benedettos' eldest daughter looked close to marrying age. That meant the mother was about 30, only four years older than me but a lifetime away in terms of babies and chores, wrinkles and dowdiness.

Mr. Benedetto also seemed ancient and perpetually tired, but his exhaustion took another sort of toll. If ever the shouting or crying — and somebody was always crying — went on for too long or became too loud, Mr. Benedetto would step outside with his belt doubled over in his hand, buckle gleaming, and wallop somebody. The beatings brought the noise to a level I couldn't tolerate, so I usually shut the windows and practiced my piano when one started.

The morning I was to take food to the pool, I opened my door to find five of the children waiting in the yard with a rusty wagon and a wheelbarrow cushioned with garden soil. They must have seen me cooking, because they'd come prepared to help deliver food. Two casseroles covered with cloths were already in the wagon. We piled two hams, two pans of fried chicken and three salads around them then nestled three cartons of deviled eggs into the wheelbarrow. As we set off down the street, the children leading the way, I imagined we looked for all the world like a Woman's Christian Temperance Union parade. They always stuck the children up front as a kind of sympathy ploy.

I asked one of the boys, I think his name was Antonio, about his youngest sister's whereabouts. He pointed behind us, and there was Mrs. Benedetto pushing the grandmother in her invalid's chair, with the golden sunflower riding regally in her lap.

Mick McKenzie, owner of the Yack-Yack Club, was on that day's work crew, and he gave us a tip of his ever-present black fedora as we marched into the park.

Art was driving a team of horses attached to a metal earth scraper. It was exhausting, dirty work, especially for a man in his condition. He made another circuit then jumped down and limped over to where we were setting up the food table. Behind the dirt caking his face, his eyes held the brightness of a low-grade fever. I didn't bother asking if he'd consider taking the afternoon off; I just set the food up buffet-style on a picnic table and settled myself on a blanket in the shade of a tree to wait and watch. It's what I'd always done for Art over the years — wait and watch.

The screeching of the invalid's chair announced the arrival of the last group of Benedettos. Mrs. Benedetto went to the food table and uncovered the two casserole dishes her children had placed there. I was curious about what she'd fixed and started to get up, but by the time I unfurled myself from the blanket, the entire crew had hurried over to help themselves.

Mr. Benedetto and several of his sons walked past with plates filled with steaming ravioli. Art and Mick from the Yack-Yack Club came to sit by me. They too had filled their plates with ravioli and, perhaps in a nod to me, one deviled egg each.

Art shoveled stuffed pasta pockets into his mouth as if

he hadn't eaten in a week. "This is delicious. Jules, get Mrs. Benedetto's recipe for these noodles."

Mick grunted in agreement. "Those fortune-tellers telling fortunes tonight?" He ate his deviled egg in one huge bite.

"I've stayed clear of the boardinghouse," I said. "Mrs. Wisenheimer wrote in her column that they are leaving today. Anyway, they're full of bushwa. Now, let me get you some of my all-American fried chicken."

"Thanks, Jules, but I'm stuffed to the brim with Mrs. Benedetto's noodles," Mick said.

"Me too," Art said. They jumped to their feet and headed back to work.

I cruised along the food table, noting that the dishes of ravioli were nearly empty. Naturally, most of the eggs and a good portion of the ham and fried chicken were also gone. I picked at a scrap of ravioli and stuck it in my mouth. It was delicious — a burst of basil, tomato and creamy cheese in a single bite.

I turned to compliment Mrs. Benedetto just as Mrs. Grundy and Fanny arrived. The Grundys had donated $175.50 to the project, with the stipulation that the pool be named after Mrs. Grundy's deceased mother, Penelope Peterson. Mayor Trinkle was quoted in the Tribune as saying that the contribution was so generous, the proposed name so lovely, it would be more fitting for the small hot dog stand that would be erected once the pool was finished. The headline on the story — "Mayor scraps P.P. Pool" — provoked Mrs. Grundy into writing a series of letters to the editor, threatening to withdraw her donation if an apology wasn't forthcoming. Mayor Trinkle submitted a written apology that miraculously warranted front-page placement but did not give in to changing the pool's name.

At the food table, both Grundy women looked as warm and perspiration-drenched as the last of the fried chicken settling into a puddle of grease at the bottom of my pan. Fanny wore a skirt that bared her knees, matching stockings and a blouse with a sailor collar. Over it all, she'd layered a letter sweater bearing the initials of her college in Fort Hays. Mrs. Grundy was swathed head to toe in one of her black moral dresses.

"Hello, Jules," Mrs. Grundy said. "You don't mind if we help ourselves to the food, do you?"

"It's for the volunteers," I said.

"I know. You're so very generous."

Mrs. Grundy scraped the last of the ravioli onto her plate while Fanny winked at me from behind her mother's back. It was another valuable skill she must have learned at college.

"How are your classes going, Fanny?" I asked. The girl was only a few years younger than me but clearly traveling down an altogether different path, one that led to her M.R.S. degree if her mother had her way.

"Oh college is the bee's knees. I passed all my classes, with A's in 'Husband and Wife' and 'Motherhood,'" Fanny said. "I'm home on summer break."

Mrs. Grundy looked at her daughter over the tops of her spectacles. "The bee's knees?"

"That's right, Ma. You know — the berries."

Mrs. Grundy sighed. "I don't know why your father insists on continuing to pay for your education when you're only learning to exasperate me. Nevertheless, he's hard at work at the store earning said money, so I'll fill him a plate here and take it over."

While her mother filled a second plate with food, Fanny smiled at me. "Have you heard what they say about the pool? It'll be bigger than a football field, with waves that lap across it like an ocean. Imagine an ocean, right here in the middle of the Bible Belt."

I had to laugh. "It's pretty exciting, even though I'm deathly afraid of the water. Not many people in Garden City have seen an ocean."

"I did once," she said, nibbling on a chicken leg. "We went to California. It was keen."

"I've seen photographs. Maybe someday I'll get there myself. I'd like to see it in person."

"You know it!" Fanny said. "By the way, I heard that the fortune-tellers are leaving Cora Mae's today. Ma visited them three times, just to reassure herself that they really were frauds. She wouldn't let me step near the place, though. Do you think they were on the up and up, Jules?"

It was an odd turn of events — the college deb asking for bug-eyed Betty's opinion. I hesitated, thinking about what Madam Isabella Luna had told me about houdinizing and watching for the boy where the boots line the rail. "I'm still trying to figure out how they got their inside information," I said. "You should have seen the letter of introduction they claimed was from Sir Arthur Conan Doyle himself. It was a wrinkled mess. But your grandpa's death — how did they know about that?"

"I'm sorry to have missed visiting with Grandpa Grundy. I heard they wouldn't give a reading to Art. Why's that?"

My hackles went up as they always did when somebody seemed to slight my brother. "You had to have been there to get the full story," I said.

"I wish I had been," she said. "Maybe next time."

"The fortune-tellers are from New York City," I said, the lie slipping through my teeth like butter. "They won't be coming around again."

MOTHER SEES DEAD SON WALKING THE GANGPLANK

Here's another one of the many pranks played by fate. A few weeks ago, a young man — a stranger — came to Garden City taking orders for stereopticon views — pictures taken of scenes and incidents during the first few months of the Great War. The views were from training camps, aboard the ships, on the battlefronts and in the hospitals.

Mrs. Kelsey Groening purchased a set of the views, and when she looked at them, she readily recognized her son, Anthony, who was killed in France not long after the United States entered the war. The picture was taken from the New York harbor and showed Anthony walking up the gangplank as his regiment boarded the ship to sail. Mrs. Groening says the picture is plain and her son easily identified. It's the last photo she has of him.

CHAPTER 7

Fate's Pranks

To understand my protectiveness toward Art when people made comments like Fanny's or Madam Isabella Luna's requires a journey back four years before, to the fall of 1917. It started on a morning so cold Art could barely get his motorcycle started in time for his farm jobs. He'd bought it used a few months earlier and was frustrated that it took a few tries before it moseyed to life.

As he left, I saw that two frozen tire furrows had burrowed into the ground where he always parked outside the parlor window. It was late September, when the weather in Kansas could come or go.

I remember that the sky was ominously white that morning, as if it had lost the battle for color with whatever swirled in the clouds. I washed the breakfast dishes before going to my piano to rehearse for Melba Swanson's wedding. I was working through the second verse of Gershwin's "Someone to Watch Over Me" when I saw snowflakes floating outside.

I decided to walk to Grundy's Market before the storm worsened. We needed flour and eggs for a cherry pie I wanted to make for dinner. By the time I pinned up my hair and pulled galoshes over my shoes, the snow had thickened.

A few folks were out, scooting chickens into coops and latching shed doors, but judging from the tangle of footprints in front of Grundy's, half the town was at the market. The crowd was so thick the windows were fogged over.

Inside was a strange, muffled tableau. Everyone was whispering, so the little bell over the door sounded like a church bell when I arrived. The Fondale brothers were a huddled mass of denim overalls. There were four of them in those days, all with protruding gooseberry eyes and floppy ears.

Mrs. Grundy, who'd not yet launched her morality campaign, wore a gauzy linen blouse. I remember her clutching its lace collar with both hands as she stood behind the counter, looking frightened.

"What is it?" I asked. "Are we going to war?"

President Wilson had narrowly won reelection the previous fall based on a pledge of continued neutrality, but everybody had feared it wouldn't last and we'd be dragged into the war in Europe. Everybody was right. The United States had officially jumped into the fray in April. Now I braced myself for more bad news — another political assassination, another passenger ship torpedoed — but it was worse.

"The Mexicans are attacking," Mrs. Grundy said with a quiet urgency to her voice. "They're on their way up the Santa Fe Trail."

Pinky was on the other side of the room watching Hooch strike a match, light hand-rolled cigarettes for his three brothers then strike another match to light his own. In those days, Hooch's superstitious bent had only just begun. Pinky, on the other hand, talked as he always has — like a cheese grater dicing up words until they were no longer recognizable.

"The Krauts want the Spics on their side," Pinky said. "They could be here by morning, or at least in the encinity."

Mr. Grundy stepped from behind the counter wearing his butcher's apron, speckled with the blood of somebody's meat order.

"It looks like war, Jules," he said. "The Mexicans have moved artillery into Arizona. The New York Times that came with today's mail says the British intercepted a telegram the Germans sent to the Mexicans. They want Mexico to attack us."

I looked around the room, wondering why Mexico would attack us. My social studies would have been better if I hadn't stopped school after eighth grade. Still, I'd stayed in school longer than most of the people here, and I continued to stay informed through the Tribune, Collier's and my Zane Greys.

Doc Trumble was there. Back then, he was a newcomer to Garden City who treated mostly animals. His soothing, gentle voice may have been the reason his patients agreed to sit beside dogs, cats and chickens in his waiting room.

"It sounds like the Germans have promised the Mexicans the return of Arizona, Texas and New Mexico — all the territory our grandfathers won in the Spanish-American War," he said. "You know, the Mexicans are familiar with the Santa Fe Trail from their trading days."

"Good heavens." Mrs. Grundy spoke as if she were on her last breath, and Mr. Grundy put his arm around her waist. It was a smooth move that he wouldn't dare try in a few years, but that day Mrs. Grundy snuggled against his shoulder.

Mr. Grundy's voice rose with anger. "If this doesn't get the president to declare war, I don't know what will. This is what happens when you let foreigners speak gibberish rather than American. They tell secrets."

The Fondale brothers nodded so fervently their ears waggled. "You're right, Mr. Grundy. I'm in complete concurment," Pinky said.

The news was so disturbing that nobody mentioned the storm outside, which was growing fiercer. I made a few unplanned purchases — a bag of chocolate-covered raisins and Zane Grey's book "The Lone Star Ranger" — completely forgetting the flour and butter I needed.

Snow crept into my galoshes as I walked home. When I looked across the street to where the Benedettos had recently moved, all I could see was the outline of the house and flickers of gas lamps burning in the windows. Art and I had installed electricity the previous year. The current was weak and frequently died during storms. The light was reassuring, though, so I turned on the bulbs in every room before I put away the groceries and brought in wood for the stove.

For half an hour, I stood at the window watching for Art to come puttering down the road on his motorcycle. He worried me. The measles that had taken my parents had left him so weak that he caught every sniffle that came around. I had no choice but to wait it out, though. Art had sold our horse and buggy to buy the motorcycle, and I wouldn't have gone out in this weather anyway.

In those days, the nearest telephone was at Grundy's Market. But there was no one to call because none of the farmers had installed telephones. I told myself Art would spend the night with one of the farmers and catch a ride home in the morning.

I remember watching from the window as Mr. Benedetto and his sons struggled to reach their horse barn. I tried to picture Art in a warm kitchen at Shorty Torgerson's or Old Man Willie's. He'd be drinking coffee and using a slab of cornbread to mop up the last swirls of tomato soup from his bowl. My stomach growled, and I thought about heating up the leftover stew in the icebox for my own dinner.

Instead, I drew a rough map in the window fog, tracing the Santa Fe Trail with my finger. The Mountain Branch over Raton Pass would provide more concealment, but the Cimarron Cutoff was shorter and led straight to Garden City.

A chill edged through the gaps in the window frame.

I loaded the stove with wood, and even though it was mid-afternoon, I opened my folding bed and climbed in, bringing with me every blanket in the house, my chocolate-covered raisins and "The Lone Star Ranger."

Zane Grey was a highly respected, prolific author who managed to bring the West to life with just enough lust to keep it interesting. With a promise to myself to eat only one chocolate raisin per page, I opened the book.

Thirty pages later, I was out of chocolate raisins, but I stood on the untamed prairie with Buckley Duane, a darkly fervent, passionate cowboy who burned with strife but was calm in the face of danger. He'd unwittingly arrived at a table of Mexican gamblers who were quiet, intense and heavily armed. I got up to look out the window. The lamps still burned at the Benedettos'. I could see people moving around. I loaded more wood into the stove and made popcorn with lots of butter and salt before returning to my book.

When I looked up again, it was nearly dark. The storm had grown worse. The furrows left by Art's motorcycle had turned into long loaves of fluffy snow. No one had tracked through the snow for hours, but Cowboy Duane had been shot in the arm by outlaws. He was hiding in a stand of willow trees, so close to his pursuers he could hear them singing around their fire. He waited out a ferocious rainstorm and in the fog that came afterward, slipped away.

I comforted myself by thinking that Mexican outlaws would very likely avoid marauding when it was cold and damp. I relaxed a little, made more popcorn and returned to my reading. Zane Grey's books were somewhat predictable; the lustful part would be any page now. Cowboy Duane met Kate Bland, whom Zane Grey described as a strong, full-bodied woman with full lips and a full-blown attractiveness. She was about my age but married to an outlaw. Duane thought Kate was bitter and overly emotional, but he might make love to her, if only to win the freedom of Jennie, who was younger and unspoiled, with a bosom that swelled under her ragged dress. To this day, I keep my copy of that book on my nightstand with that scene earmarked. I consider it an example of Zane Grey's finest writing.

That night, I marked my place with a shred of candy wrapper. It was nearly midnight. The snow had stopped, the tire tracks were indistinguishable from the yard, and the lights were off at the Benedettos'. I put on three pair of socks and loaded the stove with the last of the wood I'd brought inside.

I dreamed I was Kate Bland — full-bodied, full-lipped and emotional. Cowboy Duane was making his way through the snow to reach me, but the Mexicans were closer, and I cried so much my pillow was soaked.

The next morning, I padded back to the window, shivering. On the street, the wind had created a rippled blanket of white, speckled by the paperboy's footsteps. He'd managed to make it to every house on the block.

I sipped coffee as I searched for news about the Mexican attack. Even back then, the Tribune printed every sliver of Garden City gossip, but it took weeks, sometimes months, for us to get news from the outside world. We could read the morning Tribune and watch its stories unfold that afternoon in our neighbors' yards. But the reverberations of the universe took time to reach Kansas.

I was reading about the early snowstorm when the whine of an engine made me look up, and there came one of the farmers in his truck. I can't remember now who was driving, but I knew Art was sick from the way he got out and stumbled toward the house — hunched over with his arms crossed. At the kitchen door, he didn't bother to stomp the snow from his boots, and little clumps trailed him across the linoleum to a chair where he dropped down, a cocoon of smelly, wet wool.

"Shorty Torgerson is dead," he said.

"Dear Lord, what happened?" I asked.

Shorty and his wife, Ruby, had taken over his father's farm up north after the old man and four of Shorty's brothers died during a cholera outbreak. I knew the young couple had three little boys, although I hadn't seen Ruby in town for years, and when I tried to picture how she looked, all I could see was Zane Grey's Jennie with her swelling bosom.

Art was shivering, so I wrapped him in blankets and poured him coffee. I remember how old he looked as he told me what had happened. He'd pulled a green, moth-eaten wool blanket over his head and trembled so severely, the coffee shook in its cup.

He said a section of the Torgersons' fence had fallen under the snow's weight, and right before sunset, a dozen cattle got out. Shorty led a group of hired hands and neighbors on horseback, and right away, they came upon half the herd, nearly frozen, their rear ends facing straight into the storm.

The men split up. Some rode west to look for the rest of the herd. Art and two others headed back to the farm with the cattle they'd found. Along the way, it got dark, the temperature plunged and the wind picked up. Nobody could see more than a few feet, Art said.

By 8 o'clock, everybody but Shorty had made his way back to the farmhouse. The men in his group said they'd lost track of him in the blowing snow.

Ruby stationed her three boys at the window while she served the fellows coffee and pie. For an hour, they talked about the war, the weather, the war, the weather. Finally they went back out, this time in pairs, roped to their horses so they wouldn't get lost. Ruby wouldn't let the youngsters go, which was good, Art said, because it didn't take them long to find Shorty. He'd gotten lost in the storm and frozen to death less than 100 yards from the house.

Art set his coffee cup on our kitchen table and pulled the blanket higher. He started crying, which I hadn't seen him do since our parents died. He lowered his head into his arms on the table, and I noticed his bald spot had grown to almost the size of my hand. I smoothed his fringe of brown hair. His skin felt feverish, and when he looked up, his eyes were glassy and not quite focused.

I made him eat a bowl of leftover stew and put him to bed. An hour later when I checked on him, he was gone with the fever, muttering nonsense and wrestling with the sheets. All night, I sat beside him, covering him with damp cloths and reading my Zane Grey.

The next morning, Art talked more sense but couldn't get out of bed. He said every joint in his body was swollen, achy and hot. I rubbed mentholated liniment on him with such vigor that he howled in pain. Anxiety still does that to me, replacing the little bit of patience I have with a drive I can't contain.

Mr. Benedetto and his sons were shoveling a path to the street, and I called to them from the back door. Being newcomers to the neighborhood, they must have thought I was a lunatic the way I shouted and waved my arms. "My brother needs a doctor. Send one of the boys to the doctor's house. Dr. Livermore, not Doc Trumble."

A tomb of snow muffled my voice, and Mr. Benedetto's face pulled in on itself in confusion. I'd forgotten that he spoke only a little English. One of the boys looked up, so I shouted "doctor" and pointed in the direction of Dr. Livermore's house. He nodded and shouted at another dark-haired boy. They left a few minutes later, breaking a path in the snow.

A while later, Mr. Benedetto and another son shoveled a tunnel wide enough for a car to drive into our front yard. I handed them a plate of cookies — sugar and pecan, as I recall — then hurried back inside, where I paced between Art's bedroom and the front window for what seemed like hours.

Art was talking gibberish again by the time Dr. Livermore's Locomobile came fishtailing down Fourth Street. Behind the driver's wheel was a bug-eyed Hooch Fondale — he could see in those days. He shimmied the car straight into the snow tunnel and jumped out, nearly falling on the ice as he swung open the double doors on the passenger's side. There lay Dr. Livermore, stretched out on the gurney as if he were fast asleep.

Hooch nudged the doctor's arm to wake him then helped

him out of the automobile and across the snow to where I stood. I opened the front door wide, but only the doctor came in. He greeted me as Julianne Rose, the name only my parents had used, then went straight to the bedroom and pulled the door shut behind him. I listened to their murmured conversation, debating whether to make coffee, when the door opened, and Dr. Livermore waved me in.

He pointed to the foot of the bed to indicate where I should sit, and I remember doing so as gingerly as possible to avoid jostling Art. The doctor and I were so close our knees bumped, and I noticed, as he rifled through his leather bag, that the hairs on his head were perfectly aligned with one another, as if he'd trimmed them only moments before, while Hooch drove along the snowy streets. Such good looks seemed wasted on a man like the doctor.

Art looked at me with shrunken eyes, and I hoped Dr. Livermore's bag might offer up a syringe or powder to dull the pain. Instead, the doctor pulled out his textbook, "Man's Strength and Woman's Beauty." I'd listened to him recite from the book so many times that I'd almost memorized sections. I always marveled over the well-handled leather of the cover and the title that flowed in golden letters like those on a book of fairytales. The doctor fanned backward through the brittle pages, pausing occasionally to run a nicely manicured fingernail across the words then clucking his tongue with obvious aggravation before fluttering in the other direction. Each shuffle of the pages sent out a moldy whiff.

Dr. Livermore lit a cigarette, and I envisioned the book erupting into flames, its only rescue lying inside the partially filled bedpan at Art's side. Tiny ashes flew as he turned the pages, and I chased them with my hands, whacking them dead when they landed on Art's sheets, causing my brother to cry in pain. Finally the doctor spoke.

"It is as I suspected — hereditary rheumatism. Passed along when both parents have unsound bodily constitutions. Your parents seemed prudent. However, they obviously were hiding something."

My mind fumbled. "Truth be told, doctor, rheumatism is an old man's disease, and Art is barely into his 30s."

Dr. Livermore gazed at me through gold-rimmed spectacles. "Clearly, in this case your parents passed over before the onset of the affliction. It follows the same hereditary law that allows for gout, insanity, imbecility, scrofula and consumption. Such conditions begin earlier with each generation and manifest themselves differently in men and women."

Art moaned and rolled slowly toward the wall. When the doctor turned to look, the sun caught his hair, which shimmered with enough pomade to wax my parlor floor.

"Your brother has inherited an unsound bodily constitution, Julianne Rose. You undoubtedly have as well. You may soon begin to notice symptoms of another kind. Certainly both of you should both take precautions about whom you marry. Seek the racehorse, not the farm horse. Marry into the same eccentric race from which you came, and your offspring will be genetically doomed."

Art raised his hand, the finger joints swollen. "What can you do for the pain, Doc?"

"A strict diet of cabbage, with occasional servings of bread and cheese. Julianne Rose must plant your garden with cabbage this spring." He snapped his book closed and looked at me without blinking. "In the meantime, apply hot towels to the joints, and don't be stingy with the liniment. The symptoms will come and go as capriciously as the weather or perhaps the Mexicans and Germans."

Dr. Livermore put the book inside his leather case, and I followed him through the house, out into the snow, where Hooch scrambled out of the Locomobile. At the car door, the doctor leaned toward me and I felt a surge of magnetism. But when he spoke, his breath was so foul it failed to crystallize despite the freezing air.

"Don't forget, Julianne Rose, marriage and motherhood complete the development of the female organs. Seek the racehorse, not the farm horse."

I pulled my sweater tight and hurried back inside.

The Mexicans never attacked, but the United States was fully engaged in a war, in a far-away place that most of us had only read about in books. In April, President Wilson had proclaimed that the United States had a moral obligation to join the war in Europe. Over time, he would draft all men from 18 to 45. Not everyone was happy to participate, moral obligation or not. In the big cities, folks picketed against the war. In Garden City, however, half the downtown store windows featured a recruitment poster showing a girly-man hiding behind the curtains of his mother's house while the soldiers marched past. The Tribune concurred, with a headline that read: "A young man is either a patriotic citizen or a traitor to his country."

First to sign up was the entire Garden City band of 32 trained musicians, half of whom were too young to serve. Next, the Fondale brothers signed up. Pinky later said he'd served on behalf of his hero, Babe Ruth, who was 22 and spoke fluent German but was never called into service. Art filled out his draft card at the courthouse. Later, he told me that under "disabilities," he'd penciled in "none."

Overnight, it seemed, German was no longer allowed to be taught in schools or spoken over the telephone lines. In nearby towns, German businessmen and farmers were tarred and feathered or forced to march around town half-naked. In Garden City, a huge family of German-Russians named the Heidlemyers quit coming into town.

The Tribune reported about a German conspiracy to terrorize Kansas farmers. Three German agents posing as peddlers were caught selling bandages coated with what were originally thought to be leprosy germs and later downgraded to suspected tetanus germs. Until the guinea pigs died, nobody knew for sure.

One day later that month, I came home to find Art inside, with all the curtains shut, looking too much like the man on the recruitment poster. He showed me the rejection notice he'd gotten from the military. On the line seeking the reason for dismissal, someone had written "physical or moral deficiency."

The leafy heads of cabbage in my garden that summer grew into an off-kilter pattern that looked like the Finney County boys practicing marching formations on Main Street. I spent hours weeding, watering, watching and waiting. One week, the sky filled with white speckled butterflies. Too late, I followed the Tribune's advice to kill their freshly laid eggs with a dusting of powdered lead arsenate and flour. I used what the cabbage worms left behind to make sauerkraut. Out of respect for our boys fighting the Germans, everybody began calling it Liberty Cabbage.

We still called it that in 1921, even though the war had been over for three years and prosperity had returned to the point that Garden City was building a swimming pool that resembled an ocean.

GARDEN CITY TRIBUNE · FRIDAY, JULY 1, 1921

PROFESSIONAL FLIRTS FACE ARREST IN GARDEN CITY

Handsome gents who stand on the street corners or parade the streets in automobiles and accost women and girls ought to be arrested for such acts, the sheriff's department states. Several incidents of this nature have been reported recently in Garden City, and the law has determined to make the life of the professional flirt and drugstore cowboy uncomfortable.

CHAPTER 8

The Man with the Yellow Shoes

In the four years since Art's decline began, I hadn't found a husband, but I had grown purple, red, green, spring, summer and winter cabbage in my garden. I'd made cabbage croquettes, scalloped cabbage, cabbage soup and cabbage pork tenderloin. I'd added coleslaw to sandwiches, salads, applesauce and roasted duck. I'd even found a cabbage dessert called Hungarian Sweet Cabbage Strudel, which tasted awful.

Art improved in spite of my meals. He started courting the widow Ruby Torgerson, partly out of guilt over Shorty's death, but mostly because she was a nice lady with three little boys and very little money. Several times a week, he went to her farm. I was fairly certain he wasn't taking a penny for his labor.

One day, I found him checking the fuel level on the motorcycle. He was struggling to screw the cap back onto the tank, reminding me that he'd complained lately of a permanent ache settling in his hands.

"You're going to see the widow?" I asked, and he nodded.

With his driving goggles pulled over his eyes, Art looked like one of the locusts that plagued our harvests every summer. He sputtered down the road in a cloud of brown dust.

I picked up the Tribune from where it had landed in the center of the front porch, impressed by the notion that although the newspaper's editors were challenged to get the facts straight, the paperboy's accuracy was almost absolute. I could only remember one windy day when the newspaper had ended up in the bushes rather than on the porch.

It wasn't a job I could handle. In addition to having concave arm muscles, I'd never learned to ride a bicycle, despite their being all the rage. Art had tried to teach me once when we were younger. I'd fallen right in front of Grundy's. I remember crying over my torn dress and skinned knees while the Fondale brothers tittered.

I'm ashamed to say that I hadn't tried again. The humiliation and pain kept me from enjoying the exhilaration the sport so obviously brought to others.

Maybe I was one of the genetic misfits the scientists were always talking about in the newspapers. I wanted thrills, but I feared their consequences.

That's probably why I hadn't married, although a lack of proposals also played a role. I was curious about the unfolding a man could bring to my world; I wasn't so sure I wanted children. I didn't say that in public, of course, because only peculiar women didn't want children, and they usually just said that because they were barren. As I've said, though, I wasn't one to jump into anything with both feet. The stars needed to align just right for that to happen, and so far, I'd mostly witnessed a bunch of falling stars.

It's possible I was too choosy. Most women in their mid-20s like me were married, with two or three or a half-dozen children. Lately I'd worried that I was becoming the Bernice in F. Scott's story — no fun at a party and so boring that the boys only asked her to dance out of sheer obligation.

I used Grundy's quarter-page advertisement to make my grocery list: liniment for Art, buttermilk and ginger for a cabbage bread recipe I'd found. I also needed more candy. Without the privacy provided by Cora Mae's porch, I'd had to let up on my cigarette habit while the fortune-tellers were in town.

I did the breakfast dishes and washed my face before pinning my hair up off my neck. On the walk to Grundy's in the heat, I worried about Art's plans for the future, which the fortune-tellers claimed was set in stone. He'd courted Ruby for three years now, and I doubted he'd even kissed her. On the other hand, if Art married Ruby, I would become the old maid aunt living on the farm, raising somebody else's children and somebody else's chickens.

I'd worked myself into a sweat by the time I reached the market. Mr. Grundy's electric fan whirled on the counter, and I leaned into it, letting the air tease my hair.

Mr. Grundy nodded a greeting then reached under the

counter and spread candy before me like a deck of cards. It was embarrassing to be so predictable. On the other hand, the smell-feast of cocoa, butter, sugar and peanuts muddled my brain. Which delectable treat did I want? Squirrel Nut Zippers and peppermint sticks would be the longest-lasting; Tootsie Rolls were the cheapest; and Necco wafers offered the greatest variety.

The bell over the door jingled, and in swaggered Pinky Fondale dressed like Babe Ruth, in a long-sleeved, striped shirt and a banded straw hat. The baseball player was making a name for himself, not only on the field but off it. He liked fancy clothes, women and liquor. Pinky had the same affectations but zero skill with a ball and bat.

"Well, if it isn't the Sultan of Swat," Mr. Grundy said, and Pinky grinned.

Whatever words they exchanged next were lost on me because of the man who followed Pinky into the market. He was so handsome he had to have just arrived in town, or I would have heard about it. He was stocky — not fat, but muscular — with a warmth that didn't come entirely from the soaring temperatures outside. He wore big-city clothing — yellow leather shoes and a fashionable, lightweight blue serge suit over a white shirt with a flapping, unstarched collar — and he carried a small leather valise. He tucked his hat under one arm, reached into his suit pocket and pulled out a small black comb, which he raked across his well-oiled hair.

Pinky was jabbering to Mr. Grundy. "The New York City coppers claim Babe was going 27 miles per hour up Broadway. Judge says this time he's tossing him in the clink."

He and Mr. Grundy laughed, but Pinky's friend seemed oblivious, wandering around the store, examining the merchandise. I checked my reflection in the glass display case. Rivulets of perspiration crept down my face, and my hair was a frizzy mess.

"Who's your friend, Pinky?" Mr. Grundy asked.

"This is Jiggs Hilsdorf, just arrived from Kansas City by way of Rosebush. Jiggs, this is Mr. Grundy, and that's Miss Jules Greer drooling over the candy counter." Pinky looked at me with a click of his tongue and a wink, a habit I found to be the most annoying of all his irritating behaviors.

I glanced back just in time to see Jiggs pause at a display of cowboy boots, and the heebie-jeebies crawled up my spine when I remembered Madam Isabella Luna's prophecy to watch for the boy where the boots line the rail.

"Welcome to town, Jiggs. Are you here to help with the harvest?" Mr. Grundy said.

"No, sir, I'm here for the Independence Day picnic." He had a strong voice, like Cowboy Duane's.

"Entertainment, amusement and whoopiment," Pinky said. "Jules will be there, and Cora Mae with her special cake that she fixes every year." He wink-clicked again, and despite myself, I felt my birthmark growing warm.

Jiggs smiled at me as he picked a boot from a long wooden display shelf supporting half a dozen samples of similar yet different footwear. He had brown eyes and a full set of straight, white teeth.

"Jiggs is on his way to California, where they got endless miles of perfect highways," Pinky said. "He drives a 1917 Willys

Knight touring car, a beautilicious machine. When I saw him drive up to the store, I just had to introduce myself."

"Nice car. Must have cost a lot of dough," Mr. Grundy said. "I hear they have golf and tennis in California."

"Beaches too." Pinky sauntered over to stand beside me. "What are you buying, Jules? Snirkles are my best. What's your best, Jiggs?"

Jiggs came over, and with huge hands that were as creamy and smooth as the white keys on my piano, picked up a candy bar wrapped in red and white paper. "I'd say Baby Ruths are my best."

"Of course they are. Named after the world's greatest ballplayer," Pinky said.

Mr. Grundy cleared his throat. "As I recall, they were named after President Cleveland's daughter. Little Ruth Cleveland died in the White House when she was just 12 years old."

I nodded, having read the same article in Life magazine.

"That's ridiculatious," Pinky said. "The girl died years ago; the ballplayer is everybody's hero now. Here, I'll take one of them for my friend and a Snirkles for me." Pinky used a grimy finger to push a dime across the counter.

"Make that two Baby Ruths, Mr. Grundy," Jiggs said. "One for me and one for my new acquaintance. What is your name again, miss?"

"Jules," Pinky said with a grin.

Jiggs stacked five pennies on the counter, and, with his huge hands, delivered the red and white package to me. Our fingers touched, and the wrapper crackled like fireworks on the Fourth of July. I smiled and held it to my nose in what I hoped was a delicate movement. I didn't sniff but breathed in deeply. "Thank you, sir. It smells delicious."

"Named after the baseball player, who I might add is the people's choice for president. That's a singular fact." Pinky held his Snirkles bar to the side of his mouth where he had the most teeth and took a giant bite. "Speaking of presidents, you hear the latest on President Harding? He got his girlfriend knocked up." I blushed, and Jiggs looked away, seemingly taken aback by Pinky's brashness. "It's an actual fact from the Tribune. He and his girlfriend were caught in the act right there in the Circle Office."

"You mean the Oval Office?" I asked.

"That's right, caught in the closet," Pinky said. "Tribune said the Duchess, Mrs. Harding, didn't approve. What did she expect, though, her being a divorcee married to a man five years younger than her?"

He looked at me. "You playing at the Yack-Yack tomorrow night?"

"It's the first Saturday of the month, so I'll be there." I said.

"You'll want to witness the Yack-Yack Club, Jiggs. I can guarantify that. We'll see you there, Jules." Pinky wink-clicked, and I noticed a sugary fragment of candy bar edging its way out of his mouth, onto his shirt and, in a final burst of energy, toward freedom on the wooden floor of Grundy's Market.

———————

I spent most of Saturday working in the garden, pausing occasionally to nibble from the Baby Ruth bar in my pocket. It was a delicious mix of peanuts, chocolate and caramel that stuck in my teeth. A little bit could last a long time.

Art continued to complain of pain in his hands, so for an early supper I made his favorite dish — smoked ham stuffed with cabbage and pineapple — before I was due at the Yack-Yack Club. I cut his food into bite-sized pieces before serving him.

While we ate, I told Art about the new fellow in town without mentioning his nifty good looks, smooth-as-silk hands or expensive touring car. In other words, I didn't tell him much. But the few details I shared gave me an opening to ask about his future with Ruby and her boys.

"They're fine." He grappled with his fork, spearing a chunk of ham onto it, but the meat slid off halfway to his lips and tumbled to his lap.

"Let me help." I stood, ready to clean the mess with my napkin.

"I got it." He used his fingers to retrieve the chunk of ham and stuff it into his mouth. "What would you say if I asked Ruby to marry me?" he asked.

I should have expected the question, and for once, I thought for a moment before I answered. Ruby wouldn't be the world's worst sister-in-law, but how would she deal with Art's rheumatism? I'd visited her on the farm a few times, but she hadn't once accepted my invitations to Sunday supper. Art said it was because she didn't like cabbage, which made me wonder whether she'd keep up with his special diet and rub liniment on his hands and feet. With three growing boys, would she have time?

Finally, I spoke. "That'd be spiffy. She'd be a fool to turn you down. Would you move to the farm or live here? She doesn't seem to take to town life much."

Art shrugged. "First, let's see whether she wants me. Wherever we live, you'll be welcome."

"As the spinster aunt? That sounds dreary, and Ruby might agree. Don't worry about me."

I worried about me, though, especially when I glanced in the mirror that evening as I dressed for the Yack-Yack Club. I looked like somebody's spinster aunt. My face had plumped up, no thanks to the cigarette diet, and my hair was wispier than I remembered. I pinned my unruly waves into place and draped a string of beads around my neck. A puff of rouge and a stroke of lipstick, and I was ready.

I knocked at Art's bedroom door and peeked inside. Art sat in bed, absorbed by a book I'd recently checked out for him at the Finney County library. Despite all the damage inflicted by the fortune-tellers, Sister Margery had done us a favor when she mentioned the artist, Renoir. He was an Impressionist painter who lived with crippling rheumatism. He'd died only a few years before. His paintings in the book were blurry, but his photograph showed no obvious signs of the disease, so I'd given the book to Art, who seemed intent on reading every page.

When I bent to look over his shoulder, he pulled the book away with a glare. He had a Kansas farmer's tan — skin that was dark below his eyebrows and pale above them, where his hat kept out the sun. His hair smelled in need of a shampoo.

"I'm going now," I said. "The Benedettos are home. You'll wave the flag if you have another attack?" He reached for a flag

I'd made — a white pillowcase tied to a stick — and gave it a little wave.

"Don't forget to keep it on your bedside table," I said. "The Benedettos promised to come over if they see it fluttering from the window."

I grabbed my cloche hat on the way out the door. It was a classic summer evening in Garden City — the air thick with damp heat, the crickets chirping. A horse-drawn wagon clattered by, bits of hay drifting from its bed like fireflies, and an automobile's horn twanged a few blocks away. My beads bounced as I walked, each step easing the tension around my shoulders. Rosebushes dipped under the weight of their blossoms, their heavy scent sweetening the twilight as it deepened on every corner. Half a block from the Yack-Yack Club, I could hear laughter and clinking glasses, and smell the rich, buttery aroma of popcorn in the air.

SHERIFF LOCKS UP OLD MAN WILLIE, SPIRITS AND NEGRO

Mr. Willie Armstrong, 72, has been convicted of running an illicit still, fined $400 and sentenced to the Finney County jail for four months. A man his age should be thinking of true spiritual matters rather than the extraction of spirits from sour mash. The sheriff also raided the old Johnson property, now occupied as a colored rooming house. He captured a still that was just ready to be put into operation. The Negro who owned the outfit was locked up in jail.

CHAPTER 9

The Yack-Yack Club

The Yack-Yack Club was named after Yack-Yack bourbon, moonshine out of Chicago that blended iodine with burnt sugar. The crispy, sweet medicinal smell that gave the place its name was masked by the popcorn, which Mick, the owner, kept sizzling all night.

Mick served "near beer," which contained the legal limit of less than one-half percent alcohol. A glass cost 25 cents, which was the same hourly wage he paid me.

Yack-Yack patrons had to work at getting pie-eyed, or they could risk bringing their own refreshments in slim silver flasks that slipped neatly inside pockets, handbags and waistbands.

Mick took the extra precaution of hanging a canvas

awning over the front door and plastering the windows with posters advertising Grundy's Market, the Kansas State Bank and the Electric Theater. The Tribune story about Old Man Willie's arrest had half the town on edge. Mick had installed a screen door for the summer, but the temperature inside still soared with body heat and cigarette smoke.

Mick, wearing the same fedora as he had at the pool, pushed an icy glass of lemonade across the bar toward me when I walked in. He was a sober-looking man, considering his occupation.

I took a sip. "Farmer's Almanac says it's too early for it to be this hot."

He gave me a worried look. "It'll get even hotter when Dr. Livermore shows up. Did you hear he's appointed himself chaperone for the night?"

Occasionally one of our local pastors or city leaders would sweep through the Yack-Yack Club, double-checking that everybody's hands were where they should be and that nothing more than near beer was being served. Apparently tonight was Dr. Livermore's turn.

"Good Lord. That'll put a damper on the dancing," I said.

I put my hat on top of the upright piano, re-pinned my hair and got comfortable on the bench. My warm-up songs drew polite applause. After a while, I launched into crowd-pleasers such as "Toot, Toot, Tootsie! Goodbye." A few couples took to the dance floor.

I loved the piano, the way the keys clipped under my fingers, creating full-scaled songs without the need for any other instrument or a vocalist. My fingers pulled sounds from

10 keys at once while my beads clattered over the keyboard, and my hat shivered on its perch. I was nearing the end of Louis Armstrong's "Heebie Jeebies" when the front screen door slammed and the crowd quieted.

I looked toward the door and hit the wrong chord. Dr. Livermore's spectacles flashed as the crowd opened around him. He wore a freshly starched white collar, a gray bow tie and a black suit with the trousers creased on the sides. He stroked his glistening hair into place.

"Carry on, folks," he said. "The Yack-Yack Club has been the subject of countless complaints of corruption, degradation and prostitution. I'm here as a beacon from the past, to remind you youngsters that dance is the dry rot of society if it fails to follow acceptable moral codes."

Mick cleared his throat as he handed the doctor a sweating glass of lemonade. "Just so we're up to date on that code, doctor … what's not allowed?"

"Cheek-to-cheek dancing, neck-holds and public lovemaking." The doctor read from a pamphlet he'd pulled from his coat pocket, his voice growing louder. "Jazz music with its jerky, immoral steps. Men who cling lustily to their partners, advancing with every passing hour further below the waistline, and the young ladies who provoke such attentions."

"Who invited the fire extinguisher?" a woman whispered.

The doctor swung around, and there was Fanny Grundy, wearing a feathered boa and a plunging neckline.

"You must know, young lady, that goiter is augmented by every inch of neckline exposed. Over time, the thyroid swells until the neck puffs up like a penguin." Dr. Livermore's bow tie shivered with the weight of his delivery. "Boas muffle the throat, creating sore throats and quinsies. The sooner they are discarded, the better."

Fanny's red lips puckered as she fingered the black and white feathers of her boa then the pink flesh of her neck. She laughed and shrugged at her friends. "Then I shall cast off my quinsies." And with a display of drama peculiar to college girls, she draped her boa around the neck of the nearest man, who happened to be Mick, and used it like a lariat to pull his face toward hers until it appeared that she would kiss his lips … then his cheek … then, as it turned out, his earlobe.

Dr. Livermore glared, smoke seeming to eke from the top of his head. Fanny slipped away, however, and I sent her silent wishes for a lifetime of good health requiring few doctor visits. Mick returned to his place behind the bar, took a swig and drummed his hands on the bar's wooden countertop. "Jules, got a few tunes you could play?"

I shuffled through my sheet music while the doctor circled the room, sniffing people's drinks and occasionally patting men's shirt pockets in search of flasks. The crowd remained subdued, and the dance floor emptied. Before I knew it, Dr. Livermore stood behind me, watching as I rejected one song after another.

From the top of the pile, he plucked the music to "Baby Face" then asked, "How is your brother managing on my cabbage diet, Julianne Rose?"

"Sleeping peacefully, thank you. The neighbors are watching over him tonight."

The doctor clucked his tongue, tossing the sheet music

back onto the pile. "It's disappointing that you cannot find joy in the home, a woman's kingdom, where her happiness and contentment reign like sunshine on all whom she serves. Household duties are a source of happiness for women. The want of such occupation creates discontent, sin, disease and barrenness. No wonder Art has health problems."

I didn't understand how such a handsome head could contain such awful thoughts. My birthmark glowed as the doctor moved to the dance floor, calling over his shoulder, "Just watch what you play on your ivories of indulgence."

I sorted through the music again. An hour remained before the Yack-Yack Club closed, and an uncomfortable silence filled the room. People started to leave, and Mick looked at me with eyebrows like question marks over the dark circles of his eyes.

I glanced at my hat, wishing I could grab it and run. Instead, I plunged into the national anthem, which I knew by heart. The song brought nervous laughter as one by one, Yack-Yack Club patrons stumbled to their feet. Dr. Livermore led the singing, his well-manicured hand over his heart.

I played every patriotic song I knew. By the time I reached "Battle Hymn of the Republic," the crowd had thinned. Just as I reached the crescendo, I saw two men moving against the departing crowd. It was Pinky and his new friend.

Pinky surveyed the vanishing crowd, while Jiggs pulled his comb from his pocket and ran it over his hair. They ordered near beers and carried them over to where I sat.

"Splendific music, Jules," Pinky said. "Very much enjoyed by me and Jiggs."

"Thanks," I said. "I think I'll wrap it up with Irving Berlin's new song, 'God Bless America.'"

The two men leaned against the piano while I played, Pinky humming along and toying with my hat. I finished and was reaching for my sheet music when Jiggs took my hand, pulled it close to his mouth and supported it from beneath with his other hand. He leaned into our clasped hands, studying them closely, as if he hadn't seen such elegance since arriving in Garden City. He gently brushed his lips across my lower knuckles.

A sheet of scarlet burst down my face, which was moist with sweat. The scene felt unreal, like we should have been on the big screen. I looked back to where Dr. Livermore was slumped in a chair with his eyes closed, a cigarette burning between his fingers. Jiggs rested his foot on the piano bench, his toes inches away from my backside. His yellow shoes looked freshly polished.

"Where you'd get them golden shoes?" Pinky asked.

"Kansas City," Jiggs said. "Babe Ruth has the same ones."

"Why are you wearing Babe Ruth's shoes?" Pinky asked.

Jiggs laughed. "Lots of folks say I look like the Babe, only more solid, like Jack Dempsey."

"That must be more than one man can stand," Pinky said. "Babe Ruth says you can give up drinking, and you can go to bed earlier, but you can never give up the women, no matter how much money you're offered. 'They're too much fun' — that's what he said."

"You must have read a lot about the Babe to be able to quote him like that," Jiggs said.

"No, no. Babe Ruth says reading is bad for the eyes. He

couldn't hit home runs if his eyes went bad, so he gave up reading and so did I."

Jiggs gave me a look that sent a thrill right through me. "See you at the picnic day after tomorrow," he said.

"Make sure Cora Mae brings one of her special cakes," Pinky said.

As I watched them leave, I couldn't stop thinking about how Jiggs had kissed my hand. Finally it came to me: It was a scene straight out of Rudy Valentino's latest film, "The Conquering Power."

INDEPENDENCE DAY FESTIVITIES AT CITY PARK

Two Bands! Patriotic Address by Dr. T.W. Livermore! Picnic Dinner at City Park! Free Lemonade! Plenty of Shade! Two Big Baseball Games! Doctors vs. Lawyers and Elks Lodge Teams! American Legion Wrestling Match! Grand Fireworks Display!

CHAPTER 10

A Celebration of Independence

Cora Mae's cake for the Independence Day picnic went beyond the wildest dreams of anyone in Garden City. Early that morning, I walked over to see if she needed help. The heat wave seemed to have ended; the air was heavy with moisture, and a bank of clouds was moving in from the north. It would be a shame if it rained on the picnic, but anybody who complained did so quietly. The farmers needed the moisture. They always did.

Outside the boardinghouse, yapping dogs surrounded me. I shouted the names most likely to bring a reaction — Blackie, Brownie, and Whitey — and all but one backed off. I'd never seen this dog before. It had a big dog's head, a small dog's body and the piercing bark of a Mexican Chihuahua. When I tried to swish it away with my shoe, the dog latched onto my shoelace, tussling with it like it was a rattlesnake.

The shoes were new — recently ordered from the Sears catalog. They were pink leather with white ribbons that laced around the ankle. The catalog called them Mary Janes and claimed they were popular among women my age and younger.

Cora Mae stuck her head out the front door. "Tin Tin! Bad boy."

I hobbled toward the house, sweeping Tin Tin along with each step. Finally Cora Mae ran out, dressed in a coral silk robe, her hair in pin curls. When she pried the dog from my shoe, the shoelace snapped.

Cora Mae cuddled the dog, gently tugging the ribbon from its jaw. "Sorry you had such a rough introduction to my new dog. Tin Tin, meet Jules. He's usually all sweetness. He's named after Rin Tin Tin, the screen star. Those aren't your new shoes, are they?"

"They were." I bent over to inspect the damage.

The shoelace was in two pieces. While Cora Mae searched for a replacement, I decided to take a peek at this year's cake. The little dog followed me down the hall and through the door. The kitchen looked like a Renoir painting gone mad. The countertops and floor were cluttered with trickles of colorful frosting, sliced cherries and carrots, white rice and daubs of marmalade. But everything came together in the center of the table, where Cora Mae's cake presided. It was a swimming pool — a miniature replica of the one being built at the park.

Construction was already lagging on the real pool, which so far looked like nothing more than a giant earthen hole.

Cora Mae's cake made it real.

I leaned over for a closer inspection. The center had been cut out and filled with waves of aqua frosting. Patches of dirt were fashioned out of blackberry marmalade. Grass was made of oats dyed green. Rocks were raisins, and bushes were parsley. She'd even used sticks of chewing gum to make a dressing room and a hot dog stand labeled "PP's." Most amazing were the tiny people sitting on Necco wafer picnic blankets. There was the mayor in his peanut top hat, Pinky and Hooch driving by in their newly purchased strawberry Packard, and Dr. Livermore holding a cigarette made of rice. Half the town was standing in the water, with shreds of carrots and maraschino cherries standing in for hair and bathing caps.

Cora Mae came in with my new shoelace, which didn't match the other but would have to do. "What do you think? I've been working on it for days. It'll be my contribution to the pool effort."

"This is wonderful. You've gone overboard again," I said.

She clapped her hands. "Look, here we are, resting on a pink Necco. We're opening our picnic basket."

I shook my head in amazement. "Did I go in the water? You know I'm afraid. What was I thinking? And what on earth are we wearing?"

"You jumped in the water with both feet, and we're wearing one-piece swimsuits, of course."

"Dr. Livermore will have a kitten," I said, although truth be told, I was more interested in how Jiggs would react to seeing me in so few clothes, even if I were just a mixture of sugar and almond meal.

"You know they're wearing swimsuits in the beauty pageant back east. The Fall Frolic?" Cora Mae fussed over the cake.

"It's now called the Miss America pageant," I said, "Which reminds me, have you heard about the new fellow in town? I saw him at Grundy's on Friday and again Saturday night at the Yack-Yack. He's handsome. Only, he's friends with Pinky."

"Pinky's a regular fella," she said. "He's a bit of a goof, but he drives the finest automobiles in Kansas."

I gave her a quizzical look, and Cora Mae tightened the belt of her robe. "Let's go sit on the porch. I want to hear about this fellow. Let me get my hope chest so we can have a smoke."

We settled into our usual chairs, the strange dog resting his head on my foot while Cora Mae rolled two cigarettes.

"He drives a fancy car and comes from Kansas City. I'd say he's got the charisma of Babe Ruth and the solid darkness of Jack Dempsey," I explained. "He's about our age. You should have seen the way he held my hand at the club." I described the scene.

"Jesus H. Christ!" she shouted. "That's straight out of Rudy's latest movie. It was the actress Alice Terry's hand he kissed like that. This fellow isn't one of those professional flirts the Tribune warned about, is he? What's he doing here?"

"He came to town for the picnic."

"I mean what does he do for a living?"

"He didn't say. He could be a lawyer, from the spiffy way he dressed."

"He's not a vacuum cleaner salesman, is he? The Tribune said a new fellow has taken over the Garden City territory."

"Not possible. He's got hands as smooth as silk. Maybe

he's a doctor. He carried a valise. In any case, he'll be at the picnic."

"You'll talk to him, right? Maybe even sit with him on your Necco blanket?"

"I just met him, Cora Mae."

"Jules, we've had this conversation before. You're 26. You could wait your whole life for the right man to come along. The pickings are slim in Garden City, and you're way too picky. Just don't wait too long, or we'll be out here in our rocking chairs smoking pipes like a couple of prune pits."

I never knew whether to trust Cora Mae's advice. She'd been married, so she was experienced. But she also believed that dreams and fortune-tellers could predict the future. On the other hand, she was knowledgeable and a good friend.

"Where did this dog come from?" I asked, scratching behind his ears.

Cora Mae lit the cigarettes and handed one to me. "It was a gift from Pinky."

"Are you carrying a torch for Pinky?"

"A little bit. He's funny, and he's, I don't know, swanky."

"Says you." I'd suspected Pinky was spending time at the boardinghouse, but picturing him with Cora Mae didn't settle well with me. It did, however, give me the opening I'd been seeking since not long after I'd started working at the boardinghouse.

"Cora Mae, you and I are the same age, but you've been married. I've read your True Story magazines and my Zane Greys, but truth be told, I really have no idea about ... you know." My birthmark gushed like a volcano.

She grinned. "Don't believe what you read in your Zane

Greys. I've got drawings upstairs that can explain it. If you do decide to … pet … just relax and let him take charge. If you … go farther … expect it to hurt a little, but don't worry because it can't happen the first time."

I must have looked as bewildered as Fitzgerald's Bernice right before she bobbed her hair, because Cora Mae reworded her explanation.

"The very first time you go all the way, you can't get knocked up — your menses out of kilter — with a baby. After that, it's a matter of luck. It's illegal to send anything obscene through the mail, which of course means anything related to not having babies. All you can get is homemade, shoddy stuff — pessaries, womb veils, douches."

I was about to ask what a pessary, womb veil and douche were, but Cora Mae interrupted. "Don't believe what you've heard about disinfectant douche. Nothing that can clean the tub should be used below the waist, and Lydia E. Pinkham's compound? I've heard it can take a woman into or out of motherhood. Know what I mean?"

I nodded, sucking expertly on my ciggy.

"After the first time, make him wear a skin. The soldiers brought them back from Europe, along with some nasty diseases, although I've heard those can be spread through sharing towels too. Who knows? Just in case, make him use one."

I lifted the little dog onto my lap and kissed his big-dog nose. His breath smelled horrible, and I realized with a shiver of disgust that for the first time, I'd kissed an animal.

GARDEN CITY TRIBUNE · MONDAY, JULY 4, 1921

FREE DEMONSTRATIONS OF NEW APEX SUCTION CLEANER

To the many friends of the Apex Electric Vacuum in Garden City: Come to the Fourth of July celebration today for a free demonstration of the little, 10-pound Apex. Just $10 will put an Apex in your home with almost a year to pay the balance.

CHAPTER 11

The Importance of a Bow

We were late to the picnic. Cora Mae had to dress herself and rearrange me because the ribbon on my hat was wrong.

"True Story says a bow tied like an arrow means you're single but in love. A firm knot means you're married, but a flapping bow shows you're unmarried. If you want a beau, Jules, you need to flap."

I rolled my eyes, tucked my hair beneath my hat and let the scarlet ribbon flap. Pinky and Hooch drove us and the cake to the picnic. It was the safest way to move Cora Mae's swimming pool cake, so I buttoned my lip and sat low in the seat.

The park was crowded. Adults and children competed in contests and games. Dr. Livermore was hopping through the grass in a potato sack, every hair on his head still in shining order. The Garden City band performed on stage while folks sat on the lawn or milled about visiting or examining merchandise sold in booths along the perimeter.

We were headed to the food tables when a rumble of thunder made me look up, and there was Jiggs, handing out pamphlets at the Apex Electric Suction Cleaner sales booth. Good Lord, Cora Mae was right. He was a vacuum cleaner salesman, wearing the same blue serge suit and vest he'd worn the two times we'd met. It still looked fresh.

I pretended not to see him, instead drifting to the next booth over where Fanny sat in black and white checkered stockings, selling merchandise from her father's store. She showed me a new game from China called mahjong and a book of crossword puzzles, which she said were all the rage. "See my stockings?" she asked. "They're a crossword puzzle."

Jiggs came over, smiling with his perfect teeth. "Good afternoon, ladies. Great day for a Fourth of July celebration if those storm clouds don't roll in."

I introduced him to Fanny as I reached for a peppermint. "I didn't know you were in sales, Jiggs," I said.

"Apex Electric Suction Cleaners," he said in a businesslike tone. "The strength and command you women demand."

Fanny giggled. "It's a shame you can't leave your merchandise for a little while. You really should see Cora Mae's swimming pool cake. I hear Jules is wearing a one-piece bathing suit."

I turned crimson, wondering how on earth word had already reached Fanny, who I don't believe had left the booth since we'd arrived less than 10 minutes before. I pulled my hat down to cover my birthmark, and the ribbon flapped in a gust of wind.

"Cora Mae owns the boardinghouse where I work," I said. "She makes the best cakes in town, and every Fourth, she comes up with a different one that's more elaborate than the one before it."

"That explains what's on your cheek." Using two fingers, he cupped my chin — I hoped he couldn't feel the heat it was generating — and with his other hand, dabbed beneath it lightly with his handkerchief. He smiled before holding it up for me to see. It was smudged with aqua frosting, part of the swimming pool. "Listen, Jules, I'm sure my exhibit will be just fine, situated as it is next to the trustworthy Grundy family. Let's go see this cake."

I didn't look up once as we walked through the park, although I could feel a hundred eyes on us. Ahead, a crowd stood at the dessert table, gawking at me sprawled across a wafer, wearing next to nothing. I grabbed Jiggs by the upper arm — it was bulging and steely — steering him instead toward the spicy smell of fried chicken coming from another table.

"That chicken smells heavenly. We should have some before it's gone," I said.

We filled our plates with chicken, watermelon, hard-boiled eggs, corn on the cob and pickled beets, and wandered around looking for a place to sit. Every blanket was occupied except the one where Pinky sat, waving wildly in our direction. He and Hooch were stretched out on a chewed-up blanket with three plates of fried chicken between them. The overwhelming aroma as we settled in, however, was not that of spicy chicken but of yeasty fermentation. I pulled my hat closer to my eyes.

"How's the suction cleaner business?" Pinky asked Jiggs.

"No sales yet, but they'll pick up after my demonstration. That always happens."

"Not according to my brother here. Hooch doesn't think anything good will happen today. Isn't that right, brother?"

Hooch shrugged and stared at us with rheumy eyes.

Pinky carried on. "What happened is, Hooch and I was driving along last night when an animal runs right out in front of us, and plunk, Hooch runs over it, his eyesight being not so good. Never would have guessed such a small animal could make an automobile jump so high."

Hooch gave a horselaugh that turned into a graveyard cough, and Pinky waited for him to stop before he continued.

"Hooch thinks without doubt it's a black cat he's extermined. He stays up half the night worrying about the bad luck headed his way. He even wakes me up, saying we should cancel our plans for Rosebush. Well, this morning on our way into Garden, we see a dead animal in the ditch. Hooch checks it out, and guess what? It was a raccoon."

Jiggs laughed. "Rosebush, you say? What were your plans for Rosebush?"

"What's that?" Pinky opened his mouth wide, so I could see dark pink gums where teeth should be. He shoved in an entire biscuit, squinting at Jiggs.

"You said Hooch wanted to cancel your plans for Rosebush?"

Pinky squinted at Jiggs. "Why you asking about that?"

"I drove through Rosebush on my way here, that's all. There's a diner on the main street — Reddy's it was called — that has the best peach pie in Kansas. A sweet little gal serves it too."

Pinky's eyebrows danced. "Babe Ruth says curiosity killed the cat."

Cora Mae joined us, and I introduced her to Jiggs. When he leaned over to take her hand, I thought he was going to repeat the Valentino scene, but it was only a polite handshake. I caught a whiff of his hair creme as he straightened back up.

"I hear you've made a spectacular cake," he told her.

"That's right." Pinky wrapped his arm over Cora Mae's shoulders, making me shudder. "Jiggs will most defiantly want to see that cake, especially the picnicking gals."

A low rumble of thunder made everybody look up.

"I'll have to see it later," Jiggs said. "Better check on my display and get ready for the demonstration."

Cora Mae and I nibbled on hardboiled eggs as we watched him walk away.

"He's as handsome as you claimed," she said. "A little Jack Dempsey, a little Babe Ruth."

Pinky waved a chicken leg in her face. "Hey now, don't be making googly eyes at nobody else but me."

———

Probably half the homes in Garden City didn't have electricity, but everybody hoped that would change someday soon, so nobody wanted to miss the Apex Electric Suction Cleaner demonstration. Black wires stretched farther across town every day, accompanied by dreams of everything electric — overhead lights, toasters, washing machines, and, if Jiggs had his way, Apex Electric Suction Cleaners.

The wind had picked up. Folks fretted that a storm might

ₑe the crops, but they were also worried it might lead
ₑancellation of the night's fireworks show, a once-a-year
ₙt that thrilled the whole town.

Jiggs had disassembled the suction cleaner into four
ₑections, each of which anchored a corner of the blanket
against the growing wind. Piled in the center was a stack of
twigs and dirt. While one of the Benedetto boys handed out
Apex pamphlets, Jiggs straightened his tie and gave his hair
a last-minute combing. He'd replaced the yellow shoes with
traditional brown wingtips.

From the first words of his presentation, I could tell he'd
dedicated it to memory, an impressive skill. "Ladies of Garden
City, do you worry about unsanitary conditions in your
homes? Do you want a home free of disease-bearing dirt?
Do you view cleanliness as next to godliness? Then the Apex
Electric Suction Cleaner will bring heaven to your home. For
only $10 or ten easy payments over a year, you can have one
today. See for yourself how lightweight it is."

With three fingers, Jiggs hefted the hulking bottom section
of the machine and held it aloft as if it weighed no more than
the oversized kitchen funnel it resembled. He tried to hand it
to Dr. Livermore, who crossed his arms, shook his head and
said, "You folks should know that such devices are the ruin
rather than the salvation of women. For if household duties
be well looked after, a woman's house becomes a paradise, and
she the ministering angel to her husband."

"Ah, yes." Jiggs pulled his hand back. "However, doctor,
you must admit that the ministering angel who's lucky enough
to own an Apex can use the time she saves to perform her

other household duties, such as cooking your favorite cake. What is your favorite cake, doctor?"

"Sour cream," Pinky said in a stage whisper, and a low murmur of laughter erupted as the doctor, his hands balled into fists, turned and walked to the edge of the crowd. Hooch's giggles flared into a fit of coughing and wheezing, further delaying Jiggs' presentation.

Finally, Jiggs cleared his throat and spoke with distinction. "Ladies and gentlemen, with your permission, allow me to demonstrate the Apex Electric Suction Cleaner. Even without electricity, she performs miracles, which I will demonstrate this afternoon before your very eyes. But first, I'll need a volunteer from the audience."

An excited buzz rose up, especially from the Benedettos, who as Catholics believed in miracles. Even the grandmother flapped her fingers in the air, and the sunflower baby in her lap did the same.

Jiggs rubbed his huge hands together as he looked beyond them into the crowd. "Mr. Hooch Fondale, how about you?"

Hooch stood, swiping his mouth with a handkerchief, his protuberant eyes floating over the crowd as if he hadn't heard. Pinky latched onto his elbow and pulled him to the front.

"We'd be happy to volunteer for such a remarkaworthy cause," he said.

I fidgeted with the ribbon on my hat, thinking that Jiggs might have made a big mistake in his choice of assistants, but he looked confident as he shook hands with the brothers before turning to the crowd. "Two trusted citizens of Garden City have agreed to prove, without benefit of magic spells, potions or even electricity, the suction power of the Apex."

Pinky gave a little show of his arm muscles. "The Babe always says not to let the fear of striking out hold you back, so here I go, I guess."

Thunder rolled overhead. People ducked and glanced up anxiously, but Jiggs never hesitated. "Even the good Lord seems to approve of the Apex. Observe, if you will, my handkerchief — white as the driven snow."

"Except for that blue spot. What's that?" Pinky pointed.

It was the frosting Jiggs had wiped from my chin earlier that afternoon. Jiggs chuckled. "It's only a splash of Miss Cora Mae's swimming pool. Nothing compared to what you'll witness if you two gentlemen will just kneel here on the blanket."

Pinky sunk to his knees, put his hands together and pretended to pray. Hooch wobbled, resting one hand on Pinky's shoulder as he lowered himself to the ground. When lightning forked across the clouds, Pinky crossed himself — backward. Hooch grasped the rabbit's foot hanging from the center pocket of his overalls then bent forward to kiss the ground before him. I knew in that moment that Hooch must be the second Spiritualist interviewed by the Tribune.

Jiggs picked up the section of the suction cleaner that looked like a funnel. He placed a handkerchief over the large end then centered it on the pile of debris on the blanket.

"Now, Mr. Hooch Fondale, I'll have you go first. Very gently put your lips to the small end of the funnel." With his hand on the back of Hooch's head, Jiggs pushed gently until Hooch had wrapped his lips over the metal opening. "Now, ever so gently, suck through the handkerchief, just as the suction machine would do if it were plugged into your wall at home."

Hooch pulled away with a frown, not noticing that he had knocked over the funnel. "We don't got electricity at home," he said, and Pinky added, "That's an actual fact."

"That's fine. I just need you to show the fine folks of Garden City what happens when the Apex's magnificent, forceful draw of suction — as replicated by you — is put to work."

Pinky looked at Jiggs. "You want my brother to be a suction cleaner?"

"Precisely," Jiggs said, righting the funnel. "He should inhale lightly, though, as if he were enjoying a cigarette."

"I'd rather have the cigarette," Pinky said, grinning into the crowd.

Hooch leaned over to put his lips on the funnel, but apparently nobody but me noticed that the handkerchief covering the dirt pile had blown away. I was about to say something when a huge bolt of lightning streaked from the sky toward earth, hitting a nearby tree and blasting pieces of steaming bark into the crowd. People screamed, covered their heads from the rain that came next and ran in every direction.

Pinky nearly knocked me over in his panic to escape. When I looked to see whether Jiggs was injured, I saw Hooch rolling on the ground, gasping for air in quick, noisy bursts. His cheeks collapsed, his eyes bulged even more than usual and his face grew red then ashen.

Jiggs was bundling the vacuum parts inside his blanket. He ran after his pamphlets, which were blowing in every direction, then gave up and sprinted toward his car. I was about to head home when Cora Mae grabbed my hat just as it blew off my head. She handed it back to me, shouting over the thunder, "If you want a beau, Jules, you've got to flap."

I hesitated while the rain went from pattering to pounding. When I ran after him, it was like being in one of Cora Mae's dreams. I ran as fast as I could, shouting at him to stop. But my feet skidded in the wet grass, and my hat almost blew off again, and the thunder drowned out my voice. Jiggs was tossing the blanket carrying his suction cleaner into the trunk of his car when I caught up. Neither of us spoke as he opened the car door and I crawled inside.

GLADYS WISENHEIMER'S
Garden of Tidbits

The unmarried ladies will want to read the latest True Story article about men whose instincts overcome them. Such an article, titled "Don't Touch Me, You Beast!" won't be reprinted or even addressed here. It should serve, however, as a cautionary tale before this evening's Independence Day festivities. Watch out for those drugstore cowboys, ladies.

CHAPTER 12

Uncle Sam Protects

Jiggs and I roared down Main Street in the rain, going well above the 12 to 15 miles-per-hour speed limit. I tried not to care about who saw us, and it helped that the streets were empty. We passed Grundy's Market and Dr. Livermore's house. When we drove near my house, I strained to see if Art's white flag fluttered, but the Electric Theater blocked my vision. Surely a few of the Benedettos had returned home from the picnic by now.

Jiggs and I looked at each other and laughed, but neither of us spoke until we'd passed beyond the Garden City limits. I searched my skirt pockets and found two soggy candies. I hated being low on supplies, but I stuck one in my mouth anyway.

"Guess I'm not much of a salesman," Jiggs said.

"You weren't bad. I'd have bought an Apex from you if I had the money. Besides, the Fondale brothers needed to be brought down a notch or two."

Jiggs grinned and searched through his shirt pocket with his giant hand. He pulled out a tobacco tin and a packet of soggy rolling papers, both of which he passed to me.

"You know how to roll?" he asked.

"Not really." I fingered the tin then returned it to him.

As we drove into the countryside, he snapped open a pocket on the car door, pulled out a flask and held it toward me. I tried not to hesitate when I sipped, but my face puckered, and it was difficult swallowing. It was bootleg whiskey.

"You live in this town your whole life?" he asked.

"Oh, no. I was born in Rosebush." I handed back the flask, and he took a mouthful.

"Funny. I've been hearing that name a lot lately." He switched gears, accelerating. "I guess Pinky told you that I'm headed to Hollywood. All my life people have told me I ought to be in the films. I've decided it's time to give it a try."

It was my turn with the flask, and I already felt an edge coming on. I looked out the window. The rain pounded the dirt road.

"I suppose a salesman with your talents could do whatever he wanted," I said.

He looked at me sharply with his dark brown eyes. I hadn't meant to be crude, so I changed the subject. "Watch the road here; it jumps up at you."

"Have you seen ZaSu Pitts in the movies?" I asked.

"She's a Kansas girl. From Parsons, I think," he said. "I'm looking her up when I get to Hollywood."

I nodded and said, "Better slow down. The road gets bumpy here." Why was I such a worrywart? I wished I were like Cora Mae, all smooth and natural. We passed the flask a few more times as the countryside whirled past. We were headed north, weren't we?

We passed the Heidlemyer place, a decomposing sod house that looked as tragic as its history. The entire family of 12 had perished in the 1918 influenza pandemic. A row of splintered wooden crosses lined the yard. Art had gone to school with the mother, Florence. She'd had a baby every year for 10 years, nearly dying with the last few, and now every one of them was buried in the weeds.

"You lose any family to the influenza?" I asked Jiggs.

His driving arm stiffened, the muscle flexing against his sleeve. "Myself, almost. Over at Camp Funston, where I was stationed, over a thousand of us got sick and a bunch died."

"Pinky was there too. Truth be told, he didn't even get sick."

"I suppose I was lucky. I was only there for a month before they sent me to France." He took another swallow from the flask. "I was still sick when I shipped out. It helped that the French women were almost as pretty as you."

I gave him a little smile, no doubt fueled by the contents of the flask. But I realized then that Cora Mae was right. He was a drugstore cowboy. He rested his arm on the seat behind my neck. "I had nine brothers. Never even slept in a bed by myself until I joined the Army, and then I discovered that it's lonely sleeping all alone."

Suddenly he turned off between wheat fields onto a dirt path used by farmers to check their crops. I watched out the window as the rain lightened and condensation crept up the glass.

"We could get stuck in here," I said. "Some farmer will be out here soon with a shotgun."

Jiggs drove another few yards then turned off the engine. Harvest was a few weeks away, and the wheat stalks brushed against the car, whispering and bending forward a few at a time to peer curiously inside before springing back into place. Jiggs tossed the empty flask into the back seat and pulled another from the door pocket.

"That's strong stuff," I said.

"I call it lubrication."

He rolled himself a cigarette and lit it. I wanted one desperately but didn't even ask for a drag off his because, after all, I wasn't a total floozy.

Jiggs blew smoke in my face, making me laugh and hiccup and tear up at the same time. He patted my back gently then moved his hand to my shoulder, making me go rigid with nerves. Only a few men had touched me like that. I turned my attention to the car, running my hand along the smooth leather of the door's interior.

"This car must have cost a bundle," I said.

"I got it on credit from the bank. It's like the suction cleaner — only a few dollars to bring one home and years to pay the balance."

We climbed out of the car into the wheat field. Wherever we were, they hadn't had as much rain as Garden City. The dirt path was only damp. The nutty smell of wheat came from the fields. The sun had disappeared. Jiggs went to the trunk and pulled out his blanket. The vacuum cleaner parts clunked to the car floor.

"Where does a person sleep when he's driving from city to city?" I asked.

"Places like this or traveler's campgrounds. They're free. The tents are set up ahead of time. There's a real nice one on the road to Rosebush. Maybe I'll take you someday."

"But aren't you going to Hollywood to see ZaSu?" I said teasingly, watching him spread the blanket over the ground. He sat first then reached for my hand and pulled me down. The ruts made it uncomfortable. He kissed my fingers like he had at the Yack-Yack Club then looked into my eyes. "You've got an awfully kissable mouth."

I recognized the line from Fitzgerald's story "Bernice Gets a Bob." An admirer of Bernice's cousin had used it on Bernice in an attempt to let him kiss her. It was a comment he'd used on girls at college proms when the time was right. And how had Bernice responded? She'd turned an ungraceful red.

I looked into Jiggs' chocolaty eyes, wondering if he had any original lines, then put my arms around his strong neck and said, "No one has ever said such a thing about me."

"Then no one is a fool." His breath smelled of cigarettes. "Cash or credit, sweetie? Kiss me now or later?"

I didn't answer, raising my face toward his until he kissed me, slowly tracing his incredibly soft lips over mine. I'd never felt such tenderness, and it stirred me to my very depths. I could have gone on like that all night, but suddenly he lowered me to the blanket and pulled himself on top of me. He was heavy, making it hard for me to breathe. I forgot about that when he nuzzled my neck with his lips.

"Your perfume smells delicious. You know they banned perfume from the Miss America contest?" he said.

"Poor Miss America, but I'm not wearing perfume."

"They say it swayed the judges, made them use poor judgment. You ever use poor judgment, Jules?"

I was dizzy with poor judgment, so I repeated myself. "The farmer will be coming at any moment with his shotgun."

"You have a beauty mark right here." He touched my forehead then ran his finger down my face and inside my blouse. I looked at him closely. His hair was still perfectly placed, his luscious hair creme smelling like lilacs.

I wondered what Zane Grey's Kate Bland would do in my situation. With her full lips and full-blown attractiveness, would she use common sense or head full-on into a precarious predicament?

"Are you a drugstore cowboy?" I asked.

"Maybe," he said. "I've got a few girls around who call me sweetheart. Is that bad, though? It only means I've perfected the techniques that can make a lady lose her mind."

I tried to sit up. "I'm not sure I want to lose my mind. You should know, I've never done this before. I'm not sure I should."

"Baby, it's 1921. Time to live it up a little. How old are you, anyway?"

"I'm, well, old enough, I guess."

"Then we'll take it nice and slow, Kate. I guarantee no regrets."

"My name isn't Kate," I said.

"Damn. My apologies. You look like a Kate, that's all. You know, rough and ready."

"I don't look like a Bernice?"

"Lord, no. That's my mother's name. Let's not think about her right now." He started unbuttoning my blouse.

"You should know, I don't want a baby," I said, slipping back down on the blanket.

"Trust me, doll. It can't happen the first time. Besides, I've got big plans that don't include babies or weddings."

The muffled explosions of fireworks came from the direction of Garden City, followed by the crowd's appreciative murmurs.

"Is that coming from the park?" I asked. He listened for a moment then nodded as he pulled something from his pocket that crackled like the Baby Ruth bar he'd given me.

"Let's have our own fireworks display, sweetie."

Later, on the quiet drive back to Garden City, my mind drifted to Gladys Wisenheimer's column in that morning's paper. I'd read the True Story article she'd mentioned. The man had a slick, handsome head with blue eyes and thick lips that repulsed the young woman. She'd fled him once, but he'd returned to find her in the dead of night, alone and wearing a negligee.

The man may have looked something like Jiggs, only with blue eyes instead of brown, and I'd found Jiggs anything but repulsive. In fact, I had no regrets. I had houdinized. I was 26 years old and might never have another chance. Now I knew what the other women whispered about, what the books and magazines intimated. Only a tiny swirl of concern turned in my stomach.

"You're sure I won't have a baby?" I asked.

Jiggs smiled, handing me a cigarette he'd rolled specially for me. "Like I said, it never happens the first time. But just in case, that crackling noise you heard? It's a little guarantee against slip-ups, straight from France, compliments of the United States military. The French women like to say that Uncle Sam protects."

GARDEN CITY TRIBUNE · WEDNESDAY, AUG. 10, 1921

KANSAS NATIVE "FATTY" ARBUCKLE AT ELECTRIC THEATER

Roscoe Arbuckle was born in Smith Center, Kansas, at the grand weight of 13 pounds! He does remarkable stunts, despite his bulk. See him in his new film, "The Life of the Party," at the Electric Theater today!

CHAPTER 13

Fatty Arbuckle's Girlfriend

Jiggs disappeared from Garden City after Independence Day. I wasn't sorry to see him go. All along, I'd known he was a drugstore cowboy. He'd told me as much that night in the wheat field, and I'd played along because in truth, I wanted to see what it was like. I had no desire to marry him, but I also didn't want to wither away and die without ever having experienced it. Actually, it was easier not having him around town, not having to make eye contact.

I tried to focus on what little excitement Garden City had to offer. Roscoe "Fatty" Arbuckle's film "The Life of the Party" was showing at the Electric. Cora Mae and I had looked forward to seeing it all summer, and we'd made plans to meet at the theater for a Wednesday matinee.

I made Art cabbage rolls for lunch, adding twice the amount of nutmeg called for in the recipe, until the sweet nuttiness almost overcame the sourness of the cabbage.

"Are you going to Ruby's today?" I stuck half a roll in my mouth.

"I don't know. Stop fussing," he said, picking at his food.

Art had been especially quiet lately, which meant the house fairly rang with silence. I wondered if his courtship with Ruby had gone sour, but decided not to ask.

"Want me to see if the library has another book on that painter?" I asked.

"No," he said, and pushed away from the table.

I worked in the garden, sorted through my baking supplies and made a list for my next trip to Grundy's before heading downtown to the theater.

Cora Mae arrived 15 minutes after our pre-approved time with an unapproved guest. Pinky's presence made me feel like a third wheel. The theater was packed, so Cora Mae and I went in to find seats while he got refreshments.

"Why do you go out with him, Cora Mae?" I glanced around to see who else was there.

"Don't be a flat tire, kiddo. We talked about this before. He's a got a few quarters in his pocket, which makes him a big cheese. Plus he's good for a few laughs." Occasionally she talked like Madam Isabella Luna, which was irritating.

"He's a big cheese that smells bad," I said.

Pinky brought popcorn, candy and soda. Cora Mae and I sat together. The seat we'd saved for him was next to her. He wanted the middle seat, though, and stood there with his fanny in our faces until I moved to the empty seat. With a satisfied grin, he nestled between us then whispered in my ear. "I got you one of them Baby Ruth bars named after the ballplayer. You might have heard he made his 25th homer."

"Thanks, Pinky. It's been front page news in the Tribune for a while."

"I guess you also heard my phonyfeit friend Jiggs took off for Hollywood. Guess he figured his chances of doing business in this town got swept away when his 10-pound suction cleaner nearly put my brother 10 feet under."

He paused as if expecting amusement or empathy, but Cora Mae was preoccupied with opening her candy, and I was in a bad mood. The lack of response didn't faze him. "Maybe you heard that Jiggs forgot his valise at the picnic. Left a message for me at Grundy's that if it showed up, I was to send it to his company's headquarters in Kansas City."

Cora Mae was listening now. "Did it show up?"

"Mailed it off yesterday, minus my reward." With a grin, Pinky looked down, and Cora Mae and I followed his eyes. He was wearing Jiggs' yellow leather shoes.

The movie sputtered to a start, and I settled into my seat, trying to forget about Jiggs, Pinky and the yellow shoes. In a single smooth motion, Pinky stroked his pomaded hair and put his arm around Cora Mae.

"Can you see them words on the screen, doll? I forgot my cheaters." He spoke in his street voice, and two rows ahead of us, both Mrs. Hunter and Mrs. Garofalo turned around to glare. Pinky couldn't read; he hadn't finished third grade. Cora Mae just nestled her head on his shoulder and whispered the words into his big, fleshy ear.

Fatty Arbuckle faltered across the big screen. I bit off a chunk of my chocolate bar, and an unsettled feeling came across me. I usually relished being at the Electric, with its plush velvet seats and freshly polished floor. Today, the seats felt lumpy and the floor varnish overwhelming. A stickiness on the floor snagged my shoe. I tried not to think about what it might be. Cigarette smoke drifted across the flickering screen like black clouds in a dry lightning storm. The cabbage rolls turned in my stomach.

I whispered to Cora Mae that I'd be right back, then hurried toward the lobby, nearly blinded by the movie projector's light, and barely reaching the water closet before upchucking into the toilet bowl, which on previous visits had seemed so pristine.

After the movie, Pinky drove us to Grundy's Market in his maroon Packard. It was no mystery how Babe Ruth could afford his, but I shuddered to think of how Pinky might have acquired one. It probably involved bootlegging. Downright theft or bank robbery, rampant as they were in Kansas, seemed beyond the mental capacities of Pinky and Hooch.

We sat on stools fastened to the floor near the counter while Mr. Grundy spooned acidic-smelling powder into tiny bottles. The smell made my stomach jump. The place reeked of perfume, cigarettes and medicines. Pinky ordered a sundae for he and Cora Mae to share while I tried to keep up the conversation. "Did either of you read in the paper about Fatty Arbuckle's trial?" I asked. "They're saying he killed that actress in San Francisco, violated her in a hotel room."

"Probably smothered her," Pinky said. "The fella weighs 320 pounds. That's an actual fact."

"True Story said that the girl got knocked up," Cora Mae

said. "She must have paid somebody to ... you know, straighten out her menses. She must have been desperate."

"A girl could get that way, I suppose," I said.

Mr. Grundy had finished with our order and returned to measuring powders into bottles. I wondered if whatever he was working with could stop the rumbling of my stomach.

Pinky took a bite of his sundae and opened his mouth to speak. A cobweb of vanilla ice cream stretched across his tongue, and blood-red maraschino cherries peeked from the crevices of his teeth.

"Why'd she let that happen to her?" he said. "Fatty is a decent fellow. The Tribune said it was a singular fact that the actress was a floozy. Said she'd had operations to remove more than one illegible bastard, if you know what I mean."

"That's a hateful word, Pinky," Cora Mae said.

"What's so bad about illegible?" Pinky said.

"You know what I mean," Cora Mae replied. "Besides, maybe Fatty shouldn't have left her alone to face the scandal. If he really is a salt-of-the-earth-type fellow, maybe he should have done right and married her. He's already married, though, isn't he?"

"I don't think Fatty is the type to marry every gal he flings with, and my guess is he told her that from the start." Pinky gave his disgusting wink-clink. "Anyways, why would he tie the knot with a girl like that? Ruin his career in Hollywood."

CHAPTER 14

The Girl Who Loved Not Wisely But Too Well

Cora Mae sifted through a stack of True Story magazines
to find the article that had guaranteed it couldn't happen the
first time.

"True Story?" I asked. "That's where you got the
information?"

She ignored me, and I realized then that her missing-out-
on motherhood advice had indeed come from a magazine that
also gave tips for talking to little green men from Mars. My
monthly curse was five weeks late. I'd always been as regular
as clockwork, but now all that was regular were my trips to the
outhouse with fingers crossed to see if my cycle had returned.

Cora Mae's iced tea soothed my nervous stomach. I drank slowly, watching the sky lower the sun earthward. I'd removed my stockings and shoes, which pinched after a day of housecleaning, leaned back into the leather armchair and propped my feet on a wooden grocery crate.

"This was a goodie." Cora Mae, wearing a sky blue robe, handed me a magazine, its page earmarked to a story called "Mother or Murderess?"

"Abandoned," it began. *"The joy of love — nothing left but the cold ashes of disillusionment! Frantic with fear and shame — sneered at by her friends, cut out by her family — was this young girl, with a clear soul, to turn, cowered and criminal, because of the prejudice of a hypocritical society? Shall the rottenness of the man she loved and worshipped force her to go through life with the 'crimson brand' on her brow? The choice must be made and with the whole world looking on. It is a pitifully tragic story, as old as the world. The story of a fresh, innocent, beautiful girl who loved not wisely but too well."*

The story's character was me — a little bit, anyway.

Cora Mae waved another magazine over her head. The cover portrait showed a young woman with blond hair swept into waves against bare shoulders that peeked through a sheer scarf. She had rosy cheeks, lips that curved into a shy smile and eyes that were bluer than any color found in nature. The headline was "Wedding belles share first-night secrets."

Cora Mae's shimmering robe sent the magazine skating across her lap as she turned the pages. She paused a few times to center it before finally tossing me a triumphant look. "Here it is — the wedding night story: 'Dora was an unspoiled bride, thus liberated from the worries of fructification on her wedding night.'"

She gave a small shrug of satisfaction, and if I hadn't been about to cry, I would have laughed. People call me naive. "Fructification? Does that mean what I think it means?"

"It's like in the Bible — be fruitful and multiply. It means calendar fear. Look, there's even a photograph of the people in the story."

"Let me see that." The photograph showed a well-dressed couple gazing into each other's eyes. He frowned sternly; she beseechingly clasped his hands in hers. "These people are models, Cora Mae. The magazine paid them to pose like this. How many times have I told you that everything in here is made up? In fact, I recognize this girl from another issue. Remember 'Don't Touch Me, You Beast'?"

I held up the magazine so Cora Mae could see the girl's face. "You're right," she said. "The girl was named Marjorie, and the fellow couldn't keep his hands off her. Which month was that?"

She flipped through the pile of magazines again while I turned the pages of the one I held. There was an advertisement for three different styles of sham, look-alike wedding rings that could be ordered through the mail for a free 10-day trial. According to the magazine, the payments were so small and easy, the money wouldn't be missed.

"Maybe I should buy one of these cheap wedding rings and tell everybody I eloped with a traveling salesman, which is only half-lying," I said.

"I've seen that advertisement. I like the middle one best,"

Cora Mae said.

I sunk lower in my chair. Everyone had reassured me that a baby couldn't happen the first time. So much for the good life I was destined to create.

"Good Lord, what should I do?" I asked Cora Mae.

She crossed her legs and sat silently for a few moments. I wiped my eyes on my sleeve. The ocean of tears I'd shed lately had made the skin beneath my eyes chapped.

"I think you went all the way with Jiggs because you subconsciously remembered Madam Isabella's advice to houdinize," Cora Mae said. "Maybe you were thinking this was your one big chance."

"Don't psychoanalyze me, Cora Mae. Plus, you're the one who told me I needed to flap."

"But Freud says dreams are wish fulfillments and that the subconscious mind … "

I interrupted her. "I never dreamed of getting knocked up, and my subconscious was unfortunately being informed by a ridiculous magazine. I knew Jiggs wasn't the marrying type. He was handsome. I was tipsy. I wanted to experience … the experience."

"Pinky gave me the salesman's address, for what it's worth. His boss might know where to find him." Cora Mae pulled a crumpled calling card from the pocket of her robe and handed it to me. It was the address for the Apex Electric Suction Cleaner headquarters in Kansas City. On the line where the name belonged, someone had written: Southwest Kansas District Salesman.

"I'm not even certain Jiggs is his real name. Probably not,

because who'd name a child Jiggs? He told me his mother's name is Bernice. Jiggs must stand for something else. Anyway, I'm sure he'd deny the whole affair. I was just a flash in the pan to him."

"He should at least give you money, unless he's some kind of lounge lizard, which he probably is. Did he use anything that night?"

I gave her a puzzled look, and she added, "To avoid fructification."

"Yes, of course; he used a skin. Like I said, I'm not a dumb Dora. It didn't work."

Cora Mae fingered the magazines in her lap as if the answer was there if she could just find the right issue. Her uncertainty made me feel worse. I paced across the porch, pausing to stare into the yard, where an eternity ago the fortune-tellers had stood. We should have sent them away. Look where their visit had taken us.

Cora Mae patted my chair so I would sit again. Tin Tin jumped onto my lap, and I wrapped my arms around him. I cried into his fur, but the dampness made him smell worse than he already did, so I checked my emotions.

"What if I die trying to get rid of this baby, like Fatty Arbuckle's girlfriend?" I said. "What if I die having it? My aunt died that way after three days of excruciating, unbelievable pain. The baby died too."

Cora Mae nodded. "My cousin knew a lady whose baby was as big as Fatty Arbuckle when he was born. The doctor had to pull it out with pliers."

"Pliers? Jesus H. Christ." I craved a cigarette, but the

thought made me nauseous.

"Something like that," Cora Mae said. "The baby's head was dented on both sides, and its brain was completely squashed. They kept it alive at an asylum for a few years."

"This kind of talk isn't helping, Cora Mae. I'm already seeing myself as a canceled stamp for the rest of my life."

"It won't be that bad. Have you tried moving furniture or taking a little tumble down the stairs? I've heard that can work."

"I've rearranged the parlor twice. I even tried moving the piano. What about Lydia's Compound? I'll bet Mr. Grundy carries it at his market."

"I told you there's nothing like that you can count on. Can you butt me, kiddo?" Cora Mae said.

"What you?" I asked.

"Give me a ciggy," she said, pointing to a tin of cigarettes she'd already rolled. We both lit up and my stomach took a dive. Cora Mae leaned her head back against the chair and was quiet for so long, the tears started to bunch up in my eyes again.

Finally, she spoke. "I know a lady in Topeka who sets women right. She'll want $50 cash up front. It doesn't always work, and it can go wrong, but it's better than nothing."

I felt a sliver of encouragement for the first time in weeks, although I'm not sure why. With train fare, a visit to Topeka would cost my life savings and maybe my life. I'd heard about girls who'd died having the operation. The big city newspapers that arrived in the mail at Grundy's published the names of the women involved and printed more stories if they were charged with a crime.

Cora Mae poured herself another iced tea. "Remember the family that lived north of town? The Heidlemyers?"

I thought about the house with the crosses out front that Jiggs and I had driven past.

"I remember. The influenza took the whole family."

"That's not what happened." Cora Mae pulled on her cigarette. "The old man and nine of the 10 children passed from the influenza. Florence suffered an altogether different death — a miserable, unnecessary, evil death."

I leaned so far forward in my chair that Tin Tin nearly fell out of my lap. I held him tight while she told the story.

"Florence had a funny hitch in her walk. I don't remember it because she never came to town, but Doc Trumble told me about it. He said it was from having too many babies. She got torn apart and never healed. He helped her deliver the last few and every time, she almost died. But her husband wouldn't leave her alone. So of course, right after the influenza took him and all but one of the children, Florence figures out she's expecting again."

Cora Mae tightened the belt around her robe and continued. "She asks Doc Trumble to help her. He's done the operation on horses and cows, but he's afraid he'll kill Florence. He asks Dr. Livermore for help, but that was a mistake. Dr. Livermore calls it murder — a crime of the deepest dye. When Doc Trumble tells Florence nobody can help, she goes blooey.

"Anyway, one afternoon I'm at Doc Trumble's office with Little Whitey. Or was it Old Goldie? It doesn't matter. The cat had gotten her foot caught in my neighbor's mousetrap and had an awful infection. Doc was looking her over when a little boy — the only child of Florence's not dead from influenza — comes tearing up on a bicycle. He's smeared with blood and runs to me for a hug, crying about how his mother is dying.

"We jump in the doctor's pickup and go out there. You think that place looks miserable from the road? Well, it was worse inside. Trash was piled up, and the animals hadn't been let out or fed for days. Worst of all is the blood. It's everywhere. Florence is bathed in it from head to toe. She's on the floor, naked and dead, and — this is awful — there's a crochet needle sticking out from between her legs. She'd been digging around inside herself, trying to get rid of the baby.

"All Doc and I can do is say a little prayer and mop the place up, although the smell was enough to bring up your breakfast. We buried Florence in the yard with the rest of her family and put the boy on a train to go live with an aunt in Iowa. Everybody thought the entire family died of influenza. Doc Trumble and I just never disagreed."

I gripped Tin Tin's fur. "Wasn't Dr. Livermore suspicious?"

Cora Mae shook her head. "It was during the influenza pandemic. Remember, he was going all over the countryside trying to help people and his own son died? Dr. Livermore came down a few notches on the ladder of self-righteousness when that happened. Needless to say, seeing Florence like that gave me nightmares for weeks. They were a hundred times worse than my vampire dreams. But one night she appeared, floating and white and not a bit bloody. She said it was criminal that she'd had to take such drastic measures and that no woman should be forced to do what she did. I didn't disagree, and that's when I started making inquiries and came across a helpful lady in Topeka. I've sent more than one girl her way."

I shook my head in disbelief. "I'd always thought of Florence as a saint, fighting to her death for those children."

Cora Mae's robe swished as she crossed her legs. "I'd say that's exactly what happened."

The sun was starting to set, and Art would need dinner soon. I told Cora Mae I'd think about my options over the next few days.

"Don't take too long," she said. "The lady won't do it after the baby comes to life."

"And when is that?" I asked.

"Five months, I guess. When you feel it moving."

On the way home, I sucked on a piece of peppermint candy to clear my tobacco breath and, if I was lucky, my head. I couldn't believe I'd gotten myself into such a fix, and I had no idea what to do about it.

I didn't want to force marriage on Jiggs or whoever he was. It would be OK if he heard about my situation from Pinky and returned of his own volition. No one would know of my indiscretion if we married right away. He could sell vacuum cleaners; I could give piano lessons. We could buy a house in Garden City or move somewhere interesting, like Kansas City. If he wanted, we could have more children who would inherit their father's handsome looks and my musical abilities. But what if Pinky found Jiggs, and Jiggs told me to mind my own yard? I wasn't sure I could stand the humiliation. I was also pretty sure that I didn't want to marry a man who had a bunch of girls calling him sweetheart.

If I had the baby, nobody would hire me to play for weddings or funerals. Mick down at the Yack-Yack Club wouldn't mind, if I used discretion. But who would take care of the baby? I'd have to give it away to strangers. I'd never heard of a woman keeping her out-of-wedlock baby.

I looked at the stars as I walked, wondering if my parents somehow knew of my predicament. My father would have been outraged at the blight on our family name. My mother would have insisted I leave town until afterward. Every once in a while, a Garden City girl disappeared for six or seven months then reappeared as if nothing had happened. Everybody knew why, though.

At home, I tried to fix Art's dinner but ended up upchucking in the outhouse, which was the worst place to get sick because the smell came right back at you. Art worried that it was serious, and although he was right, I told him it was just the cabbage smell making me sick.

It was still early evening, but I stretched out on my folding bed, looking forward to a few hours of nothingness. I'd just drifted off when Art called me into the kitchen. He'd set the table with our mother's lace tablecloth and finest china, and he served me a bowl of steaming chicken rice soup.

"Maybe this will help," he said.

I should have dispelled his worries right away. I regretted that I didn't as events unfolded. The soup did help, despite being from a can. Art headed to bed, so I read about poor Franklin Roosevelt in the newspaper. He'd been diagnosed with infantile paralysis and wasn't doing so well either.

I heated water on the stove, washed the dishes and stacked them to dry on a towel. My mother's lace tablecloth made me melancholy. I wiped a few tears on it before tucking it away in a drawer. Then I turned off the light, climbed from the kitchen chair onto the table and jumped.

CHAPTER 15

A Cobweb Against Danger

My landing was awkward — one ankle bent unnaturally when I landed. I must have hit my head too, because the next thing I knew, Art was kneeling in front of me, holding a glass of milk.

"What on earth?" he asked.

I propped myself up on one elbow, reaching behind with the other hand to explore the folds of my skirt. They were as dry as if they'd just been brought in from the clothesline. Not a trace of the sticky wetness that would have returned my life to normalcy. My head and left ankle, however, throbbed. Art set his glass on the floor, and the look of fear on his face made me summon up every last shred of my purported naivete.

"I must have fainted from exhaustion, or maybe it was a mouse. Have you seen a mouse in here lately?" I couldn't look him in the eye.

"Damn!" he shouted. I'd never heard Art curse, and my eyes grew wide with genuine surprise. "Well, I'll set a trap for it later. We need to get you to Dr. Livermore's hospital."

"What?" I protested. "No, no. Really, I'm fine. Just a little twist of the ankle."

"You were out cold, Jules. Does it hurt too much to move? I could get the Benedetto boys to help me carry you. It's awful late, though."

"I'm OK. Just help me stand." Art helped me up, but the pain was sharper than I'd imagined, and I collapsed, lightheaded, into a chair.

"Stay right here, Jules. I'll bring the motorcycle around."

I clung to Art as we rode the empty streets, the sputtering of the motorcycle cracking the nighttime silence like a shotgun. Dr. Livermore's hospital was on the first floor of his home, only a few blocks away. Even at its top speed, though, Art's motorcycle didn't go fast enough to stir up a breeze.

Garden City folks joked about how the doctor made his nurse, "Maudlin" Maude Murphy, answer the door and tell patients to wait in the foyer, sometimes for hours. The night we arrived, it was after midnight, and the doctor opened the door himself. In all the years I'd been Dr. Livermore's patient, I'd only been in his house once, and that was to fetch him when my parents were sick. Most of the time he made house calls.

So it was disorienting when he instructed Art to help me down the hall to an examination room that must once have been the doctor's dead son's bedroom. The room smelled like a young man's sweat and hair tonic. An eye chart and diagram of the human body hung on the wall as well as a drawing of the night sky and a banner with the Fort Hays State College mascot, a lunging tiger. The boy had been a student there when he'd died.

Art helped me to the bed. For once, he was downright chatty, although his timing couldn't have been worse.

"I was getting a glass of milk when I found her under the kitchen table, doctor. She must have fainted and hit her head. She's been sick a lot lately, upchucking in the outhouse. She blames the cabbage, and it does stink the place up. You don't think it's the influenza, do you?"

"I'll give her a thorough examination, Arthur." Dr. Livermore motioned with his head for Art to leave the room.

Now I was the one chattering nervously. "You know how Art worries unnecessarily. I fainted because a mouse ran through the room and right across my shoes. Between you and me, that cabbage diet of yours works miracles for Art, but the smell doesn't sit well with me, which is why none of this is necessary."

"I'll decide what's necessary, Julianne Rose." I despised him calling me that. He unlaced the shoe on my uninjured foot and, without removing my stocking, kneaded the bones of my ankle and toes so gently it almost tickled. I gave a little shriek when he moved to the injured side.

"I'll have to cut the lace to get your shoe off," he said more to himself than to me. They were my pink Mary Janes, and it hurt to see them damaged further, especially by him. I rose up on my elbows, watching him work and bracing for the pain, but he gently snipped the lace — the one Tin Tin had torn — then eased the shoe off and peeled away my stocking. My ankle was purple. He probed it slowly until I was at the very edge of relief. But what happened next made my stomach plunge.

Dr. Livermore grasped the hem of my dress and folded it neatly to my upper thighs. He inspected my bare calves, my knees and thighs, and I dropped back onto the bed, staring at the ceiling in humiliation. He'd promised a thorough examination, but this was too much. Without lifting my dress higher, Dr. Livermore kneaded my stomach and pressed against my innards until the air left my lungs. Surely he couldn't tell.

He walked to his desk, and I realized for the first time that he wore an Oriental robe and slippers. His college textbook, "Man's Strength and Woman's Beauty," rested on his desk like a cherished family Bible, and while he turned its pages, I tried to recover my dignity, sitting up with my feet hanging over the edge of the bed and rearranging my dress. He shimmied a pack of store-bought cigarettes from his robe pocket, and I badly wanted to ask for one. Instead, I retrieved a single, blessed peppermint from the depths of my skirt pocket. I stuck it in my mouth just before he looked at me and spoke.

"The basis of the female character is gentleness. Woman has less violence in passion but greater depth of feeling, which provides the foundation for the divine virtues of love, faith, hope and fidelity."

The unlit cigarette bobbled in his mouth as he spoke. I watched, mesmerized. "Woman lives not for herself but to serve others, just as the fruit tree serves its fruit." His voice rose like a minister's whose congregation was sleepy.

He finally lit the cigarette, and I inhaled deeply. "Julianne Rose, since the day I diagnosed your brother's hereditary degenerative disease, I have anticipated the escalation of your own. Do you remember that day?"

"Of course. Art's rheumatism has responded nicely to the diet." *Where are my shoes? My almost new shoes?*

"And now here you are, carrying the fruit of your sinful ways in your womb, doing what you can to shake that very fruit downward to an early death. How dare you?"

My Mary Janes were damaged, I know, but my other pair of shoes had thinned at the toes. I wouldn't leave my new shoes at Dr. Livermore's.

"Indeed, an unhealthy tree like you will bear unhealthy fruit. Nevertheless, to attempt, as you've done, to further damage the fruit in your womb is tantamount to murder, and if you continue on such a path, I'll see that you pay the price."

My feet touched the floor. With or without my shoes, it was time to find Art and hobble forth.

"Art, let's go," I called to the ceiling. "Doctor, can I please have my shoes?"

"Jumping off a kitchen table is a timeworn choice of women like you, Julianne Rose. Such women are unwilling to face the consequences of their actions. It's a symptom of the moral decay and weak-mindedness of the out-of-wedlock mother."

Suddenly I was as enraged as the tiger on the wall. I might have been an out-of-wedlock mother, but the only smell of decay in the room came from the yellowing pages of Dr. Livermore's old textbook. Dr. Livermore read aloud from it: "An attempt to procure an abortion is a crime of the deepest dye, a heinous murder, attended, moreover, with fearful consequences to the mother's own health. If these fearful consequences ensue, such a woman ought not to be pitied. She richly deserves them all."

So I deserved the twisted ankle and whatever other injuries I might have to suffer during the pregnancy and birth? And the doctor was my self-appointed judge and jury? Out of the corner of my eye, I saw my shoes by the door, the severed lace of one tucked inside it. I limped over to pick them up, calling again for Art.

"Your child will inherit your feebleminded genes!" Dr. Livermore shouted. "Morons beget morons. Insanity runs in families. Did you read the story in today's Tribune about the three family members who simultaneously went insane? They were once my patients."

"Now that makes a lot of sense," I said. I slipped my injured foot into the shoe with the torn lace, tying it around my ankle as best I could, then slipped on the other one. I'd have to hop out of there.

Dr. Livermore stood nearby, watching. Smoke came from his mouth in an angry whoosh. He inhaled again deeply, this time keeping the smoke down.

"Your baby's father — the vacuum cleaner salesman, am I

right? He's also feebleminded."

I reached the door, resting one hand on the knob. "Listen, doctor. I didn't expect to find myself in this condition. Truth be told, it was my first time, and he used a preventative."

"A condom? Condoms are the breastplate against pleasure and mere cobwebs against danger, Julianne Rose."

"Just don't call me Bernice," I said, smiling at his puzzled expression. "In fact, don't call me Julianne Rose either. My name is Jules."

Suddenly Art opened the examining room door — I wondered if he'd been listening — and I grabbed his arm to steady myself. "Let's go," I said, nodding toward the front door and trying to lead him, hopping on my one good leg with the shoe flopping around on the other. But Dr. Livermore was shouting, and Art turned to listen.

"I'll deliver your bastard, Julianne Rose, as a favor to Arthur. Even bastards have a place in this world, if only to remind us of our mistakes. We'll find a family to adopt it. Keep acting out, though, and I will have you locked up in the Rosebush Home for Hopeless Women."

———————

For three days, Art didn't speak to me. He spent a lot of time at the widow's farm, coming home to eat dinner then heading to bed by 8 o'clock. I hopped around the house on my tender ankle until one day, Cora Mae stopped by with a rhubarb pie.

Over coffee, I told her about the midnight visit to Dr. Livermore and his threat to send me to the Home for Hopeless Women. It was an asylum built in Rosebush after we moved. It was for insane and feebleminded women as well as unmarried mothers.

"That man is a sap," she said. "I know somebody whose aunt was sent there because her husband claimed she was nuts. He got a doctor to agree, and she never came back."

Cora Mae was the person I could depend on the most to help me through the difficult months to come. Her stories were hard to hear, though. "Enough already," I said. "You're giving me the heebie-jeebies. It's bad enough that the doctor will be watching my every move, so I'll be having this baby whether I want it or not."

She nodded, looking around the kitchen. "What stinks in here?"

"It's cabbage. It helps Art's rheumatism." I opened a window and heard the Benedetto children screaming.

"Let's have some pie. I used the last of my rhubarb to make it," she said.

I made coffee and got out plates. "Nobody will hire me to play for their special occasions, and at some point, I'll have to quit the Yack-Yack Club."

"Weddings might be a problem, but what's to keep you from the funerals?" Cora Mae was opening yesterday's Tribune. "Looks to me like you should be busy in the very near future."

"Really? Who?" I asked.

When she rustled the newspaper, I could smell the ink. "Mrs. Grundy's mother has whooping cough, and, Jesus H. Christ, Old Man Willie cut off two of his fingers with a saw. That's not always fatal, though. But listen to this. Little Johnny Wilson's mother poisoned him. She left a can of fly poison on a windowsill, and the baby drank it."

"Good Lord," I said. "Some women just aren't fit to be mothers or, as Dr. Livermore would say, fruit trees." It occurred to me that my baby could end up in such a home. Maybe Dr. Livermore would go so far as to replace Little Johnny Wilson with my child.

"How do you suppose the doctor will decide who should have my baby?" I asked, my throat tightening with tears.

Cora Mae spoke from behind the front page. "You've got enough problems of your own, kiddo. Don't worry about the adoption. Does Dr. Livermore even know people who aren't supremely righteous like him?"

"Dr. Livermore knows you and me, and he thinks I'm a moron," I said. "What if he punishes me by giving the baby to somebody who's cruel or hateful, or who leaves poison lying around the house?"

"He is spiteful, no doubt. The beauty of it is, you'll never know. He'll never tell, so you'll just have to trust that the baby is leading a happy life … which reminds me … " She shuffled through the newspaper. "J.C. Penney is having a sale on girdles. We can order you a maternity girdle that will get you through Thanksgiving. After that, we'll sew panels into your dresses."

"Everybody will be able to tell anyway, if they don't already know," I said.

"True, but everybody, including you, has to pretend that it's not happening. Otherwise Dr. Livermore will lock you up, right?"

A worm of worry wiggled across my belly. It might have been flatulence, but it definitely wasn't the baby. The Benedetto children screamed, louder than usual, pulling Cora Mae and me to the window.

"They're just over-excited," she said. "Children are always over-excited."

We watched as the children kicked a ball back and forth, the sunflower baby toddling along the sidelines.

"Did you ever want a baby?" I asked.

Cora Mae looked at the floor. "I was newly pregnant when my husband was killed in the war. The baby died a few weeks after he did. The timing was all wrong."

"That must have been awful, Cora Mae. I'm so sorry."

She shrugged, picking up the dishes from the table. "How about you? Have you thought about having children — once you're married I mean?"

I looked out the window again, watching the baby wobble across the yard, intermittently falling, crying then pushing herself to her feet again.

"Would you think I'm peculiar if I said I didn't? I like children, of course, but I'm not sure I'd be a good mother. I mean, look at the mess I've already made of this child's life." I ran my hands over my stomach. "I wouldn't mind a husband, but the stars have to be aligned just right, and that's not likely to happen given my current situation."

"I can't stand children," Cora Mae said, putting her arm around my shoulders. "Let's be old maids together. Grow old with me, darling. We can have some fun along the way."

"I suppose," I said, but I lost my battle against my emotions, and tears came streaking down my cheeks.

"It'll work out, sweetie," Cora Mae said, offering me a

handkerchief. "Keep your head up and your shoulders back. Now, I'd better get back to the boardinghouse."

Not long after Cora Mae left, Art came home. For dinner, I fixed his favorite dish, which got him speaking to me again. We talked about that day's weather, yesterday's weather and the fall weather forecast. Over a piece of Cora Mae's pie, he said, "If Ruby and I marry, we could raise your child as our own."

"Have you asked her to marry you?" My heart thudded.

He shook his head. His fork wobbled, and he set it down on his plate.

"I'm having a girl, by the way. I can tell," I said.

Art gripped the arms of the kitchen chair to push himself into a standing position. His rheumatism must be acting out in his knees. "I wouldn't mind having a little girl around the house. We'll see what comes."

I nodded as I started to clear the dishes from the table. Later, I picked up my new copy of Zane Grey's "The Mysterious Rider." For the first time, the author let me down, with a plot about a poor lady whose father is forcing her to marry. Not my favorite topic.

I stayed up until midnight, sweeping, polishing and waxing the kitchen floor, thinking about how a suction cleaner might have lightened my burden.

GARDEN CITY TRIBUNE · SATURDAY, SEPT. 10, 1921

GLADYS WISENHEIMER'S
Garden of Tidbits

Garden City has endured a number of unfortunate events the past few weeks. First, the youngest Mason girl fell headfirst into a bucket and drowned in 3 inches of water. Mrs. Mason had gone to the barn and left the children alone in the house. When she returned a few moments later, the baby's legs were sticking out of the bucket.

As if that weren't enough, Freddy Wintermote celebrated his 13th birthday on Sunday, and on Monday, he fell ill. By Wednesday, Freddy knew he was dying and approached it in the same pleasant, cheerful way in which he had lived, his father said. The boy gave what belongings he had to his family and friends.

CHAPTER 16

Happenstance

What happened the next week in Garden City proved my point that Madam Isabella Luna and Sister Margery were only beating their gums during their stay in Garden City. The horrific nature of the incident should have at least caused a flicker of light to cross their crystal balls. Cora Mae argued that bona fide fortune-tellers only draw attention to the unusual events of a lifetime — the events that alter our souls.

Unfortunately, the death of a child was not unusual.

Everybody knew somebody who'd lost a child. The cemeteries were filled with little nubs of rock, half of which didn't even bear names. The prevailing attitude seemed to be: Why waste a good name on a dead child? Maybe I coped better with those children's deaths or with the recent deaths of the Mason baby or Freddy Wintermote because I didn't know them. But what would happen later that week in my own neighborhood would rearrange my very depths.

It must have been a hundred degrees out, making my nausea worse. I'd taken a break from weeding the garden to drink a glass of lemonade turned warm as soup in the kitchen when I heard the noise coming from the Benedetto children across the street. I leaned out the window until I was certain they could see me, which sometimes brought their screams to a temporarily tolerable level. They were noisy children, after all, not rude.

Across the street, four boys were playing tag, but they were uncharacteristically dispirited. Nobody seemed to want to chase the others.

They shouted — *fretta* — over and over again, and I didn't know what it meant. But another sound raveled through the clamor to catch my ear. It was coughing — relentless and breathtaking — and it came from a group of children lying on a frayed quilt beneath a sprawling oak. They squawked with each inhalation, and the noise took me back to my youth, when Art and I had been stricken with the same disease. However, as was true with any ailment, it hit him harder.

It was whooping cough, named after the cries of cranes.

But, in my opinion, it sounded more like the cackles of chickens. When one of the girls coughed so hard she vomited, I shouted, "Is everybody all right over there?"

One boy, I think his name was Giuseppe, paused, then ran across the street to where I stood. Snot jelled below his nose, which I'd come to expect with the Benedetto children, but his eyes were red and watery, and it took him a few minutes to speak because he had the same dry cough as the others.

"We have trouble. Please come," he finally managed to say.

Part of me wanted to pull my apron over my face to ward off their affliction. A better part sent me across the street, where the boy ushered me through the front door and into the parlor. It was odd walking into the same floor plan as my own house but with different, strange furnishings.

Everything was layered, draped and drooping. Fringed shawls hung over a chair and table. Lining nearly every wall were sleeping cots, each piled high with blankets, clothing, toys and books — apparently whatever possessions its owner could claim.

I followed the boy into the bedroom, which was filled with heavy, dark furniture — all of it draped and fringed. The room was heavy with the scent of mentholated ointment. In the same corner where Art had situated his bed stood theirs, shrouded in floor-to-ceiling curtains. From within the folds came the sound of weeping.

"Mama," the boy whispered. He pulled back the curtain.

Mrs. Benedetto was lying on the bed. She wore a nightgown, more gray than the chalky white it might once have been, and her coarse black hair, which she usually braided and pinned, had unraveled on the sheets. She was curled into a half circle, her arm stretching a corner of a blanket across the child lying there. It was the youngest Benedetto, the sunflower baby. Her skin was blue, her chest unmoving, and her unblinking eyes were filled with blood vessels jagged from coughing. The wispy blond hair that had made her stand out among the flock was so dark with perspiration that she looked, at last, like one of them.

I'd seen death. I'd wiped pus oozing from my mother's ears and eyes. I'd listened to my father chatter with fever to the people he claimed were waiting for him just beyond a garden gate. But this death was different. This was the theft of a lifetime, the stealing of a soul who had done nothing, nothing at all. She'd barely learned to walk, to view the world from a standing position. It was so sorrowful that I didn't want to let it in my mind for fear that it would never leave. I didn't even know this child's name, and I didn't want to. Here we were in this house that so resembled my own, surrounded by a grief I hoped never to know. Another reason never to have a child.

Mrs. Benedetto pushed herself up on an elbow and looked at me with eyes swollen and red and not quite focused. Her chin trembled as she spoke to the boy, who interpreted for me.

"She says Papa will be returning from his trip tonight and that in the meantime, if you could, please fetch the professional," he said.

"She wants me to bring Dr. Livermore?" I asked. "Or Doc Trundle?"

Mrs. Benedetto spoke again, her words trailing on far

longer than the boy's interpretation. "No," he said. "She wants a photographer."

I didn't stop to ask why. I ran home and busied myself fixing food to give the Benedettos and to send with Art. He quickly packed a bedroll on the back of his motorcycle and set off for Rosebush, where we'd heard there was a man who worked on Sundays. I stayed up all night baking loaves of bread, meatloaves and three kinds of cookies. Afterward, I cleaned the kitchen — taking everything out of the cupboards, wiping the canned goods clean, alphabetizing the spices and lining up the jars according to height.

I told myself to shut out the grief, to think about peach pies and planting potatoes, peas and parsnips. I was pretty sure Mrs. Benedetto had served up the last slice of her soul.

But early the next morning, there she stood in their front yard when Art sputtered up with the photographer and his equipment. She'd pinned up her hair and dressed in her Sunday clothes with a fringed black shawl draped over her shoulders. Mr. Benedetto shouted at the children while the photographer fumbled with his equipment. Later, Art told me he was surprised the man could operate the camera so well because one of his hands was missing two fingers.

I watched from our kitchen window as he told them where to stand. The sick ones leaned against the others; the grandma — her lap achingly empty — was wheeled to the center; and on either side of her, Mr. and Mrs. Benedetto sat in kitchen chairs. At the last minute, while the others waited restlessly in the heat, Mrs. Benedetto ran into the house and came back with the baby, wrapped in the shawl and looking for all the world like she was asleep. The photographer snapped their portrait.

Afterward was the funeral. They put the baby in a wooden box and gathered around her while a Catholic priest talked Italian. Art took the photographer home, so I was the only one there without a clue as to all the kneeling and crisscrossing. I must not have messed up too badly, because when it was over, Mrs. Benedetto had one of the boys ask me to do something that I was familiar with: play my piano. I opened every window in our house and struck the chords without mercy until the notes floated across the street.

GARDEN CITY TRIBUNE · WEDNESDAY, SEPT. 28, 1921

BABE RUTH PROVES WHAT WE ALREADY KNEW: HE'S SUPERNORMAL

Intelligence tests conducted on the baseball player Babe Ruth have shown he truly is superhuman. Mr. Ruth's vision proved to be sharper than the average human's by about 12 percent. His ears function at least 10 percent better than those of the ordinary man, and his nerves are steadier than those of 499 out of 500 persons. In attention and quickness of perception, Mr. Ruth rated one-and-a-half times better than the average human. In intelligence, as demonstrated by the quickness and accuracy of his understanding, he was about 10 percent above normal. Mr. Ruth was given tests similar to those conducted by the U.S. Army during the Great War.

CHAPTER 17

Babe Ruth Visits Garden City

I had a sliver of a moon growing between my rib cage and hips. I'd started wearing the maternity girdle — a wretched strip of elastic held in place with belts and buckles that were supposedly adjustable for growth. It was suffocating, like the corsets my mother had worn, and the elastic absorbed my perspiration, creating a smell that wouldn't wash out. I probably didn't really need it until the next month, but I was self-conscious.

Nobody mentioned the shadow growing beside me. That fall, Babe Ruth was everybody's everything, and it's true that he brought more than a little excitement to Garden City.

Ruth was shown to be superhuman by intelligence tests, the newspapers reported. He'd met with a mentalist at the Hippodrome Theatre who'd accurately predicted the number of home runs the star expected to make that year. He'd received his second speeding violation in three months and spent jail time playing craps with the other inmates.

I wasn't a baseball fan, but Babe Ruth had spent part of his growing-up years in an orphanage, and I'd heard those places were like prisons — run-down and overcrowded. Ruth was overblown and overpaid; he was Pinky's role model. Still, I had empathy for the man, and I wasn't about to miss hearing him and the other players when, for the first time, a World Series would be broadcast on the radio.

Pinky had assembled the best radio set in Finney County, so Cora Mae organized a party for the "Invisible Audience," which was how the New York Times described the estimated 5 million of us who'd listen to the game outside of the Polo Grounds in New York.

Earlier that week, Cora Mae told me she'd dreamed about the baby and me. A dinosaur with giant teeth was chasing us through a cabbage patch. The baby was bundled in a pink blanket, and I was holding her tight, when we rounded a corner and there was a valise, lying open and filled with candy. Nestled near the center was a pocket-sized camera, and when the dinosaur caught up with us, I snapped its photograph. Frightened by the flash, it ran off. It was another of her ridiculous dream stories, but thinking about it reminded me of my dwindling supply of candy. I needed to go to Grundy's

FINDING BABY RUTH

after dinner.

I nibbled on a peanut butter and jelly sandwich while I caught up with my latest Zane Grey, "Wildfire." The heroine, Lucy, had lips the same sweet red as an Upland rose. In the last chapter I'd read, she'd spurned a young man who'd been kicked in the face by a horse. He was threatening to strip her naked and tie her to another horse. I earmarked the page, made another sandwich and kept reading. Three chapters later, I looked up to find that dark clouds filled the sky.

I buckled myself into my maternity girdle and pulled on my bulkiest sweater for the walk to Grundy's. Leaves crunched under my feet as I walked. A chill perched in the air. Zane Grey would have said autumn had shaken the wrinkles from its cloak.

Mr. Grundy greeted me excitedly, waving me to the back of the store. "Come look, Jules. It's unbelievable. Hooch found it down by the river. It weighs 16 pounds." I followed him to where Hooch and others were gathered. They'd spread an old Tribune over the glass counter, and on top of it was a rock the size of a well-grown cabbage. It was more gray than yellow, with cracks running down the sides. Hooch was going over it with a handheld broom.

"A dinosaur tooth," he told me. "Needs a good brushing."

"Sixteen pounds — we weighed it," Mr. Grundy said. "A science teacher from the college in Fort Hays is on his way, but when we described it to him over the telephone, he said it's probably from either a mastodon or a mammoth. Can you imagine that kind of monster lurking around Garden City?"

I could only imagine Cora Mae's dream, and it made me

shiver to think that once more, she'd predicted the future in a strange way.

The dry spell we'd been having shattered into a downpour as I carried my groceries home. I couldn't run with my hands full, and the maternity girdle squished the air right out of me. So I plodded along, my rain-drenched wool sweater adding to my overall smelliness until I could hardly stand to walk with myself.

My self-pity peaked when I got home just as Art pulled up on his motorcycle. He hadn't worn his waterproof alligator coat, so he was soaked, shivering and undoubtedly about to complain of aching in his hands, feet, knees, or maybe all three. Soon, he'd want dinner — some kind of reeking cabbage dish. I put away the groceries in silence as he skulked off to his bedroom.

"Do you want dinner?" I asked, but he didn't answer, so I changed into dry clothing and checked the icebox for leftovers. Nothing looked appealing, so I poured a can of vegetable soup into a pan and put it on the stove to heat. "Wildfire" was beckoning. I opened it where I'd left off, just as the man with the kicked-in face came close to carrying out his bareback riding scheme with Lucy, who fortunately fought back. Meanwhile, her true love was searching high and low for her.

I looked up when I heard Art stir in his bedroom. It was dark outside, and the rain had stopped. Dinnertime was long past. The soup sat cold on the stove. I'd forgotten to light it. I figured Art had fallen asleep, so for once, I fixed my favorite meal: a box of chocolates that I'd bought at Grundy's.

Back at the ranch, Lucy's true love found her, half-naked and tied to a horse. He noticed her bruises, her pale face, her breast heaving against his, but he didn't see her half-nakedness until she asked to borrow his coat. I looked up, mostly because I didn't believe anyone could be so blind but also because I might have heard a noise coming from Art's room. It was quiet, though, so I finished the last few chapters in which Lucy, wearing barely a stitch of clothing, shoots and kills the horse thief.

I listened at Art's door but heard nothing so went on to bed. That night I had a dream exactly like Cora Mae's, only it was a horse thief chasing me through the cabbage patch. When I snapped his photograph, he fell off a cliff. I thought I heard his moans coming from the canyon floor, but when I opened my eyes, the sun had risen, and I realized the moans were coming from Art's room.

I knocked, waited a heartbeat then went inside. Art looked dead, lying white and motionless on the bed with his eyes closed. He must have heard me shout his name, because when I reached the side of his bed, he muttered, "Hurts."

"What hurts, Arthur?" I touched the back of his hand, and he yelped like one of Cora Mae's dogs. I pulled back, fighting tears. Dear Lord, what was wrong? He could scarcely open his eyes. They looked like slivers of shiny green marbles. "Everything hurts," he whispered.

"Have you been like this all night?" My voice wrenched with guilt, and he nodded imperceptibly. "It must be your rheumatism acting up. I'll send for Dr. Livermore."

A white cotton blanket was folded at the bottom of his bed,

but when I pulled it across him, he cried out. Tears struggled across the bristles of his cheeks.

"Listen, I'll be right back, Arthur." I reached out to reassure him then caught myself and pulled my hand back. I grabbed the white flag off the table instead. Across the street, the Benedetto children were playing, so I stuck my head out the door and waved the flag. They ran over in a pack, sweating and breathless. I still had on my nightgown, and I shielded my pooching belly with the door, trying to remember the tallest boy's name.

"Lou?" I said. The boy nodded.

"Lou, run as fast as you can to Dr. Livermore's house. Tell him my brother's rheumatism is on its worst rampage yet, so he'd better hurry over."

I wasn't certain he understood all of what I said, but he must have gotten the intent, because he grabbed another boy by the arm, and they ran off.

I took Art a glass of water, but he seemed to be sleeping, so I left it on his bed stand. I dressed, dusted and swept the parlor then waited at the window. It didn't take long before the Locomobile came rattling down the middle of Fourth Street.

Dr. Livermore was driving himself this time. He spent an eternity parking — backing up then pulling forward, trying to get the car straight — before hurrying inside with his bag. He went straight to the bedroom, and just as he had during Art's attack four years before, sent me out. I waited nearby, listening, until I was allowed back in. Art lay facing the wall. A hypodermic needle and the doctor's book were on the bedside table.

"Your brother has suffered a setback of the rheumatism, brought on by your debauchery and exacerbated by not eating enough cabbage. I've given him an injection of morphine."

"Thank you, Dr. Livermore. He was in so much pain."

"Morphine is habit-forming, so I use it only when no other alternative is viable."

"I swear I've tried the cabbage diet. We eat it almost every day in one form or another."

"I noticed. It smells awful in here." The doctor fanned his hand in front of his Roman nose. "Make Art drink the brine each morning."

He stared at my stomach bump, and although I knew it was useless, I sucked in my breath. "I presume you're taking care of yourself, Julianne Rose. Abstaining from alcohol, which inflames the blood and creates puny infants; getting plenty of fresh air and exercise to prevent a laborious labor. "

I nodded, rearranging Art's bedding, careful not to brush it against him. "I'm being extra cautious. I was wondering, though. You won't put my baby in an orphanage will you?"

"I will do my best to avoid an orphanage. They're breeding grounds for incorrigibles. I think I've found a young couple willing to take the baby straight from my hospital to their home."

The news set me back a minute. It seemed too soon to be making such permanent plans. "Do I know them?" I asked.

Dr. Livermore smoothed his hair. "You do not, and you will not. You only need to know that they are God-fearing Christians."

"But are they kind and careful? They don't leave poisons lying about the house, right?

"As I said, they are God-fearing."

"Well, I suppose that's good. I was wondering, though, does your book say whether it's possible for a mother to know whether she's having a girl or a boy?"

"It does. The tests are absurd. A mother must take what she is given."

I couldn't believe he was questioning his own book's sacred advice, and oddly, it made me uneasy. I wanted a knowledgeable, certain doctor, even if his ideas were a hundred years old.

Dr. Livermore returned his instruments to his bag, shut it with a decisive snap and headed out. In the parlor, a pile of Tribunes sat on the coffee table. He paused, and I could see over his shoulder that he was reading the story about Babe Ruth.

"You know, Julianne Rose, these tests offer insight into the functions of the human mind. It's quite obvious, for example, that Mr. Ruth has more intelligence than the normal man. The examinations confirm that."

"He can certainly hit the home runs," I said, thinking about Ruth's time at the orphanage. "So what do I owe you, doctor?"

"I'll take the rest of that apple pie I saw on the kitchen table," he said.

For three days, Dr. Livermore returned to give Art injections. His visits kept me on edge because I never knew when he'd show up. I kept him supplied with baked goods, and he never asked for a penny.

On the third day, while Art slept soundly from the morphine, I strapped myself into my girdle and went to

Grundy's. I needed to call Ruby with the news about Art's setback. Thank heavens she'd finally had a telephone installed.

When I arrived at the market, Mr. Grundy was unloading a shipment of goods from Kansas City. "Would you mind placing the call yourself, Jules?" he said. "Just keep your lips a good inch from the mouthpiece, or whoever you call won't be able to hear you."

I'd made a few telephone calls — three to be precise — so I was a little excited and a lot uncertain as I went through the steps. I held the receiver to my ear and positioned my mouth roughly an inch from the mouthpiece.

"Hello, hello?" It was Melba Swanson, the switchboard operator. I'd played at her wedding a few years before, so we took a few minutes to reminisce about what a lovely ceremony it had been and how lovely she'd looked and how she and her fellow were expecting their second child any day now. When I asked Melba to put me through to Ruby Torgerson, she spent another few minutes explaining that Ruby was on a party line with two neighbors who liked to eavesdrop.

"They're only supposed to pick up when they hear their special ring — two longs for the Gilberts, one short for the Taylors, and two shorts followed by one long for Ruby. They can't seem to get it straight, though. Everybody picks up every time. It's exasperating, but it's the only choice we have until the phone company installs private lines around here. Just don't say anything you wouldn't want everybody to hear."

"I understand," I said, pushing the receiver closer to my ear. I heard the phone ring: two shorts followed by one long.

"Hallow. George Gilbert here."

Then Ruby's voice. "Hello?"

And lastly, an old woman. "Who's there?"

The man said, "Ladies, I think this call is for me. It was two long rings."

Ruby disagreed. "I'm sorry, Mr. Gilbert, but my ring is two longs followed by one short, I mean two shorts followed by one long. You have to let it ring completely through more than once."

"She's right." It was Melba, the operator. I didn't realize she was still listening. "The rule is to let the phone go through its ring cycle at least twice before answering. I have Miss Jules Greer on the line for Mrs. Torgerson."

"My apologies," the man said. "I'll hang up now."

The old lady spoke again. "Who's there?"

"Mrs. Taylor, is that you?" Ruby said.

Silence. "Mrs. Taylor?" Ruby said more loudly.

"You've reached the Alvin Taylor residence. Who's there? You'll have to speak up. Put your lips right next to the mouthpiece."

Good Lord, I thought. I could have delivered my message faster by walking to Ruby's farm. I moved my lips closer to the mouthpiece and shouted, "This is Jules Greer calling for Ruby Torgerson! Ruby, are you there?"

Mr. Grundy walked by carrying a case of canned goods. "You don't need to shout, Jules. One inch, remember?"

I nodded. "Sorry."

"I'm here," Ruby said. "Mrs. Taylor, you can hang up now.

The old woman's voice crackled. "I'll need an open line soon to call my son."

"We'll make it fast then," Ruby said.

Still no disconnecting click, but I went ahead anyway.

"Ruby, Art is sick again with the rheumatism. He's worse than he's ever been."

"Oh dear," she said. "I was afraid this was going to happen again. He drove home in that terrific rainstorm without his alligator coat. How bad is he?"

"He can hardly move. The pain is horrible. Dr. Livermore comes by every day to give him morphine shots."

"That's just awful. I'll have to see if I can find another man to help out in the meantime."

"I was thinking it might help if you could come by. Could one of your boys bring you to town?"

She hesitated. "You want me to bring Art's money? Is he finally going to let me pay him for his labor?"

"I'm not sure about that. I thought it might cheer him up to see you."

"Gosh, I don't know. It's awfully busy here with all that needs to be done for the move."

"I didn't know you were moving."

"Art didn't tell you? Heavens, it's no secret. We're moving to Stockton. I'm marrying a fellow up there."

I couldn't speak for a minute. Tears locked up my throat. Now I understood why for three years Ruby had never once visited our house, why their relationship had never progressed. Art's talk of marriage had been a fairy tale. Ruby probably didn't even know about my baby.

She rushed to fill the empty air. "Don't be hurt, Jules. I would have asked you to play for my wedding if it wasn't happening so far away. By the way, the house here is for sale if you know anybody who might be interested."

"I'll ask around."

"Give Art my best. I'm sorry to hear he's so bad off. I'll send one of the boys by your place tomorrow with his pay."

"Yes, thank you. I'd better hang up now so Mrs. Taylor can make her call."

The old lady coughed. "Cabbage works miracles for the rheumatism."

The next day Art was sleeping when Ruby's son showed up with an envelope of cash. I tucked it inside my piano to use during those last couple of months when even my maternity girdle wouldn't allow me to leave the house.

I never told Art about my conversation with Ruby. He would have been ashamed. I saw no harm in letting him have his dreams even while my own were withering. On my folding bed that night, I felt a roiling deep in my gut. Was it my distress over Art, or could it already be the baby? I didn't know, but thoughts of both scenarios kept me from sleeping that night.

CHAPTER 18

The Great Escape

The day the World Series began, Art got out of bed. I was grateful that he was better. I was equally grateful that I could go to Cora Mae's party and hear the first World Series game ever broadcast, even if it was on Pinky's radio. The newspapers reported that 30,000 people would pay $1 for tickets to attend the series. Thousands more would listen to it on the radio. It was a Wednesday, which I thought was a ridiculous day for such a momentous occasion. Later, I realized it wouldn't be the most earth-shattering event of the day.

Before I left, I loaded up Art's bedside stand with a glass of water, another library book about Renoir and the white flag. I rubbed liniment on his shoulders, noticing for the first time that his hair was graying. When he looked at me with teary eyes, I thought for a moment the rheumatism was back.

"Are you sure you want to be alone?" I said. "I don't mind staying."

"I'll be fine." He waved the white flag. "If not, I can always surrender."

"I'll be home before dark. There's a sauerkraut meatloaf in the oven and sweet potato pie in the icebox."

He smiled. "You're a real sweet sister, Jules. You've always been good to me."

I touched his shoulder, and he gave my hand a little sideways kiss.

"Tell the Babe to hit one out of the ballpark for me," he said. "Tell him to hit it all the way to Garden City."

As I left the house, I was glad to see the Benedettos were home. The children were playing baseball in the yard, caught up like everybody else by the hysteria over a stick and ball.

Cora Mae's boardinghouse was more frenzied than usual. In addition to the usual brood of animals running in and out, Hooch stood on the roof adjusting an antenna, his position so precarious I was afraid to startle him by saying hello. Across the street, Mrs. Grundy was hanging laundry. I stood a little straighter when she peeked out from between two of her black moral gowns.

The party was to be held upstairs in the room where Madam Isabella Luna had told her fortunes last summer. If any of the spirit guides lingered, they'd better be Giants fans. Tin Tin the dog followed me to the kitchen, where Cora Mae, wearing a dress for once, put the final touches on a Polo Grounds cake that was almost as amazing as her swimming

FINDING BABY RUTH

pool cake. It was round, with stadium seats made of crackers and piped frosting around the diamond. The Giants players were candy corn; the Yankees were peppermints; and Babe Ruth was a chunk of a milk chocolate.

Pinky shouted that the game would start soon, so we hurried upstairs. The room was filled with the Fondales' no-good buddies and a few of their girls. They'd pulled chairs from the other rooms, although three of them were stretched out on the bed and one had hoisted himself up to sit on top of the dresser.

Pinky wore his version of a baseball uniform — a pinstriped shirt and knickers, a billed hat, and Jiggs' yellow shoes. He was on his knees, cursing and fiddling with the radio box he'd made just for the game. It was the size of the telephone at Grundy's, settled inside a lidded oak box that was studded with buttons and levers.

The men placed bets on the game, which I'm pretty sure was as illegal as the bootleg whiskey they drank and the store-bought cigarettes they smoked. Dogs raced about, barking and snatching pieces of cheese from peoples' plates. When they knocked over a liquor bottle, Pinky made Cora Mae put them outside.

It was stuffy because of the smoke and the sheer number of sweating, nervous folks piled into the room. The windows were closed and the curtains drawn. I was grateful my nausea had tapered off. Pinky's face glistened with perspiration as he turned knobs and flipped switches, trying to get reception. "Shut your traps, everybody!" he shouted.

Straightaway, the room grew silent except for Hooch's

wheezy breathing. From the radio box came a motionless, crackling noise. It seemed ceaseless, although occasionally a high-pitched whine would interrupt. Pinky put his fleshy ear next to the box and slowly rotated the knobs until suddenly, a tiny voice came from out of nowhere.

The whole room leaned in, putting our best ears forward and exchanging wide-eyed grins of astonishment as the voice grew sharper and louder. "This is WJZ Radio in Newark bringing you on-the-spot reporting for the first time ever of the World Series being played at the Polo Grounds in New York City."

At that, the room erupted. Everybody laughed and clapped and stomped their feet. It was one of those moments you never forget. In the same flicker of time, the whole nation — from President Harding to Zane Grey to us — was united. Each of us sat scrunched in front of a box, trying to make out an announcer's high-pitched, wavering voice. We were together, alone.

Pinky made a toast to Babe Ruth, the "phenomenable Sultan of Swat," then rotated knobs until the voice emerged again from the static. The starting lineup was introduced. The Yankees had Babe, Carl Mays and "Long Bob" Meusel. The Giants had High Pocket Kelly and Emil "Irish" Meusel — Long Bob's older brother. The Yankees would be first at bat.

After the first hit, I didn't pay much attention to the game because I didn't understand the rules. Cora Mae tried to explain, but I was more interested in what Pinky described as "studio noises." The crack of the bat, for instance, was really the snap of a wooden matchstick inside the New Jersey radio

FINDING BABY RUTH

studio. The radio announcer himself wasn't really at the Polo Grounds in New York, Pinky said. He was at a studio, relaying whatever was telegraphed to him by sports writers on the playing field.

After a few innings, I walked over to admire Cora Mae's cake. I waited until everyone was riveted to the radio by an exciting play then stuffed the chocolate Babe Ruth into my mouth.

I was cleaning up in the kitchen when Pinky came in carrying a piece of cake and rubbing his wrist. When he sat down at the table, I saw that he'd taken the piece of the Polo Grounds cake with the most frosting — home plate.

He shoved a forkful into his mouth before speaking. "Had to take a break from the static. Too many things floating through the air creating inferences."

I nodded and handed him a cup of coffee.

"Thanks." He took a sip. "What's your name for that baby?"

I hesitated. My baby wasn't usually discussed in public. "Why should I name it?" I said. "I want to forget it as soon as it's born. I won't be able to keep it, so why bother?"

"I was just thinking about what I'd name my baby if I had one."

"And what would that be?"

"I don't know. That's why I'm asking you."

Pinky was the strangest man I'd ever met, except perhaps for Hooch. It was nearly impossible to carry on a conversation with either of them.

He took another bite of cake. "Cora Mae says your baby is a girl, so I was thinking you could name her Bernice."

"I hate that name, Pinky," I said. "It reminds me of a character in a story I once read, and the mother of a man I once knew."

"How about Ruth then? After the baseball player or the candy bar, either one. That's what I'd name my daughter if I ever was to have one. That's a singular fact."

"I suppose that's as good a name as any, if I was to give her one," I said. "By the way, the vacuum cleaner salesman who loved Baby Ruth bars — did you ever hear from him?"

"I've been meaning to tell you, Jules. I'm sorry I ever introduced you to that no-good fellow."

I didn't know what to say, so what I said was ridiculous. "You're a peach, Pinky, and so is the name Baby Ruth."

"I'd better get back to my game," he said.

The Yankees won 3-0, and after Pinky collected his winnings, he gave me a ride home in his Packard. It was later than I realized.

———————

Every light in the house was blazing when Pinky and Cora Mae drove me home after the World Series game. Darkness had settled, and while they smooched in the front seat, I leaned against the back window, staring at the house.

"Something isn't right. Art would never waste money by leaving the lights on like that."

Cora Mae pulled away from Pinky to peer out her window. "Maybe he's got company. Maybe it's Ruby."

"It's definitely not Ruby. It could be somebody from his Masonic Lodge dropped by."

I got out and spoke through the car's open window. "I'll

see you tomorrow. Thanks for the lift."

Pinky shifted into gear, but Cora Mae put her hand over his.

"We'll wait until she's inside the house, safe and sound."

I walked up the front step in the glow of the Packard's headlamps, but the door was locked, which was odd because we never locked the door. I wasn't even sure we had a key. I turned back to the car to see Cora Mae coming up the sidewalk with Pinky.

"What is it?" she said. "Why is the door locked?"

"I don't know. I'll try around back." An alarm rattled in my head as I walked to the back door and jiggled the handle so hard the windowpane rattled. I peered inside. Dinner dishes were draining in the sink just as I'd left them. The table was covered with my mother's lace tablecloth, the chairs pushed into place. But what was at the center of the table made me seize with panic: Art's white flag was stuck inside a flower vase.

I screamed his name, my ear pressed to the glass for the familiar sound of him shuffling across the room. "Art, can you hear me?" I pounded on the door with my fist. All I could hear was Cora Mae and Pinky walking through dry leaves on their way to join me.

"Jesus H. Christ, you don't suppose he fell?" Cora Mae asked.

"Maybe. I don't know." My heart raced. "Let's check the windows. At least the curtains aren't all drawn."

We fanned out in three directions, cupping our hands around our eyes so we could see inside. On such a small house, it didn't take long.

I went around to the side of the house where Art's bedroom was located, hoping to find him rumpled in the sheets, asleep. And he was there, but his arms and legs were taut and twitching. A blanket was pulled over his head, and a sheet twisted around his trousers. He was having a fit. Even his bare feet trembled. A little cloud of black smoke hung over him. A 12-gauge shotgun was near his feet.

"Dear Lord. What's wrong? Art, can you hear me?" I was screaming and pounding my fist against the glass until it cracked. Art lurched off the bed, unaware. The sheet caught his hips, so his forehead hit first. He was bleeding. A pool formed where his head battered the wood, and darkness stained the sheet that held him halfway on the bed.

Pinky was behind me, cursing. He shoved me aside and pushed up on the window, but the glass rained down in shards and cut his hands. The wreckage splintered under my shoes as I stepped closer. Without the windowpane, everything in the room was suddenly lucid. The overhead light was sharper, the sheets were paler and the puff of smoke that hung in the air smelled stronger. The blood especially was unnaturally red and profuse.

"Hang on, Art. I'm coming. Please, please hang on." I ran to the next window, the parlor window, and with both hands shoved it open. I hoisted myself up so I could crawl inside. There was a bookcase below the window, and I kicked it over when I climbed in, the books creating an uneven path that I slipped across as I ran toward Art's door.

It was locked. I took a few steps backward and was about to throw myself against the door when it opened from the inside. Pinky stood there with his torn hands wrapped in one of Art's undershirts. Art lay motionless, one foot wedged in the sheet on the bed, the other motionless on the floor. Pinky helped me to kneel so I could wrap my arms around my dead brother.

Dr. Livermore and the sheriff came to investigate. Cora Mae took me outside, and I walked in circles for so long, I could have been halfway to Kansas City mileage-wise. Pinky kept telling me to simmer down and sit down, but I couldn't. Sorrow was nipping at my heels, and if I stopped walking, it would come roaring inside. I wasn't certain I could take that.

On one of my loops, I looked through the broken window. Dr. Livermore and the sheriff were hunched over Art's body. I saw his bare foot, the toes pointing skyward, and the hair on his leg inexplicably dark against skin already drained of color.

I looked at the sky. The night my father died, I'd seen a shooting star, which I'd taken as a sign that he was OK. The evening Art died, though, milky-white clouds hung thick and low, their edges so rigid that the black sky in between them formed shapes like letters of a language I'd never seen. One cloud in particular — it was dark gray surrounded by a jagged red sphere — bulged toward me, so close I might have jabbed it with my finger. A breeze rattled the leaves on the cottonwood trees. It sounded like an audience clapping. I looked up, wondering how they could possibly applaud such a tragedy.

CHAPTER 19

A Test for Morons

The Tribune reported every snippet of Art's death except the contents of his suicide note, and everybody's knowing everything filled in those blanks. The note was written in pencil and addressed to me. I cried when I read it.

Dear Jules,

Renoir lived until he was very old. He painted from his wheelchair even when they had to help him with the brushes.

Even so, he was a lot older than me when the rheumatism first came on, and I'm already so bad. This is my choice, my decision. It's what the fortune-teller knew would happen. If I'd waited much longer, you'd have had to help me hold the shotgun in my hands.

I lied to you about Ruby. She never intended to marry me. I hope you seek out a life of your own without me. Now the baby is coming, and you have a good friend in Cora Mae. (Even Pinky and Hooch aren't too awful.) I don't think I could bear it if your baby inherits my rheumatism and other bad traits. Watch over her, Jules. If she does get sick, nobody else will know how to make cabbage in so many different ways. I want a Masonic burial, although I have to admit that at heart, I'm really a Spiritualist. That's what I told the Tribune reporter anyway.

Love,
Art

We had a graveside service. Art and I hadn't attended church for so long, it didn't seem right to impose on the Garden City pastors. Thank heavens word didn't get out about Art being one of the two Spiritualists mentioned in the Tribune's religious poll. I had enough on my hands dealing with my own grief, the turmoil of his suicide and the rumors flitting about town as folks tried to pinpoint where we'd gone wrong, thus justifying to themselves why such a horrific ordeal would never happen to them.

Not a lot of people came to the funeral. Cora Mae stood beside me, and Pinky stood beside her, and Hooch stood beside his car. Art's Masonic brothers carried his casket, just as he'd wanted. Dr. Livermore offered sympathetic words, but he kept staring at my stomach, and I knew what he was thinking: Only the feebleminded kill themselves or have babies out of wedlock.

It was hard to go back in the house, and I waited until Pinky and Hooch had replaced the broken window and cleaned up the blood in Art's room. When I did return, I watched from the window for a long time, occasionally thinking I heard Art's motorcycle puttering down the street. Cora Mae wanted me to move in with her at the boardinghouse, and I agreed. Neither of us liked living alone, and we could share expenses.

The Benedetto boys helped Pinky and Hooch move my piano, and late one night, Hooch drove Art's motorcycle to the boardinghouse while Pinky shouted directions on where to turn to him through the Packard's window.

One gorgeous autumn afternoon, I hoed up my old garden. It didn't take long to turn the wizened roots of cabbage plants back into the earth. A family from across town had bought the place. I took a final peek into the shed to make sure we'd cleared everything out and was surprised to see an old bicycle leaning against the wall. It was the one Art had tried to teach me to ride. I hopped on, wavering slightly because of my stomach but not really caring if I fell because that might solve everything, right? Once I got my balance, I rode without mishap all the way to Cora Mae's.

The days were difficult. Over and over again, my mind reeled through visions of Art wobbling on the floor, his bare foot facing skyward, the blood, the clouds, the chattering leaves. Nights were just as difficult. In my dreams, Art watched from a short distance away as I climbed through the window, held his body, planned his funeral. He never spoke.

I lost track of time. At first I didn't know whether it was day or night. I'd wake from an afternoon nap — even then the dreams held sway — and think it was time for breakfast. The shadows of the afternoon sun coming through the kitchen windows would confuse me. Eventually my sense of my time returned, but it unfolded slowly. Once I sorted out whether it was day or night, it took a while for me to remember the day of the week, the season, the month, the year.

A few days after the funeral, Dr. Livermore's nurse, Maude, knocked on the door of the boardinghouse with a letter for me. I'd only received a few letters in my life, and now I'd gotten two in one month. The first one — from Art — was the worst sort of news. I expected this one to be as well, and I wasn't disappointed. The doctor wrote that he would administer an intelligence test to me the next morning at his office. He'd enclosed a sample of the questions.

I carried the letter to the kitchen, where Cora Mae, wearing pin curls and a robe, made breakfast for the first tenant we'd had in months. He'd introduced himself as Charles when he'd arrived on his motorcycle the afternoon before. He said he was on his way to flight school in Lincoln, Nebraska. Right away, Cora Mae nicknamed him Slim because he was lanky and so tall his feet hung off the bed. Slim ate twice as much as everyone else, and Cora Mae made him extra servings of every meal. In return, he promised to come back when he finished school and take her for an airplane ride.

In the kitchen, Slim sat with his legs folded awkwardly

beneath the table as he studied a drawing of an airplane. He was a bit of a sheik, with thick, sandy hair that he kept long on top and short on the sides. He was also a mama's boy. Every day he posted a letter to his mother back home in Wisconsin.

I sat across from him and told Cora Mae about the letter delivered by Maude. My stomach wasn't huge yet, so I told Slim that I was taking the test to become a schoolteacher. Of course, Cora Mae knew how I worried about whom the doctor might pick to raise my child. She also knew that a slip-up on my part could land me in the Home for Hopeless Women. Dr. Livermore would justify such a step as saving the world from immoral lunatics like me.

Cora Mae had pancakes frying in one skillet and bacon in another. "That man is pure evil. You'd better memorize the answers to those sample questions. Pinky will be here soon. He can help. How about you, Slim? How are you with tests?"

Slim looked up from the drawing. "I flunked out of college."

"Read us the questions anyway, Jules. Let's give it a try." Cora Mae loaded a plate with pancakes and bacon for Slim, who tucked a napkin under his chin before he began eating.

"Here's the first one," I said. "An Indian comes to town for the first time in his life. As he sees a white man riding along the street, he says, 'The white man is lazy; he walks sitting down.' What was the white man doing that made the Indian say that?"

Cora Mae watched Slim eat. "What size is the town?" she said. "In a big city like San Francisco, the man might have been riding a streetcar. In Garden City, maybe he was on a horse. Or maybe the man is like Grandma Benedetto and rides around in a wheelchair."

"Maybe he's on a bicycle," Slim said. "The pedals on a bicycle go up and down like a man walking. It's not a horse because an Indian wouldn't be surprised to see a horse, and it's not a car because the man's feet wouldn't be visible to the Indian. The wheelchair could work, but it's not likely."

I smiled. I'd been riding the old bicycle a lot lately. Not in town, of course, where someone might see me, but on the dozens of dirt paths that lay just beyond the city limits. I wrote "bicycle" below the test question and turned the page. Cora Mae was pouring more batter into the frying pan when there was a knock at the door, and Pinky let himself in, with Hooch trailing behind. Cora Mae introduced them to Slim.

"Don't anybody have a real name anymore?" Pinky said.

"Slim is helping Jules study for her schoolteacher test," Cora Mae explained. "Maybe you can help with some of the answers too. Go ahead, Jules."

I worried that Pinky might question the schoolteacher story, but he just bit into a piece of bacon and looked at me like he had a deep sense of curiosity, like he hadn't quit school in third grade.

Hooch pulled a stub of a pencil from his pocket and handed it to me. "Write down the answers with this, and the pencil will remember them."

The lead was dull and the wood so chewed up it gave me the heebie-jeebies to hold it, but I needed all the help I could get. "Thanks, Hooch. Here's the next question: My neighbor has been having queer visitors. First, a doctor came to his house, then a lawyer, then a minister. What do you think happened there?"

Pinky raised his hand. "That's easy. Your neighbor is a bootlegger."

Cora Mae ruffled his hair, laughing. "Let's think now. You wouldn't need a doctor for a wedding or even for a birth, most of the time. How about a family reunion?"

"Maybe someone is dying," I said, and a flashback of Art's bare foot reeled through my mind.

"Although, you'd think they'd have settled their affairs beforehand. I mean, who calls a lawyer to his deathbed?" Cora Mae said.

"I knew a guy did that," Hooch said. "Course the lawyer was his brother."

Slim agreed with me, so I wrote, "Somebody is dying," and a little chill went over me.

"What else?" Cora Mae asked.

"Multiple choice. What is Crisco? Is it a) a patent medicine, b) a disinfectant, c) a toothpaste or d) a food product?"

Pinky took a bite of pancake before he spoke. "That's a trick question. The answer is hair product."

"Wait a minute. I've got this one," said Cora Mae. "It's a food product. Write that down, Jules."

The next question was another multiple choice. "Christy Mathewson is famous for being a) a writer, b) an artist, c) a baseball player or d) a comedian."

Again, Pinky had an answer. "Everybody knows Matty pitched for the Giants and the Reds. That was before the Krauts gave him the tuberculotis during the war."

Slim shook his head. "I'm not so certain, Mr. Pinky. Mr.

Mathewson was mistakenly gassed during a training exercise in the Great War. Before that, he was a respected pitcher, but he also wrote children's books about baseball."

I remembered the books, "Second Base Sloan," "Pitcher Pollock" and "Catcher Craig." Art had read them as a boy.

Pinky wasn't pleased. "Why did Matty bother writing books when he pitched for the Giants and Reds? What a waste."

A glob of pancake flew from Pinky's mouth onto Slim's drawing. He shook it off, but a spot of grease remained.

"These questions are impossible. What am I going to do?" I said.

"You'll do fine. Follow your instincts and use Hooch's magic pencil," Cora Mae said. Hooch, Pinky and even Slim nodded in agreement.

The answers from the sample test whirled through my head most of the night. I may have slept for a while, but when the hall clock chimed six, I was awake, dressed and ready to go. Slim had left even earlier that morning for Nebraska, and Cora Mae made me eat some of his leftover scrambled eggs and toast before Pinky dropped me off at Dr. Livermore's hospital.

"Remember what the Babe says: 'Don't let the fear of striking out hold you back.'" He gunned the car.

"Maudlin" Maude made me wait in the foyer, where all I could think about was the night Art had brought me there. I picked up a Collier's magazine and leafed through it. In between advertisements for Oldsmobiles, Goodyear tires and Schillings Auto-Camp was a story written by Babe Ruth titled

"Why I Hate To Walk." I couldn't help but wonder when Pinky would also cross walking off his to-do list.

A few pages later, I was surprised to see a story about Hutchinson, Kansas. It was the first in a new series on "How We Americans Live." Having never been to Hutchinson, I studied the photographs before skimming the story.

"Kansas is more than populism, sunflowers, prairies, agricultural weeklies, William Allen White, Prohibition, women's suffrage, grasshoppers, hot winds, wheat, corn and oats," the article reported. "Hutchinson is healthful because there are no poor there, because the neighbors would rather talk about babies than jazz, because it is still fashionable there to go to church."

The reporter might have written a different story had he traveled to parts of Kansas bloodied in those years by gangs like the Dillingers, the Cookson Hills, Ma Barker's gang and our own homegrown mob, the Fleagle Brothers. It seemed like half of the gangs either passed through Kansas robbing banks and trains, or they ended up here, at our federal prison near Leavenworth.

At last, Dr. Livermore opened his office door and beckoned for Maude and me to sit across from him at his desk. "How are you, Julianne Rose? You miss your brother, most certainly. Now, don't be afraid. These tests are simply to be sure you're on the road to recovery. Nurse will keep track of your answers."

"Dr. Livermore, I hope you don't think I'm a moron. Truth be told, I just made a mistake. You know, an error in judgment."

"You certainly did," Dr. Livermore said. "As to whether you are a moron, we'll see what the tests tell us."

He handed me a pencil, but I waved it off, instead pulling out the chewed-up one Hooch had given me.

"That disgusting pencil doesn't have all the answers, does it?" The doctor looked at me over the top of his glasses as he handed me a writing board with a booklet clipped to it. The cover read: "National Intelligence Tests, World Book Company, Yonkers-on-Hudson, New York."

"Thirty minutes." He pulled out his pocket watch and handed it to Maude.

I took my time as Slim had advised, reading each question twice before writing down an answer using my best penmanship. I didn't want to give the doctor any excuses to lower my grade. The questions were similar to the sample ones. Some had straightforward answers; others seemed to be matters of opinion.

Dr. Livermore sat across from me, smoking, while Maude fidgeted with the watch. I finished the roll of peppermints in my pocket and the test itself before Maude called time. I thought I'd done well.

Dr. Livermore put the booklet into an envelope then pulled another, larger package from his desk drawer. "I'm going to give you another test now, Julianne Rose. This one is newer and provides more accurate results."

I glanced at Maude. "My ride is probably waiting for me. Can I take this another day?"

Dr. Livermore shook his head. "It won't take long and requires relatively little exertion on your part. You simply identify a few ink sketches on some cards. No time limit."

He set a stack of cards face down on his desk, his fingernails glimmering, and slid a blank sheet of paper toward Maude. "Tell me what you see, Julianne Rose. Nurse will record your answers."

He turned over the top card, which looked like someone had shaken a pot of ink across it.

"An ink spot," I said, and Maude started to write, her red hair bobbing with each pen stroke.

"What?" Dr. Livermore looked at the card. "The test is a series of ink spots that you must identify as an image you've seen before. Look closely. What does the blotch look like?"

I reached for the card, but the doctor pulled it back, so I turned my head sideways and from the corner of my eye, saw Maude do the same.

"It's a coyote chasing a deer at sunset."

The doctor sighed and looked at the card again. He turned it sideways. "Try again."

"It could be a butterfly," I said, and Maude nodded as she wrote.

I went through four more cards that way — taking cues from Maude — until Dr. Livermore held up a card that looked like a woman with an enormous bust. My birthmark heated up, and I saw Maude startle. Dr. Livermore tapped his finger on the desk. "Don't dawdle, Julianne Rose. What does the ink spot resemble?"

I reached into my pocket, which contained only empty wrappings. I tried to see the image as anything but a bosom. Finally I said, "Truth be told, it's the Great Lakes region," and Maude wrote it down.

GARDEN CITY TRIBUNE · SATURDAY, DEC. 31, 1921

INSTITUTE RELEASES US LYNCHING RECORDS FOR SECOND HALF OF 1920

According to the records compiled by the Tuskegee Institute in the Department of Records and Research, in the last six months of 1920 there were 30 lynchings in the United States. Of those lynched, two were whites and 28 were Negroes. Five were burned at the stake; three were first put to death and then their bodies burned.

CHAPTER 20

Mahjong

Dr. Livermore explained that my tests would be mailed to Kansas City, where a team of experts would grade them and send them back. He would call for me when the results were returned. I passed the time crying, wondering why I couldn't have saved Art and eating so much that by Christmas, my maternity girdle was on its last fasteners.

We celebrated the holiday at the boardinghouse with Pinky and Hooch. Cora Mae prepared a vegetarian dinner of stewed tomatoes, cranberries, chestnut dressing, snowflake potatoes and mincemeat pie, which she reminded us didn't contain a shred of meat. We'd agreed not to exchange gifts, although everyone broke their promises.

Pinky and Hooch gave me Zane Grey's book "The Last

of the Plainsmen," about one of the founders of Garden City. Cora Mae gave me a mahjong game, which according to the Tribune was more popular than bridge. I dedicated songs to each of them on my piano, and they accepted my paltry offerings. Pinky even grew a little misty-eyed when I played him "Songs My Mother Taught Me," one of Art's favorites.

To celebrate the arrival of 1922, we planned a mahjong party for New Year's Eve, complete with Chinese food. A snowstorm swept in that morning. I watched flakes swirl through empty trees, thinking about Art freezing in the cemetery. I'd worked hard the past three months to keep away the grief. I'd repainted every room in the upstairs of the boardinghouse — silver gray with touches of royal blue, rose pink and carmine. I'd refinished an old desk of Cora Mae's and sewed new curtains for the kitchen windows.

The sadness hadn't been so all-encompassing when our parents died. Art was there to share my sorrow, and our parents had been older, with no choice in the matter.

I thought about how Art, if he'd chosen differently, could be with me right now, watching the snow fall. Instead, he and our parents had left me alone in a world where nobody else had nut-brown wavy hair or green speckled eyes or a birthmark centered on their foreheads. Cora Mae, even Pinky and Hooch to a degree, were like family, but it wasn't the same, and admitting that put my mind in a bad state.

Maybe Dr. Livermore was right about me being feebleminded. Baby Ruth was all I had now. Since Pinky had suggested giving her that name and Art had killed himself, the baby had become more real to me, more a part of me. I'd be fine as long as she was curled up inside of me. I wasn't at all sure how I'd be when they took her away. I hadn't changed my mind about becoming a mother. It still sounded depressing. It was just that somewhere along the way, Baby Ruth had become a vital part of me. I was no longer certain I could tell her goodbye.

That would be months in the future, though, so I forced my mind back to the party and the preparations that needed to be done. The Chinese New Year's Party was to be a small dinner party with Pinky, Hooch and Fanny Grundy, who was home for Christmas. Cora Mae was using an Oriental cookbook she'd found at the library.

The recipes had to be adjusted according to what was available at Grundy's Market. Nevertheless, the menu included egg drop soup, Dynasty Noodles, Nanking biscuits and three kinds of salads. Unfortunately, both the Japanese and Imperial salads included cabbage, but the Emperor's Favorite Figs did not, so I kept my eye on those. Dessert would be Peking peach pie, rice pudding and Pinky's traditional favorite, fruitcake.

Right after sundown on New Year's Eve, Pinky and Hooch arrived with three crates of moonshine. They came in through the kitchen door, stomping snow everywhere and letting the cats out. Cora Mae was dressed in the creamy peach robe that Pinky had given her for Christmas, and she made him go after the animals. When he returned a little later, he had a cat under each arm and Fanny Grundy at his side.

Fanny said she'd had to crawl out a window to escape her mother's watchful eye. She was dressed in a black cape and wore her father's cowboy hat pulled nearly over her eyes, reminding me of Cowboy Duane in Zane Grey's "The Lone Star Ranger." What she wore underneath, however, was downright Kate Bland. Fanny wasn't the "full-bodied" woman that Grey had described in the book, but in her black spaghetti-strap dress, she certainly possessed Kate's "full-blown attractiveness." The Fondale brothers whistled until she pulled off the cowboy hat. The blond hair that had tapered past her shoulders now ended at her ears and clung to her head like a cap of its own. She'd had it bobbed again.

"Like it?" Fanny smoothed a stray hair. "Mama absolutely detests it. The hair culturist at The Golden Curl styled it. I hope you don't mind that I invited her to the party too."

Truth be told, none of us had heard of a hair culturist, let alone met one. Cora Mae cut my hair, and I cut hers. Art had gone to Sam's barbershop on Main Street, and I supposed that's where Pinky and Hooch went too. I'd read about The Golden Curl's opening in the Tribune. I thought it was located on Boundary Street, the dividing line for Garden City's white and colored neighborhoods.

"Is that hair lady on the colored side of Boundary?" I asked Fanny.

She nodded. "It's the best hair salon in town, though. Posey is a real sweet gal. You'll see."

"We should have plenty of food," Cora Mae said, looking anxiously around the kitchen.

Pinky was less enthusiastic, and it occurred to me that I'd rarely seen him angry. Frustrated, stupefied, mesmerized, but rarely angry. "I'm not celebrating the beginning of 1922 with a colored. Plain and simple," he said.

Cora Mae climbed onto his lap and nestled a piece of a Nanking biscuit between his lips. "Baby boy, have you joined the KKK? They go after coloreds. They also don't like Jews, Catholics or people like us who partake in evil activities."

"I don't like the Klukkers or the coloreds," Pinky said, his biscuit half-chewed.

"But Posey Fryer is a representative colored, culturally assimilated," Fanny said.

"That culturated stuff don't mean nothing to me," Pinky said. "Dr. Livermore says colored people are feebleminded misfits who should go back South where they came from, and I agree."

"He calls me a feebleminded misfit too," I said.

"He has a whole chestful of bad words for me," Fanny said.

"He thinks we're all morons, Pinky." Cora Mae stroked the fuzz on his chin. "Seems to me that anybody Dr. Livermore doesn't like is somebody we should like."

Pinky stood up, sending Cora Mae tumbling off his lap. "I don't want people saying I'm a champithizer of the Negro. Fanny, you look like a boy with that haircut from that upstage hen coop. Hooch, load up the Packard."

Cora Mae steadied herself then hissed at Pinky. He clucked his tongue at her. Fanny pulled the cowboy hat on again, and I reached for my candy. The tension swung back and forth across the checkered tile floor so fast it was dizzying.

Hooch carried out the crates of bootleg. By the time he returned for the last one, a trail of puddles crossed the linoleum. Pinky lifted his chin. Even his ears were crimson when he looked at Cora Mae. "Seems to me you're choosing a

Negro over your longtime best sheik. That's not right, not one little bit."

"You're the one choosing," she said. "You're the one leaving."

"Horsefeathers. Come on, Hooch. Let's go find us a juice joint."

The snow was thick when they walked out. A few minutes later, the Packard's engine cranked to a start, and Hooch yelled something we couldn't hear. Then Pinky yelled and his voice came through loud and clear. "It's like Babe Ruth says, 'I hit big or I miss big. I like to live as big as I can.'"

Cora Mae ran to the door and shouted, "You are not Babe Ruth, Pinky Fondale. Not even close. Go chase yourself!"

We girls sat at the table, the clattering of our coffee cups echoing across the kitchen. We could hear the Fondale brothers' car grind into reverse and rattle backward over the snow piled in the yard. A second grinding of the gears signaled they'd reached the street, where Hooch gunned it. But the tires spun unevenly, desperately, and the accelerated growling of the engine sent out a clear signal. They were stuck.

"That man is such a flat tire," Cora Mae said with a smile. "Come on, girls."

We ran outside in our street clothes, followed by Tin Tin and the other animals. Snow filled our shoes as we hurried toward the street, and when my extra belly threatened my balance, we linked arms. The dogs circled the car, barking. Hooch pushed from behind while Pinky revved the engine, sending the car even deeper into a knee-high drift. Then we all pushed while Pinky rocked the car back and forth. Everybody was laughing except for Pinky, and even he grinned when Cora Mae fell into a snowbank. When Fanny thought she saw a window curtain move at her house, we girls decided to go back inside while the boys dug out the car.

We were crossing the yard when a bundled-up figure layered with snow approached. I thought it might be Dr. Livermore spying on me, until the person came closer, and I saw that it was a woman. A dark-skinned woman. My nerves jangled. Here I was in Garden City, Kansas, about to play a Chinese game with a Negro. I'd never dreamed of such a thing.

"Posey!" Fanny cried. "Come inside. I was worried about you out here in the storm."

Pinky and Hooch watched us until we reached the house. The snow was tapering off.

We brushed the flakes from our clothes while Posey took off her coat and hung it on the back of a chair. When Fanny introduced us, it occurred to me that Posey had every reason to view us as the misfits rather than the other way around. Cora Mae still wore her peach colored robe, Fanny had on her father's cowboy hat, and I had a melon-sized bump under my dress.

Posey Fryer, on the other hand, was the most beautiful colored woman I'd ever seen. I'll admit, I haven't seen many of them in Garden City other than the ones who crossed Boundary Street to clean houses or cook or take care of people's children. Posey had wavy black hair that fell to her shoulders, and she wore it brushed away from her face, highlighting every lovely feature, from her high cheekbones to her manicured eyebrows to her walnut eyes. She didn't say much, but she had full lips that she pressed together in a way that wasn't a smile or a frown.

We sat at the kitchen table, listening to the Packard's tires spin. Cora Mae said Pinky and Hooch would rather freeze to death than come inside, so we'd start the party without them.

We agreed. We were starving.

Posey jumped up, insisting that she should have the privilege of serving the food that everyone else had prepared. Technically, only Cora Mae had cooked, but Posey was so smooth, so quick, that we just sat and watched. She found her way through the kitchen cupboards as if she'd been there before, only once having to ask Cora Mae where something was located. She ladled steaming egg drop soup into bowls and brought them to us on a tray without spilling a drop. She got out the salads, spooning a little of each onto four plates. The cabbage reeked, but I didn't have the heart to protest. In fact, once Posey put the plate in front of me — nudging it until it was perfectly centered — the odor stirred fond memories of Art.

We talked about motion pictures while we ate. Fanny and Posey raved about the latest Tarzan film. Cora Mae talked about Rudy Valentino, nicknamed "The Sheik," after his simmering role in a wildly popular silent film of the same name. I hadn't been out on the town for so long, I had nothing to share except for my books, and I could see their eyes glass over when I mentioned Zane Grey or F. Scott.

I helped Posey clean up. Cora Mae took the dogs out and reported back that the car and its occupants were gone. She seemed a little blue, probably because it was New Year's Eve, so I suggested we try out the mahjong game. None of us knew the rules, but that wouldn't keep us from having fun, right? Cora Mae got a bottle of hooch and four glasses from the pantry.

The game had 144 mysteriously carved bone tiles, according to the instructions on the box. We each took a handful and spread them across the table.

"These flower tiles are the bee's knees. I'll take them," Fanny said. "Would you look at these piano notes, though? Jules will want those."

I was sitting opposite Fanny, but even from that angle I could see that the symbols weren't musical. "Good Lord, Fanny, those are Chinese letters, or characters, I think they're called."

"Hold on; let me get my cheaters." Cora Mae pulled spectacles out of her robe pocket and opened the little red booklet of rules. "It says to line up for the Charleston."

"We should dance?" Fanny said, and everybody laughed.

Cora Mae flipped through the booklet, looking bored. As she neared the end, I saw her eyes light up. "Listen to this. These tiles can tell fortunes too."

I got a little dizzy then. Maybe it was the heat and smoke, but it seemed like I'd been here before, or somewhere just like it, and the results had not been good. "Let's follow the rules," I said. "That's how the game is supposed to be played."

I looked to Posey for confirmation, but she only shrugged, and Cora Mae laughed. "Come on, kiddo. Don't you want to know whether you're having a girl or boy?"

I hadn't planned to share my news with everyone in

Garden City, although I was certain they'd find out eventually. Now both sides of Boundary Street would know my secret. I rubbed my belly and smiled apologies at Fanny and Posey. They smiled back, as if they hadn't heard a word. Fanny broke the silence. "How do the tiles tell fortunes? My mother would simply die if she knew what I was doing."

"Fanny, you choose a tile. I'll be the diviner," Cora Mae said.

Fanny reached for a tile, pulled her hand back, touched her hair then picked a different tile and handed it to Cora Mae, who studied the tile through her cheaters. "Let me consult the booklet."

Fanny giggled nervously, and Posey half smiled and half frowned while Cora Mae turned the pages. "Here it is. Four circles symbolize jade, which in China is prized above gold. Jade, when taken from the ground, is a dull piece of rock. It acquires value only when work and skill transform it into an object worthy of admiration."

"Keen," Fanny said. "What's it mean?"

"It's you, sweetheart. You're supposed to polish the chunk of lead that is a college girl until she turns into a baby vamp with a manacle on her ring finger." Cora Mae's voice sounded so much like Madam Isabella Luna's, I half expected her to pull a cigarette holder from a sequined bag.

"Nifty," Fanny said with a giggle. She reached for her glass of hooch, which was half empty.

"It's Posey's turn," Cora Mae said.

Posey didn't hesitate. She plucked a tile with six circles from the table, and I noticed that the skin on the palm of her hand was almost as white as mine.

Cora Mae read from the booklet using Madam Isabella Luna's voice. "You've chosen the tile that symbolizes feminine beauty, influence and appearance. Posey, it's your beauty shop."

For once, Posey smiled. "You think so, Miss Cora Mae?"

Cora Mae nodded. "Without a doubt. The shop will be a huge success. Now it's Jules' turn."

I'd decided to play along. It would be easier than battling Cora Mae. Besides, it was New Year's Eve. We were supposed to be having fun. I picked a tile I'd been eyeing from the start. A black dog hair — it looked like one of Tin Tin's — clung to the tile, and I blew it off before handing the piece to Cora Mae.

"It's the six Wan tile. It warns of danger." The room was so quiet I could hear the dogs' nails scratching against the wooden floor.

"Pick another, Jules," said Fanny. "This is a lot of hooey anyway."

I picked another tile, waiting as Cora Mae read silently from the booklet. Her lips moved when she read, just like Madam Isabella Luna's had and her eyebrows rose upward with surprise. When she finished, she lay the booklet face down on the table. The clock in the hallway chimed midnight.

"Jesus H. Christ, it's 1922," she said. "We'd better fill our glasses."

Fanny's eyes were wide. "What's the tile mean? It must be horrible."

I grabbed the booklet and read my own fortune — aloud, unfortunately. "The North Wind tile signifies that you face difficulties ahead and are missing what you need to endure."

GLADYS WISENHEIMER'S
Garden of Tidbits

Dr. T.W. Livermore says white women these days are more concerned with the ballot box than with babies. It's racial suicide, what with the Italian and Irish Catholics – not to mention the Negroes – flooding our land with their children. We women of Nordic descent should heed the late, great President Teddy Roosevelt's proclamation from eight years ago when he said, and I quote, "I wish very much that the wrong people could be prevented entirely from breeding; and when the evil nature of these people is sufficiently flagrant, this should be done. Criminals should be sterilized and feebleminded persons forbidden to leave offspring behind them."

CHAPTER 21

The Golden Curl

Six weeks passed, and I was still contemplating difficulties followed by death. I was too bulky to play at anybody's wedding, but funerals remained a possibility, and I got 10 cents more for them. Twice I read Gladys Wisenheimer's column, wondering whether having Baby Ruth was my way of fulfilling my patriotic duty or whether I should have been forbidden from having her in the first place. Otherwise, the morning's Tribune was nothing but a harbinger of good news. Mr. Grundy's mother was recovering from a bad cold, and four of the Benedetto children had survived a potentially lethal combination of measles and chickenpox.

I missed the Benedettos, even if the children were loud and argumentative. I missed my brother. His funeral was so fresh in my mind that I really had no business contemplating playing for anyone else's.

I turned the page and noticed a 2-by-2-inch advertisement for The Golden Curl buried in one corner. Miss Posey Fryer, the owner, was a graduate of the Madam C.J. Walker Hair Culturist School, according to the advertisement. Haircuts and styling were 50 cents and shampoos a quarter.

I needed both but could afford neither. My fingers reached through the bundle of hair pinned at my neck. Tiny flakes lodged below my nails when I scratched my scalp. The baby in my stomach seemed to be sucking my skin dry, not to mention my income and overall ability to get around town.

We'd had a warm spell lately, with temperatures hovering near 30 degrees. The Farmer's Almanac predicted a snowstorm later in the week, making me itch to get outside while I could.

A newcomer to the boardinghouse brood jumped into my lap. Cali the Calico cat was still feisty from her street days, and when I tickled her ears, she raked her claws over the newspaper in my lap. I lifted her to the floor, and my heart about stopped. Cali had torn off the corner where The Golden Curl advertisement had been. The newspaper scrap had floated to the floor, and I reached for it with trembling fingertips gray from the newsprint. Was it an omen?

That was the moment I realized how much living at Cora

Mae's boardinghouse had climbed under my skin. I allowed animals on my lap, and more than once I'd kissed one. It had always been Tin Tin, but it had happened several times. To make matters worse, I'd become Hooch-like with my superstitions.

I crumbled the newspaper, tossed it into the waste bin and went into the kitchen. I'd make candy and take it to the Benedettos.

I looked through my favorite cookbook, with recipes compiled by the First Methodist Ladies' Club. The recipes were usually delicious, but the ladies weren't always precise in their measurements. One recipe called for butter "the size of a walnut," and another used "enough cream of tartar as you can hold on the point of a knife." I'd made a lot of candy in my life, though, so I was confident. I just needed to pick which type I wanted to make.

Divinity was delicious; Art had adored divinity. Cora Mae liked fondant, and I couldn't keep enough peanut brittle around the house to please Pinky, who'd forged a peace treaty with Cora Mae after their New Year's spat. I'd eaten too many of the Emperor's Favorite Figs over New Year's to make fig molasses bars.

Taffy was good in cold weather, and when I checked the pantry, we had plenty of sugar, cornstarch, corn syrup and butter. I stirred the ingredients into a pot of water on the stove until the water boiled. When I could reach in with a wooden spoon and spin a perfect thread, I added a few drops of vanilla and let the mixture cool on buttered plates until it was ready to break apart.

It was early afternoon when I finished scrubbing down the countertops and drying the last of the dishes. I arranged the taffy on a plate, wrapping it in a towel for my walk to the Benedettos. I put on a dress that I'd expanded with a fabric panel, and over that, a sweater and my coat. My rubber galoshes were a tight fit under the best of circumstances, but my swollen feet made them impossible that day. Instead I wore Tin Tin's favorite shoes — still pink, one lace longer than the other and with no traction whatsoever.

The cold air was refreshing until my nostrils started sticking together. I hadn't been by our house since Art's death, and the closer I got to it, the more I dreaded seeing it.

So I turned the other way, passing Dr. Livermore's hospital without looking. When I crossed Boundary Street, the pavement ended. I'd been down here before. My mother patronized the butcher shop for its superior cuts of beef. It was a little unnerving being alone, but I felt better when I passed the colored Methodist Church and heard piano music coming through its doors. They were probably rehearsing for Sunday services.

My feet were freezing by the time I saw the sign hanging from the front porch. The Golden Curl was painted in swirling golden letters above bold black print announcing: "Miss P. Fryer, Hair Culturist."

I climbed the porch steps slowly, holding onto the handrail to keep from slipping, and pressed my forehead against the window of the front door. The floor inside was black and white square tiles, the walls painted robin's-egg blue. Down the center of the narrow room were three kitchen chairs set before mirrored dressers. A desk held a shiny black candlestick telephone. I was surprised Posey could afford one. Maybe the mahjong tiles were correct, and business was booming.

Posey was sweeping the floor. She gave me a puzzled look when she saw me and wiped her hands on her apron before opening the door.

"Miss Jules, I didn't expect to see you here today. Let me help you with your coat."

I hated to be without the concealing shelter of my coat, but the place was empty and warm.

"I brought you some taffy," I said, handing her the plate.

"Thank you, ma'm. Thank you very much." She set the plate on the receptionist's desk and turned back to me with that no-smile smile of hers that could be rearranged for whoever stood before her.

"What in the world is that smell? Ammonia?" I asked.

"I like to say it's the smell of beauty," Posey said, her eyes sweeping around the shop.

"The smell of beauty?" I asked. "No wonder I'm a stranger to it."

We laughed as I waddled around the room in my frozen shoes. I ran my fingers along the backs of the wooden chairs and across a pile of folded cotton sheets. I paused in front of a framed photograph hanging on the wall. A Negro woman sat behind the wheel of a Model T. She wore leather driving gloves, a lace collar and a brimmed hat with a huge feather plume.

"That's Madam C.J. Walker." Posey stood behind me. "She's the one who started my hair culturist school. Her daughter carries on the business. Would you like to see her products?"

I nodded and followed Posey to a dresser, its top drawer lined with rows of jars and tins. I picked up a jar labeled "vegetable shampoo."

"Cora Mae could eat this for supper. Does it only work on colored ladies' hair?"

"Madam Walker's products grow hair in addition to keeping the hair and scalp healthy. I'm sure the white ladies will find it works nicely."

"Do you mean to say that I'm the first white lady to give it a try?"

"In Garden City, ma'm." Posey shook open a white sheet and stood like a frightened matador: elbows bent, shoulders arched into dual question marks. She raised her eyebrows — I'd forgotten how beautifully manicured they were. I looked into a mirror. My hair had never been my best feature. I hadn't washed it in a week, and my last cut was in November, when Cora Mae had been preoccupied with fixing a meatless Thanksgiving meal.

"How much for a shampoo and face treatment?"

"A plate of taffy?" Posey said, and I smiled gratefully, trying not to let my excitement show through.

She let me pick the products I wanted, and I sorted through the drawer, looking over the different designs on the labels and smelling each one. She wrapped a white sheet around me, and my stomach jutted out like a watermelon in winter. The chair tilted back so I could rest my head over a basin. Posey poured a pitcher of warm water on my hair then dribbled shampoo that smelled better than any vegetable I'd ever eaten. She made slow circles with her fingertips all the way from my forehead to my neck, and I closed my eyes. Another pitcher of warm water rinsed out the shampoo, and then Posey was rubbing my hair dry with a towel.

My voice seemed to boom when it broke the silence. "This Madam Walker, was she married?"

"Married three times, ma'm. She was the sixth child of slaves, orphaned at 7 and married for the first time at 14. The recipe for her hair product came to her in a dream."

"Good Lord, don't tell Cora Mae that. She'll work vampires into the story," I said. "Six children, though. Are you from a big family, Posey?"

"Five brothers and two sisters," she said. "Except for my sister and I, who live here, they all live in Nicodemus. You've heard of Nicodemus? It's a colored town up near the Nebraska-Kansas border."

I'd heard of it, settled by freed slaves. "Your sister here, is she married with children?"

"Oh, yes. Married almost a year and just had a baby boy," Posey said.

"Your sister made it through OK?"

"She did. She said having a baby was easy as pie."

"I hope so. Guess I'll find out for myself in a few weeks."

"You from a big family, Miss Jules?"

I was surprised Posey hadn't heard my life story from Cora Mae and Fanny. So I started talking while she arranged bobby pins across my head, and I didn't stop until I'd shared every grim detail, starting with my parents' deaths and ending with Baby Ruth's impending arrival. Maybe it was because the room was warm and Posey a good listener that made me open up with particulars I hadn't even told Cora Mae.

"Good Lord," I said when I'd finished. "Madam Walker must have stirred truth potion into her shampoo."

"Don't you fret, Miss Jules. Listening is an important part of a hair culturist's job."

The telephone jangled, shattering the room's discreet covenant. Posey kept massaging pink cream onto my face.

"Aren't you going to answer?" I asked.

She looked up. "It was two longs, right? That's Dr. Livermore's ring."

My shoulders tensed. "You share a party line with him?"

"That's right. He wasn't happy about it when the telephone company gave us the same line. Until they install private lines, though, he doesn't have much choice."

"It must be torture having to listen to that man's ring all day and night. Does he listen in?"

Posey spread cream across my forehead. "He does sometimes. I think he feels obliged to know everybody's business, him being a doctor and all. Have you ever noticed how much he looks like Rudy Valentino?"

"Never. Anyway, you should complain to the authorities, Posey. That's against the telephone rules. Have you asked him to stop?"

"It's not worth the trouble, Miss Jules. You just take it easy. You've been through a lot lately, and this kind of talk isn't good for the baby."

Posey wiped the cream from my face with a small square of cotton towel. She was plucking out hairpins when the telephone rang again. Two shorts.

"Excuse me. Two shorts is me." Posey wiped her hands on her apron as she crossed the room. She picked up the telephone earpiece and bent over to speak into the mouthpiece.

"Hello. This is The Golden Curl." She spoke then listened, and I listened too. "Hello, Mrs. Morgan. I'd be happy to fix your hair. When would you like to come by? Later this week? … Hold the line a minute, please. Is that you, Dr. Livermore? … Of course, you need to keep the line clear for emergencies … Mrs. Morgan, are you still there? Hello? Hello?" She hung up slowly.

"He's a tyrant," I said. "You won't be getting much business with him on the line." I watched in the mirror as she resumed taking pins from my hair. Each one left behind a tight curl.

"It'll be fine. I just hope my clients don't get frustrated and quit calling." Posey's voice was as smooth as it was the day she served us egg drop soup at the boardinghouse. She started brushing the curls, which came together in an ocean of waves.

"Have you ever listened in on him?" I asked.

The brush yanked a little as it crossed the ocean. "Miss Jules, you know that wouldn't sit well. It's against the telephone rules. Besides, what's he saying that would interest me?"

I touched my hair, which looked better than I'd ever imagined it could. Posey's face was more frown than smile when I answered, "I'll think of something.

CHAPTER 22

Birth of a Bad Gene

The storm arrived as predicted, but unpredictably, Baby Ruth arrived in the middle of it. Earlier, I'd counted down the months, anticipating a springtime delivery. I guess I didn't consider a snowstorm in early March to be spring.

The birth pains weren't bad at first, but Hooch was the only one of us with any knowledge on the matter, and he'd only witnessed the birth of a calf. I wasn't inclined to rely on him.

Mid-morning, Hooch drove me to Dr. Livermore's hospital, with Pinky beside him and me in the back seat. Under the best of circumstances, I'd have preferred Pinky drove. He insisted, however, that the roads were in perfect condition for Hooch's nearly blind driving skills, and he was right. The car slid in places, but banks of snow caught us before we went into a ditch. Pinky yammered the whole way about Babe Ruth.

"Judge suspended him for going on a barnstorming tour. Says it dishonored his contract with the Yankees. So what does the Babe do? He signs a contract to join a vaudeville act. He's a comedian through and through."

Hooch laughed, which led to a coughing spell, and Pinky reached over to help him steer until it passed.

"I got two bits of advice for you, Jules, compliments of the Babe," Pinky said, winking and clucking his tongue. "One is to always sign a contract when you give anything away, and number two, remember that every strike brings you closer to the next home run."

At Dr. Livermore's, they helped me out and across a snow bank. Neither brother would go so far as the front steps of the house, but Hooch sweetly handed me a rabbit's foot before they left.

Maude answered the door wearing her nurse's uniform: a starched white apron and a crisp white scarf tied at the back of her neck. Snippets of red hair peeked out. She led me past the doctor's office, where I'd taken the tests and into the dead son's room, where the tiger still lunged off the banner on the wall.

I was unpacking my overnight case when Dr. Livermore walked in. "Nurse Maude, how long until the child arrives?"

"I haven't checked yet, doctor, but guessing from the distance between pains, it will be a few hours."

He looked at me. "God makes birth more difficult for those who ignore His commandments. Marriage prepares a woman for childbirth by the sacrifices it demands, the obedience it instills and the virtue it bestows."

"Dr. Livermore," I said, "it would ease my mind if you could just tell me a little about the parents who'll get my baby. I just feel so alone after losing Art."

He stared at me without saying a word. I crawled into the bed and slept fitfully, the pains waking me every few hours. I got up a few times to look out the window, watching the day grow dim as the snow fell. Occasionally, Maude checked on me, and when the pains grew intolerable, she called in the doctor.

He carried a tray of shining instruments to my bedside table. There were razor-sharp scissors, a syringe, a long wire, and forceps with deep finger depressions in the handles. A mask was there too. It looked like something out of the book "Dr. Jekyll and Mr. Hyde," with its metal slats fanning into the shape of a featureless face.

The pain frightened me; the mask was worse.

Dr. Livermore lifted my nightgown to check between my legs, which was mortifying. "It won't be long now," he said. "Prepare the morphine."

Maude handed him a syringe the size of her hand, and once more, the doctor pulled up my nightgown. When he plunged the needle into my thigh muscle, the burn brought tears followed by blissful sleep.

By midnight the morphine had worn off and the tiger on the wall was the most peaceful part of the room. I pulled at sweaty sheets twisted around my thighs, screaming and moaning. I cursed, using words I didn't realize I knew, words that made me blush even as I shouted them.

Maude and the doctor returned after what seemed like

hours. Dr. Livermore came to my side. "Nurse Maude, prepare the ether."

Maude twisted open a bottle of liquid, letting loose an overwhelmingly sweet, fruity smell into the room. She sprinkled the fluid onto a square of cotton then tucked its corners under the straps of the mask.

With both hands, Dr. Livermore lowered the mask onto my face. I tried to push it away, but Maude held my arms down as the mask dug into my skin and my eyes burned. I gasped for air, suffocating. The smell was nauseating as it filled my mouth and nose, but even as I gagged, Dr. Livermore pressed down harder.

When I came to, the mask was gone and my muscles twitched uselessly. I couldn't open my eyes, but I could smell, and I could hear. The odor was overwhelming; the sounds, muffled. It seemed as if Dr. Livermore and Maude were tromping across the room, their voices echoing from the ceiling and sliding across the floor. The baby was pushing.

I heard Dr. Livermore say something about test results and the Home for Hopeless Women.

Then came Maude's syrupy voice. "I doubt she'll repeat ... she learned a lesson."

Dr. Livermore spoke again, clearer and louder this time. "Our nation's worldwide superiority is threatened by these prolific but unmarried mothers. Add to that the endless offspring of the Italians and Irish swarming to our shores, and soon enough the defectives will outnumber the rest of us."

Clothing brushed the bed sheets. A cool hand rested on my forehead, covered seconds later by a rougher, larger hand that I recognized as Dr. Livermore's. "You're an intelligent woman, Bella, and beautiful ... it's racial suicide ... true American women of Northern European descent don't want babies ... others, like Julianne Rose here, won't stop having them ... bringing down our nation."

Maude again: "Now T.W., that's ... an exaggeration."

Water splashed, something opened and closed, a match snapped, and I caught the sweet smell of a freshly lit cigarette. Small hands brushed the hair on my forehead back, and Maude said something about my birthmark. Laughter swooped down.

Someone was at my feet, lifting the sheet and my nightgown. Cool air blanketed my legs as they fell apart.

"This baby ... too much time." It was the doctor's voice. " ... asylums prescribe dental work ... once they're under, they slice away ... no more moron babies cluttering up the gene pool."

Maude said something about "the woman not knowing," and the doctor replied: "takes less time than a dentist cleaning a cavity."

Maude's hands covered my legs with the blanket again. "Doctor, do you think the feebleminded ... overwhelmed by animal instincts?"

Dr. Livermore's voice grew so soft I almost couldn't hear him. "Animal instincts ... powerful lust ... you've witnessed it, Bella."

"Don't be vulgar, T.W. "

"I'm talking about ... a man's soul ... let me show you again ... don't deny me, darling."

"You're a regular drugstore cowboy ... now is not the time."

"Please, Bella," he said, and I listened to a shuffling of shoes followed by a shriek.

"Maude!" he cried.

The sound of crashing metal and breaking glass was so near, I tried to jump but couldn't.

Dr. Livermore shouted, "My God, the ether!"

The fruity smell grew unbearable. Shoes crunched around the room, a window opened, and somebody retched. I heard splattering on the floor.

I woke from a dreamless sleep. The room was freezing. Dr. Livermore, preceded by his stale, smoky smell, was at my side again. I heard Maude cough, and somebody peeled away the layers around my legs, saying, "It's time."

Baby Ruth pushed and I saw her. She had curly blond hair and piano-playing fingers. She floated in a sea of water, waving goodbye.

The hall clock chimed midnight.

ONE IN 12 KANSAS BABIES DIES IN FIRST YEAR

Nearly one in 12 Kansas babies dies before its first birthday. Accidents and illnesses result in the deaths of nearly 3,000 babies every year. The Kansas State Board of Health is doing its bit to stop this loss of life by publishing the Kansas Mother's Manual, a booklet of 114 pages. For a free copy, write to the Division of Child Hygiene, State Board of Health, Topeka.

CHAPTER 23

Dreaming of Benjamin Button

The day after Baby Ruth's birth was as bad as the day of the birth itself. I exhaled ether until it filled my room, my bedding, my hair and my skin. The odor outdid every other smell. I retched into a metal pan, and when the smell came back at me, I retched some more. My eyes were raw; my nose constantly dribbled. Sitting and walking were difficult because of the tearing between my legs and a gut-wrenching pain from the place Baby Ruth had occupied.

It's difficult to describe how much I missed her. For nine months, we'd been one. I'd felt her movements; she'd felt mine. She ate what I ate. Our blood flowed between us. The breaking of the bond was harder to endure than losing my parents or even Art, and I suspected the empty feeling would never go away.

It took all my energy to replace those thoughts with the shaky conviction that the right step was giving her up for adoption to what I hoped would be a kind and loving family.

Maude arrived in a clean pinafore, her red hair combed into a bun. She snapped up the roller blinds, and sunlight screamed in from the snow outside. Snow was piled taller than the men I could see working to clear the streets with horse-drawn sleds.

"I'm going to change your linens now. Can you make it to the chair?" Maude asked.

I nodded, so she helped me to sit then stand and shuffle to the chair. She showed me how to sit by grasping the chair's arms from behind then lowering myself. The blanket on my bed crackled with static electricity as she folded it. She made a puddle of dirty sheets on the floor near my feet.

"Was my baby OK?" I asked. "Was it a girl, like I suspected?"

"Dr. Livermore is on his way. We'll ask him."

Sure enough, the door burst open, and Dr. Livermore came in, trailing snow across the wooden floor. He coughed into a handkerchief that he held over his mouth and nose.

"My God, that ether brings as much trouble as it resolves. Nurse Maude, crack a window."

Maude used both hands to push up a window, and a swirl of freezing air moved in. The doctor felt my forehead, the sides of my neck and behind my ears. "No signs of infection. Are you feeling well, Julianne Rose?"

"Not really. Is my baby OK?"

"The baby is fine. I would prefer that it be nursed. I won't insist, however, because of the damage created by uniting an illegitimate child with its unmarried mother. Besides, the cold weather will keep the cow's milk from going bad. In the summer, you know, twice as many babies die because insects carry disease to the milk."

"Did I have a girl?" I asked.

Dr. Livermore stroked his hair, watching Maude pull the sheets tight before helping me back to the bed. "Nurse Maude, what do you think? Does an unwed mother deserve to know whether she had a girl or boy?"

Maude looked at me, not him, when she spoke. "Jules has a right to know, doctor. She's been punished enough already."

The doctor seemed stung by her words. His shoulders slumped as he spoke. "I am not a totally heartless man. It can be injurious to give too much information in a case like this."

He watched Maude cross the room and take a writing board from the dresser drawer. When she handed it to him, his fingers rested briefly on hers, and a memory flittered across my mind. "Here's the birth certificate," she said.

Dr. Livermore gave me a half smile. "All right, Julianne Rose. You had a girl. It was as you suspected."

I hesitated for a moment, looking to Maude for confirmation, but she was staring at Dr. Livermore. "Your baby was beautiful," she said. "Blond, curly hair, just as you pictured."

"Thank you so much." I was jubilant. "Thank you for telling me. Truth be told, I knew I was having a girl. I even named her — Ruth. And did she have long fingers, like a pianist?"

"Long, slender fingers — for a baby that is," Maude said.

The baby's gender was a scrap of information, but it helped to complete the picture lodged in my mind. I had a little girl with blond curls and long fingers.

"Let's get this done," Dr. Livermore said, leaning over the writing board. "Born shortly before midnight on March 6, 1922, at the T.W. Livermore Hospital in Garden City, Kansas. Illegitimate."

He wrote with great swoops of his pen. "And the real parents will pick the child's name."

"Are they the couple you had in mind all along?" I asked.

"The God-fearing people, yes. They have agreed to take the child despite your test results, which were less than satisfactory."

"I didn't realize they'd come back. How did I do?"

"Not well, but well enough. We'll discuss them another time."

He slammed the window shut and started to leave. My courage was foundering, so I blurted, "Can I hold her just once?"

Dr. Livermore shook his head. "The weather has created bad traveling conditions for the new parents. However, they are on their way. Until their arrival, you and the child must remain separated. Is that clear?"

He looked at Maude, who was focused on folding a blanket. Not long after the two of them left the room, a newborn's wails pierced the air. They were coming from a room directly above mine.

As it turned out, Baby Ruth and I cried together for two nights and three days. Once an hour, I could hear Maude pad up the stairs and across the room. The floorboards would sway, and the cries would quiet. My breasts ached when the milk arrived. Maude said the best relief was to wrap the affected area in a paste of, what else, cabbage.

I told her a candy bar might help, and she brought me a Hershey's. I ate it as I read a Collier's, but the magazine only gave me nightmares. The main feature was an F. Scott Fitzgerald story called "The Curious Case of Benjamin Button." It was about a baby born at age 70, with almost no hair and a wispy beard. As time passed, the baby grew younger until it finally died as an infant.

After breakfast on the third day, I tried to sneak upstairs for myself, but the stairs groaned, and Maude caught me. That afternoon, I looked out to see Pinky's Packard pulled to the curb. Maude had already packed my bag, and as I walked downstairs, I nearly collided with Dr. Livermore.

"You're leaving," he said. "That's just as well. The parents will be here tomorrow. However, we will need to have you back to discuss the test results. I'll be in touch."

"You'll need my signature, though, on the adoption papers." I spoke as if Cora Mae had grabbed onto my vocal chords, but it was Pinky's advice about a contract pushing me on.

"That's questionable," the doctor said.

"It won't be legal otherwise. I promise not to make a fuss about it. I would like to see my little girl just once, though. This separation is harder than I'd thought." My throat ached.

"We've gone over this. A reunion of any sort will only make it more difficult for you, your child and the real parents."

Baby Ruth started crying, and Maude brushed past us on

her way upstairs. Pinky honked, and Dr. Livermore looked out. "You're associating with the Fondale boys? What would your brother say?"

There was movement at the top of the stairs, and when I looked up, Maude was holding a tiny bundle wrapped in a yellow blanket. Dr. Livermore gripped my elbow and guided me out the door. He handed Pinky my suitcase then opened the car door for me, leaning in at the last minute to speak.

"You should understand, Julianne Rose. There will be no more babies."

———————

At the boardinghouse, Tin Tin jumped from Cora Mae's lap to the floor when he saw me.

"Welcome home, kiddo," she said. "I've got blueberry muffins in the oven. Get us a couple plates."

I opened a cupboard, and a gray cat nestled inside hissed at me. That's all it took to open the floodgates. Cora Mae wrapped her arms around me as I launched into a full-fledged cryfest.

"I can't believe how much I miss her. It was a girl — I was right about that. If it had been a boy, I was going to name him Arthur. I could hear her crying from the room above mine, but Dr. Livermore wouldn't let me see her. Maude did. When I left today, she came to the top of the stairs with the baby wrapped in a blanket. I couldn't really see what she looked like, though."

"The baby is still at the hospital?" Cora Mae asked.

I nodded, wiping my nose with a handkerchief. "The storm delayed the parents. Dr. Livermore says they'll get in tomorrow. Don't you think I should sign something, though? How can the adoption be legal if I don't sign the papers?"

"I don't know," Cora Mae said. "Are you all right, though? I mean, what was it like when you delivered the baby? Do you remember anything?"

"Not much. They took away the pain with ether, which smells horrible. I couldn't move, but I could kind of hear and smell. I'm not sure it worked properly."

I ate a muffin, thinking until I was exhausted. I slept until dinner, when the smell of baking bread woke me. Cora Mae must have given the Fondale brothers the bum's rush because it was just the two of us at the kitchen table.

"Did you have sweet dreams?" She served bread and tomato soup the color of her robe.

"You know, I did and I didn't. I'm not certain if it was a dream or a memory that came to me. I remember glass breaking and the ether becoming suffocating. I remember the sound of kissing too."

I imitated the noises I'd heard, and each memory opened onto another until the entire miserable night rose to the surface.

"The ether must not have put me out all the way because I remember he called her Belle, or Bella. That's it. And she called him T.W. Dear Lord, do you suppose they're having an affair?"

"Dr. Livermore, a lounge lizard? He may look like an aging version of The Sheik, but Jesus H. Christ, it's sick to even imagine him ... you know," Cora Mae said. "On the other hand, this might be a chance to get back at the old prune pit.

"If he ever goes crazy, you tell him what you remember," she said. "So the baby is on the top floor? Would that be the room at the top of the back steps?"

HAMMERSTED BABY DIES WHILE MOTHER MILKS COWS

A recent house fire at the Hammersted farm outside of Garden City consumed a family's belongings, furniture and about $250 in cash. Their 7-month-old baby died of burns the next day. At the time of the fire, Mr. Hammersted was absent, and his wife was a short distance from the house milking the cows. How the fire originated is unknown.

CHAPTER 24

The Visit

A thousand stars pinpricked the sky that night as we walked to Dr. Livermore's hospital. The snow had melted, then frozen again, since my trip earlier in the day, and ice crackled beneath our feet. Tin Tin chased after us, so Cora Mae had to take him back and lock him inside. Dogs weren't allowed on this particular adventure.

It still hurt me to walk, so we took our time, finally reaching Dr. Livermore's around midnight. We tried to avoid the ice as we walked to the back stairway. It was a fire escape, narrower than I'd imagined, without a handrail. At the top was a door with a window.

Cora Mae looked around while I counted: 15 steps covered

with snow and ice.

"Dogs?" she whispered. "Does he have dogs?"

I shook my head.

"That figures. What dog in its right mind would want to live with him?"

I hugged her, fighting against my nerves, before I started climbing slowly and painfully. The snow muffled my footsteps, but the boards squeaked. I hadn't realized I had such big feet — longer than the steps themselves. Halfway up, it occurred to me that the door might be locked. When I stopped to look down at Cora Mae for a sign of encouragement, a wave of vertigo swept over me, making me reach for the handrail that wasn't there. I pulled back, took a few deep breaths and climbed to the top.

The door opened easily. I'd expected it to be locked or heavy, but it swung freely and silently. I gave a little wave to Cora Mae before walking inside.

It was the baby's room, all right. I recognized the smells of cleaning powder, slightly sour milk and laundry soap. I smelled myself too. Not my sweat or the food smells from dinner but my own particular smell that Baby Ruth had gotten from me.

I waited for my eyes to adjust to the dark. The room was used for storage. Piles of quilts, a spinning wheel and a rocking chair sat in no particular order, as if they'd been forgotten. The metal crib too looked abandoned, except for the impossibly tiny mound wrapped in a blanket and lying in the center. The little bundle rose slightly with each breath.

I crossed slowly, taking a step then bringing both feet together before taking another step. I kept my eyes on Baby

FINDING BABY RUTH

Ruth, watching for signs that she was awake and on the verge of crying. Finally my hands gripped the white bar at the edge of the crib.

Baby Ruth was on her back, her hands curled up on either side of her head. She had the long piano-player's fingers and the wispy blond curls that I'd seen in my vision right before she was born. Her fingernails were a fraction of my own, and the slivers of her lips were crinkled. She reminded me of Art, except for her forehead, which was stamped with a thumbprint of scarlet. It was a birthmark, nearly identical to the ones my mother and I had.

I'd planned to just look, but I couldn't resist fingering her silky hair, and, when that didn't rouse her, I touched her cheek, amazed at the softness. Suddenly, Baby Ruth opened her eyes. They were as brown as her father's. I held my breath, pulling my hands back to the side rail.

"Don't cry, sweet pea," I whispered. "Mama is here."

Tears drizzled down my cheeks while I thought about how easily I could take her. She'd feel like a loaf of bread in my arms as I ran back to the boardinghouse. We'd hide out until morning then take a train to Wichita or maybe New York City, where strangers would fuss over Baby Ruth and talk about how much she resembled me. I'd have to change our names, but I could teach piano lessons to pay the rent and tell people her father had died in a farm accident.

The baby whimpered, and when I stepped backward, I tripped on a wooden box, splintering the top slats when I landed in a sitting position. I cried out from the pain, and the baby's whimpers exploded into full-blown cries. I heard a door open below and footsteps on the stairs. I pushed up from the crate, scratching a finger on a jagged edge, just as Maude opened the door.

"Jules, what on earth?" She stood in the doorway.

"I only wanted to see my baby. Please, Maude. Please, don't tell Dr. Livermore." Once again, Cora Mae must have crawled down my throat to expel what I said next. "Or should I call you Bella, and him, T.W.?"

A few days later, Maude showed up at the boardinghouse. She must have been afraid of dogs because she hesitated when I answered the door with three yappers at my side. After I put them outside, she followed me to the parlor, where Cora Mae and I had been enjoying an after-supper smoke.

Maude didn't look anything like she did at Dr. Livermore's hospital. Her uniform was soiled, and her carrot-colored hair fell out of the bun at her neck. Her eyes were puffy, making me think either she was tired or she'd been crying.

I tried to be gentle when I repeated what I'd overheard the night Baby Ruth was born. I didn't want to tarnish Maude's reputation, I explained. I knew how awful that could be. And although I had no plans to kidnap the baby, I wanted to see for myself that she was in a good home. I needed to see her one more time.

"Neither of us is a candidate for Miss Garden City, but we might be able to help each other along, which is why I'm here," she said, falling into a full-blown crying spell. While we waited for her to recover, Cora Mae rolled a cigarette and handed it to Maude. I was shocked when, after blowing her nose a few times, Maude lit up like a professional, puffing away as she told her story in the syrupy voice that took me back to the night Baby Ruth was born.

"The adoptive parents took the baby two days ago. I didn't get their names because Dr. Livermore locked the papers in his desk drawer. He's suspicious or maybe just disappointed that I haven't always ... returned his affections. He asked the new parents a lot of questions. I can tell they're good people who are delighted to have a baby. They told the doctor they'd been trying for seven years to have their own."

It hadn't occurred to me that someone desperate for a baby would get mine. The idea made me feel better.

"They farm near Rosebush," Maude said. "He has a side business as a photographer."

"A photographer?" Cora Mae asked. "Did they have the name of the business painted on the side of their car? You must have seen it parked outside the hospital."

Maude kept looking out the porch window, and I suspected it was more than the dogs making her nervous. "It was a black Ford Model T," she said.

"Good Lord. Half the county drives Model Ts, and they're all black," I said. "Did it have any add-ons? You know, privacy curtains or hood ornaments?"

"They're farmers," Maude said as if that answered the question. And it did. Farmers wouldn't spend money on equipment that wasn't useful in the field.

"How do you know they were nice? What did they look like?" I asked.

"They were gentle. The father held the baby. He was

missing a couple of fingers on one hand. He wore fancy cowboy boots. Dr. Livermore asked him about his boots, and the man said he collected them."

"Truth be told, a collection of boots?" Goosebumps jumped down my arms as I recalled Madam Isabella Luna's advice to watch for the boots that line the rail. Then I remembered something else, another slip of information: the photographer who took the Benedetto family picture was missing two fingers on one hand.

Maude asked if we had liquor in the house. I didn't think Cora Mae should admit that we did, but she was gone in a flash and returned carrying three glasses. Maude tipped hers back without a sputter, and her eyes grew shiny with emotion.

"Now I need your help," she said, turning to Cora Mae. "Word around town is that you know somebody who can help a girl in trouble. Well, I'm in real trouble."

Maude and Cora Mae talked for hours while I did the evening chores, drifting in and out of the room. They got tipsy and teary, and at one point I heard Maude say, "Underneath it all, he looks nothing like The Sheik."

They both giggled, then Cora Mae turned serious. "Sister Margery predicted this, you know. That day they came to town, she told Dr. Livermore to watch for his son. Everybody figured she meant his dead son, but maybe it was this one instead."

GARDEN CITY TRIBUNE · MONDAY, APRIL 24, 1922

ROSEBUSH MERCANTILE SAFE BLOWN WHILE NEIGHBORS SLEEP

The big safe at the Rosebush Mercantile was blown up Saturday night and robbed of approximately $754.55. The thieves also carried away several silk sweaters and a quantity of men's and ladies' hosiery.

Windows were smashed, and there was considerable damage to the interior of the store, but strange to say, no one was awakened from their sleep sufficiently to realize what was going on. Two families living nearby were aroused from their sleep, but both said they thought one of their children had fallen out of bed.

CHAPTER 25

The Road to Rosebush

The robbery in Rosebush was one in a string of similar events that had occurred recently around Garden City. I'd kept track of them all by scouring the Tribune — as well as any other nearby small-town newspaper I could get my hands on — for clues to my baby's whereabouts. I'd read every birth announcement and baptismal report. I'd pored over the advertisements, hoping to find photographers seeking customers or perhaps even old cowboy boots. I'd found nothing. It was as if my child had disappeared into the snowstorm.

Pinky and Hooch had offered to take Cora Mae and me

for a drive to Rosebush, and despite my misgivings about the brothers, I'd accepted. The trip might provide relief from my worries, and I'd keep my eyes open whenever we passed a farmhouse where my baby might live. Besides, it was a beautiful spring day.

Pinky and Hooch looked like twins when they arrived that morning at Cora Mae's. Each wore a white Van Heusen shirt and gray, wide-legged flannel trousers. The only difference in their dress was that Hooch wore a fedora, while Pinky had on a New York Yankees baseball cap that he claimed had been worn by Babe Ruth himself. He'd even tucked a cabbage leaf underneath, a trick he claimed Babe Ruth used to stay cool.

Cora Mae and I had filled picnic baskets with peanut butter and jelly sandwiches, hardboiled eggs, pickled beets, fruit salad, lettuce salad, lemonade and two cakes. If all went well, the 20-mile drive would take us an hour and a half each way, meaning we'd be home that night. Still, it was better to be prepared. The road to Rosebush had countless potholes and no diners, and without a doubt the Packard would get a flat tire or worse.

Cora Mae refused to go if Hooch drove, so Pinky took the wheel while Hooch sat in the passenger seat, and Cora Mae and I stretched out in the back seat, with the picnic baskets.

A heavy rainstorm had passed through the day before, so it was unlikely the roads would be dusty. Still, Pinky and Hooch wore driving goggles as we took off down Main Street.

The last time I'd been this way, I was in Jiggs' car, terrified that someone would see me. Now as we passed Grundy's Market and the Electric Theater, I didn't put my face against

FINDING BABY RUTH

the window, but I didn't sink low in the seat either. I had less to lose on this adventure.

When we drove past the Heidlemyer place, with its row of wooden crosses, Cora Mae and I exchanged a look. Florence Heidlemyer's suffering might not have been in vain after all. Her death by crochet needle had started Cora Mae's search for the lady in Topeka. A few days earlier, we'd put Maude on a train headed that way.

Nobody said much as we drove along. Clusters of red and black cattle walked along fence lines, and birds perched on almost every bleached-white stone post. Hooch pointed out the telephone pole where he left bootleg liquor for patrons, each of whom was scheduled to pick up on a different day. The system worked splendidly unless folks got their days mixed up, which he said happened occasionally.

No sooner had we picked up to a brisk 30 miles per hour than we hit a patch of mud. The car swiveled before coming to a standstill. Pinky gunned the engine, cursing and making the tires sink further.

Hooch and Pinky took turns shoveling mud while Cora Mae and I stretched our legs. We hadn't walked far when I saw the path between wheat fields that Jiggs had driven down. So much had happened since then. I wondered if Jiggs had made it to California — whether he'd gotten stuck in the mud along the way — and whether he'd made it onto the big screen like he'd predicted. It would be strange to once again look into those dark eyes, those Jack Dempsey eyes, magnified a hundred times over.

Pinky whistled for us to return. The brothers were sweaty,

and mud climbed the legs of their flannel pants, but the car was free, so we went on.

About mid-morning, we turned off the main road onto a winding dirt path that eventually became two tire tracks in the dirt. Pinky explained he needed to visit his Ma. We stopped three times for Hooch to unlock gates made of barbed wire and tilting fence posts. He'd wait until we drove through then close and lock the gate before jumping back in the automobile. On the fourth gate, someone had posted a hand-painted sign that read: "Pedalers and sells men will be shot."

"I made that myself," Pinky said proudly while Hooch opened the gate.

The Fondale home was a new, two-story frame building that had never been painted. Not a single flower or tree had been planted, and the dirt yard emerged as little islands in a sea of floating newspapers, rubbish and Russian thistle. To reach the house, Pinky maneuvered around rusted farm equipment and broken-down automobiles.

No farm dogs greeted us, no living creature stirred, even when Pinky honked the car's horn — one long and three shorts. He and Hooch got out and bounded up the listing front steps. A few minutes later, Pinky came back for Cora Mae. She was to meet his ma; I was to wait.

I ate a sandwich, careful not to spill on Pinky's velour upholstery. I tore off a piece of cake. Cora Mae was experimenting with angel food cake recipes for the county fair coming up. She'd gotten second place for her entry last year and was determined to take first this year. She'd tried five recipes, each of which used a dozen eggs and a cup of sugar. Each had been delicious, and my sample that day was no exception. When I looked closely, though, I saw two black cat hairs sticking out. I'd need to remind Cora Mae to omit those from the recipe.

I was eating a second sandwich when the brothers came out with Cora Mae. Pinky pulled out a handkerchief and polished the car's hood ornament. It was a silver-plated angel, soaring toward heaven, her skirt hiked over slender thighs and a tiny spare wheel in her extended hands.

Pinky said he wanted to give us an auto tour of the place. At one outbuilding, the brothers loaded up crates of bootleg. At another, Hooch retrieved guns and a battered valise. Our third stop was at a grain bin. While Pinky circled in the car, Hooch went inside and, to our amazement, hoisted open a door on pulleys. The entryway was indistinguishable from the wood siding and big enough to drive a car through, which Pinky did. We sat inside, watching dust float through the air and listening to mice scurry.

"Might as well use this place for something," Pinky said with a grin. "Sister Margery gave me the idea."

I remembered her standing on the porch, dressed like a vampire and talking about how the two Fondale brothers killed in the Great War wanted Pinky to leave his car in the "tower of grains."

We continued on to Rosebush. It was a smaller version of Garden City, although it had grown since I last visited, not long after my parents died. We passed the market, post office, a half-dozen churches and three banks. I couldn't find the diner named Reddy's, where Jiggs had flirted over his pie with the waitress. At the First National, Pinky pulled over, saying he wanted to see if what he'd heard was true about the bank's president carrying a revolver once owned by the outlaw Jesse James. When he took off his Babe Ruth hat, the cabbage leaf fluttered out the window, onto the ground.

He and Hooch got out and stood arguing until Pinky went into the bank alone. Hooch came back to search the car for one of his rabbit's feet. He told us he was afraid he'd dropped it on one of his gate-opening jaunts at the farm, and we all searched in vain until Pinky returned.

The bank president wasn't there, he explained. We might as well head home.

We left town on a different road than we'd come in on. Hooch said it was a shortcut, and it was a nice change of scenery. We put the windows down as we passed field after field of freshly planted corn.

The Packard did get a flat tire, and while Hooch patched it, the rest of us sat on a blanket near the road to eat our picnic. I poured glasses of lemonade — with flecks of dust — and Pinky took a glass over to Hooch.

"I got a postcard from Slim," Cora Mae whispered. "He's coming back during the fair to take me up in his airplane. Pinky doesn't need to know."

She looked at me as if for confirmation, so I nodded.

"Wasn't that hidden garage at his place strange?" she said.

"You mean strange because no law-abiding citizen would need a hidden garage?" I asked.

"Strange because those fortune-tellers predicted it, along with a lot of other amazing things like Grandpa Grundy's passing and Dr. Livermore's baby with Maude. They even knew about Art's decision to take his own life."

"We can't be certain about that part," I said. "Maybe Sister Margery was pulling our leg. Maybe she just needed another shot of moonshine before she and Madam Isabella started telling fortunes for the night."

I swallowed a lump in my throat before I could speak again. "But remember when Madam Isabella brought your dog back, only she called it Russell instead of Russet? She said you were seeing a ZaSu Pitts film when he died, but it was Lillian Gish. She told me to watch for my boy where the boots line the rail, and that's where I first saw Jiggs, the drugstore cowboy."

"It just seems crazy that so much of what they said came true," she answered.

Pinky came back to tell us the tire was fixed. He stuffed a wad of cake into his mouth and said, "This is your best yet, Cora Mae. A grand-prize winner. The Babe says you just can't beat the person who never gives up."

The sun was setting as we drove on. I fell asleep, my head bouncing with every bump of the road. It wasn't a restful sleep, but it was deep enough that I jumped and almost hit my head on the car ceiling when Cora Mae shouted, "Jesus H. Christ, would you look at that?"

Everybody looked, and the car weaved sluggishly. Just off the road was a tidy farmhouse surrounded by white outbuildings and a red barn in back. Chickens strutted down a gravel driveway, and two horses gazed at us through the slats of a winding fence. It was a split-rail fence held up every 10 feet or so by wooden posts, and situated on top of each post was what had made Cora Mae shout. Cowboy boots had been placed upside down, to keep them from blowing away. They were weathered and worn and missing heels. Each one was different, although I supposed if you walked the entire length, you'd find its mate.

"Why'd they treat decent boots that way?" Hooch said, but Cora Mae was shouting over him, telling Pinky to turn into the driveway. As soon as he did, three big dogs came running, and Pinky slowed down until we were barely moving.

Cora Mae looked back at me. "Don't you see? It's the boots that line the rail. You're supposed to look for your boy here."

But I'd had a girl, Jiggs was long gone and the only boys I could see were in the front seat. I didn't want to dampen Cora Mae's enthusiasm, though, so I looked out the window. Behind us, where the horses stood, a sign had been mounted on a post. It faced away from us, though, so I'd have to read it when we left. It probably gave the name of whoever lived in the house.

Whoever that was must not have been home, because nobody came to settle the dogs. Pinky stuck his head out the window. He winked and clucked his tongue at the dogs. "Hey, little fellows. I'm just part of the family."

The dogs kept yapping, though, and one with a scarred nose jumped up, clawing the Packard's maroon shine.

"Damn you! You'd better not scratch my automobile." Pinky used his Babe Ruth baseball cap to whack the dog, and the dog wrapped its jaws around the hat. The dog growled and Pinky shouted. The tug of war made the other dogs frenzied.

At the sound of fabric shredding, Pinky let go, his hand

banging the door below. The dog carried the hat to the front porch and laid it down. He sniffed the ground nearby, relieved himself on a bush and started digging. When he'd reached a few inches down, he put the hat in the hole. We watched from the car as the New York Yankees crosswise initials disappeared in dirt.

"Son of a gun, that's my special hat. Hooch, reach me my shotgun."

Cora Mae grabbed his shoulder. "Don't you dare, Pinky Fondale. That wasn't even Babe Ruth's real hat."

Pinky looked at her. "But you said when you gave it to me … "

"I know. I'm sorry. I pushed the truth. I promise I'll get you another one if you just calm down."

Pinky stepped on the clutch and shifted into first gear. We drove to the back of the house, where we saw a doorway into the earth, a standard feature on most farms in tornado-ridden Kansas, as well as a freshly painted outhouse and a child's wagon. An empty clothesline stretched from one freestanding pole to another.

"Let's get out of here," I said. "It's almost dark."

Pinky nudged the car through the flock of chickens, back down the driveway to where the dog sat on the burial place of the Yankees hat.

"Come on, let's skedaddle," Cora Mae said.

Pinky tore out so fast I couldn't make out the family's name on the sign inside the fence. All I could see was a silhouette of what looked like an accordion. I puzzled over that the entire way back to Garden City. When we drove past Dr. Livermore's hospital, it came to me. The shadow was a camera with bellows, the kind used by professional photographers.

GARDEN CITY TRIBUNE · THURSDAY, JUNE 8, 1922

COUNTY FAIR PROMISES TO BE BETTER THAN EVER THIS YEAR

Come out to the Finney County Fair this week! You won't want to miss the competitions for food preparation and animal husbandry, or the fascinating displays of the latest gadgetry. New this year will be aerial stunts featuring Charles "Slim" Lindbergh. Also new will be a Better Baby Contest and an essay contest sponsored by the Kansas State Children's Bureau. The theme of the essay contest is to explain the decline of birth among Nordic women.

CHAPTER 26

The Better Baby Contest

Slim returned to Garden City as promised, only he wasn't flying an airplane, he was standing on his head between the upper and lower wings. The Tribune called him an "aerial daredevil." Most of Garden City turned out to watch in an open field east of town. On the airplane's second pass over, Slim jumped off, spiraling earthward until, at the last moment, he pulled a cord and floated down on a muslin parachute. Mrs. Grundy fainted.

The barnstorming act marked the opening day of the weeklong county fair, an annual ritual in Finney County. For days, workers had been at the fairgrounds setting up carnival rides and game booths. Rows of huge tents were erected to house displays of everything from garden produce to gopher traps to prizewinning pigs.

Dr. Livermore was to judge the Better Baby Contest and the essay contest. I wasn't certain the doctor was of Nordic descent — he looked more German than Scandinavian — but he was definitely the authority on superiority.

Cora Mae insisted we walk rather than take a ride from Pinky, even though the temperature was approaching a hundred degrees when we left at mid-morning. Her excuse to Pinky was that the car might bounce the air right out of her double-layered angel food cake. At the fairgrounds, the midway swirled with the sugary smells of candied apples and taffy. Sweat-stained barkers reiterated the guarantees of winning, and an old man called young men to step into the boxing ring with Benny "The Bulldog" Kowalski. Pipe organs at the carousel and Ferris wheel competed with each other. Chickens squawked, cows bawled and horses left a trail of grassy-sweet-smelling manure.

Cora Mae needed to sign up for the cake-baking contest, so we made plans to meet later, and I wandered into the tent where the Better Baby contest was underway. A short, bald man in a stark white suit shouted at women with crying babies on their hips and in carriages.

"The good mother doesn't play with the baby or overindulge him with kisses and hugs," the man said. "A kiss on the forehead each morning or evening is sufficient. Laughter only strains the developing nervous system."

He held up his hands, waving forms through the air. "Now, do we have a few good mothers with beautiful babies?

We'll announce winners at the end of the week. You provide your family history. We'll do medical exams, psychiatric assessments and intelligence tests."

Cora Mae was waiting for me at our prearranged meeting spot, just outside the tent marked "Discoveries." Together we went inside.

An entire wall was taken up by an exhibit of electrical gadgets for homeowners lucky enough to have their homes wired. We saw pop-up toasters, irons and a permanent-wave machine that looked like a chandelier.

Down another aisle was newfangled photography equipment. I looked through spectacles that had one red and one green lens and saw how a building in a photograph could look three-dimensional.

We reached the booths where the photographers advertised their work. One man sold postcards with photos that were obviously hoaxes. We laughed at an ear of corn the size of a train and a man riding through the sky on a grasshopper. Another man displayed pictures of buildings in New York City, Chicago and Kansas City. He'd taken a few of Garden City too, and Cora Mae paid a nickel for one that showed the Electric Theater advertising a Douglas Fairbanks movie on its marquee.

Near the tent's exit was a table covered with photographs of people, and when we looked closely, we recognized them.

"There's Melba Swanson in her wedding dress, and look at this one of Old Man Willie," I said.

Cora Mae leaned over to get a better look. "Jesus H. Christ.

Old Man Willie looks positively young. That must have been taken before he started making moonshine."

The photographer grinned proudly from where he stood behind the table. "Come by my studio someday, ladies. Have a photograph taken for your grandchildren to remember you by."

Cora Mae and I exchanged smirks before I returned to search for more familiar faces in his display. One picture in a simple black frame showed a man who looked so much like Pinky and Hooch he could have been their father, although Cora Mae insisted his ears weren't big enough. The same man was in another shot, this one in a frame that opened like a book, with hinges joining the two sides. The other half showed a woman with ears poking through her hair. Cora Mae asked the photographer about it, and while they talked, I looked through a tray of lockets in different sizes and shapes.

I sorted through a few before picking up one the size of a half dollar and clicked it open. Photos were mounted on both sides. One showed a baby holding onto a wooden chair and dressed in a knit suit and hat. The other photo showed a couple. I recognized the man as the photographer who was talking to Cora Mae. He and a woman were dressed in their Sunday best, standing in front of house that struck me as familiar. It was a typical Kansas farmhouse — two stories, surrounded by a barn, a fence and outbuildings.

"Where's your studio?" I interrupted the man's conversation with Cora Mae, and he leaned across the table to see which photograph I held.

"I operate out of my home," he said. "That's a self-portrait of me and my family."

FINDING BABY RUTH

"What's the baby's name?" I asked.

"That's Elizabeth, or it was." His voice lowered. "She ... she died not long after this was taken."

Cora Mae clucked her tongue. "I'm sorry. That's awful. We'll take one of your cards. Maybe have our portrait done someday."

The man extended his card between his finger and thumb, and I noticed with a start that he was missing two fingers. It was the man who'd photographed the Benedetto family after the sunflower baby died, the man Maude said had adopted Baby Ruth! I pulled the photograph in the locket toward me until it was only a few inches from my eyes. Sure enough, I realized that what was familiar to me wasn't so much the house but what was barely visible in the background. It was the split-rail fence with the posts wearing upside down cowboy boots.

My voice jumped an octave. "How did she die, the little girl?"

The man cleared his throat. "Spider bite. The doctor thought it was a black widow."

I gripped the table with both hands and shook it. Frames tottered and fell. Locket chains tangled. "What on earth?" asked Cora Mae.

"How could you let that happen?" I cried. "Doesn't your wife keep a clean house?"

The man looked at the scattered pictures on the table and floor, then at me. From the corner of my eye, I could see people staring and somebody sprinting toward us from across the room.

The photographer didn't raise his voice. "My wife is a

wonderful woman, a wonderful mother. We were on a picnic when it happened. But why do you ask? Are you one of those Better Baby people?"

"Of course she isn't," Cora Mae said. "We're just admiring your work. We'd better get a move on. My airplane awaits."

Cora Mae pulled me by the elbow toward the tent's opening. I was crying so hard, all I could see was a splash of daylight ahead. Then a voice came from behind.

"What's going on here, Julianne Rose?" Dr. Livermore was shouting.

We ran out, straight into the path of what sounded like a cyclone. An airplane roared overhead. Huge hailstones rained down. One hit me on the head, bounced off my nose and landed in my hand. It was red and white and attached to a miniature parachute. It was a Baby Ruth bar. The plane circled back, dropping dozens more along with fliers explaining that it was a publicity stunt for the Curtiss Candy Company. I stuck a few bars in my pocket, right next to the locket with the photograph of my dead baby.

––––––––––––

Cora Mae got her airplane ride. She said that from up in the air, the wheat fields looked like great boiling pots of oatmeal. The experience, she claimed, eased the pain of taking second place again in the cake-baking contest. I envied such simple solace.

GARDEN CITY TRIBUNE · WEDNESDAY, JULY 12, 1922

MISS AMERICA PREPARATIONS BEGIN IN ATLANTIC CITY

Plans are in the making for the second Miss America pageant, which will be held this fall in Atlantic City, New Jersey. Last year's winner, 14-year-old Margaret Gorman, is expected to win again.

The New York Times reports that Samuel Gompers, head of the American Federation of Labor, complimented the young lady by saying: "Miss Gorman represents the type of womanhood America needs: strong, red-blooded, able to shoulder the responsibilities of home-making and motherhood. It is in her type that the hope of the country resides."

Protests are expected from women's and religious groups that question the morality of a beauty contest that features bobbed hair and bare limbs.

CHAPTER 27

Miss America

Everyone I loved had been taken from me, and I wasn't sure what I'd done to deserve it. Maybe Dr. Livermore was right. Maybe I was a hopeless degenerate, and my depravity was circling back, making me steal and lie and lose my baby for a second time. I wished Art were around. He was a brother, a blood relative who'd have stuck by me no matter what. Although, of course, he hadn't.

I kept listening for Dr. Livermore's Locomobile to pull

up to the boardinghouse. Stealing the locket had sealed my commitment to the Home for Hopeless Women. It was just a matter of when he came for me.

Cora Mae gave me a chain for the locket. I only took it off when I took a bath, which became increasingly rare with each passing day. I kept out the grief as best I could, although I wasn't sure why. No one needed the strength of my soul.

I remade my dresses, removing the pregnancy panels and adding snippets of lace, which hardly reflected my mood. I sewed curtains for the kitchen, embroidering them with tiny yellow and pink flowers over 2-by-2-inch blue fabric squares that matched the linoleum floor.

I sunk into a black hole without sunlight. I slept for hours and cried so much my eyes seemed permanently puffy. I ate entire boxes of candy at a time.

I started Zane Grey's latest, "The Day of the Beast." After 30 pages, I threw it across the room. It was no way to treat one of Zane Grey's novels, which had given me so many hours of comfort. But it seemed even the author had turned against me. He'd written that Mel Iden was standing on the porch of the doctor's office. Pretty and popular before the Great War, she now wore a strained, tragic shadow around her eyes, and her full breast heaved as she spoke with Daren Lane, a soldier just back from the war. She'd had a "war baby, a nameless child." She was an outcast, just like me.

The summer had been hot and humid. Cora Mae kept the windows open, so the boardinghouse grew dusty and bug-infested. She didn't say a word about it, which made me think she didn't care about the filth or about my previous efforts to keep it spotless. When I heard her laughing with the Fondale boys, I knew they were laughing at me, because there was no other earthly reason to be happy. A few times, I thought about taking Art's shotgun from my closet, but I hesitated because of the mess it would make.

One day, Fanny dropped by to show us her engagement ring, which looked suspiciously like one of those advertised in True Story. She'd failed her class on Household Economics and dropped out of college. None of it mattered, though, because she'd met the man of her dreams. He was the son of the minister at the Wayside Church of the Lord, the church my parents had helped start, the church of the holy measles, the church where Fanny would marry at the end of the summer. She asked me to play the piano at the ceremony, and with mixed emotions, I agreed.

The next day I got up and cleaned the house from top to bottom, starting with the crapper. I washed windows, scrubbed the fingerprints from the doors and walls, and dusted everything — including the wainscoting.

I had to reacquaint myself with my piano, it had been so long since I played. It was out of tune from the move and the passage of time. I went over to the Yack-Yack Club to ask Mick if he could recommend a tuner. When I started rearranging the bottles on the shelves behind the bar, Mick handed me the card of a tuner in town and kindly showed me to the door.

A few days later, I made sugar cookies. Outside, the bicycle had been leaning in the same spot against the boardinghouse's front porch all winter, and for a moment I thought about climbing aboard. I had the cookies, though, so I walked. I didn't want to run into Dr. Livermore, whom I was certain knew about the stolen locket, so I was careful where I went. I ended up, much like I had the previous spring, on the doorstep of The Golden Curl. I needed a wash, a trim and a favor.

But when I climbed the front porch steps, I saw that the window in the door was boarded over. I knocked twice before a walnut-brown eye appeared at a crack between boards. I heard a bolt slide back, then another. When Posey opened the door, the funny smell floated out again, but something had changed. The half-smile, half-frown she'd always worn was nothing but grim. She locked the door behind us.

"What happened?" I asked. "Have you closed your shop?"

"Only for a while. Somebody tossed a brick through the window a few nights ago."

"Good Lord, was it the KKK? I read in the Tribune that their membership has grown huge, and they're more active than ever."

"Most likely. They tied a note around the brick, reminding us that lynching is still legal for coloreds who get out of hand."

"Pinky and Hooch better not be involved," I said, remembering how they'd acted on New Year's Eve, when Posey showed up at the boardinghouse. "Did you call the police?"

She looked at me from the tops of her eyes as if to say I was a fool to suggest it. I took a cookie from that plate I'd brought her.

The phone rang — two shorts, Posey's ring — and it was as if another brick had crashed through the window. Neither of us moved. We stared at the telephone as it rang over and over, until finally Posey picked up the earpiece and spoke into the candlestick base. "Hello. This is The Golden Curl."

She listened, nodded, asked questions and scribbled notes. Her half-smile was back by the time she hung up. "That was the lady who brings me supplies from the Madam C.J. Walker Company in Wichita. She's mailing my order tomorrow."

"What about the window and the KKK?" I was finishing my third cookie.

"My brother-in-law can fix the window. I don't know what I can do about the Klukkers. Live through it, I guess, just like Madam Walker and a lot of other folks did." Posey looked across the room, and I followed her gaze to the framed photograph of the woman in the Model T.

"Do you have any more of that vegetable shampoo?" I asked. "I got some bad news about my baby."

I told her the story while she pampered and poured and massaged my head. Finally, I relaxed and was half asleep when she spoke. "I'm glad you came in. I've been meaning to tell you that I accidentally picked up on one of Dr. Livermore's calls the other day. I got in a hurry and picked up before I knew whether it was two longs or two shorts."

I sat up so fast, shampoo dribbled into my eye. "Who was he talking to?"

Posey dabbed at my eye with a cotton towel. "It was long distance, all the way from Yonkers, New York. The National Intelligence Tests Company, they said when the doctor answered.

"Seems like Dr. Livermore wrote them a nasty letter about some questionable test results. He was challenging their answers to some questions. One in particular agitated him —

something about an Indian coming into town and thinking the white man was lazy because he rode sitting down."

"That was on the sample," I said. "How could he argue with that?"

Posey shook her head. "He used it as an example of how the whole test was flawed, how the answers could go every which way. He had more; I just can't remember them."

"That's OK. For once, the doctor is right. The questions were impossible. What else did he say?"

"He argued for a long time with the man in New York. The phone charges must have been outrageous. Dr. Livermore kept asking for his money back. He said he'd sent in a test that was taken by a complete and obvious moron — his words, not mine — and that when the results came back, they showed the person was above average in intelligence."

"Truth be told, I'm confused," I said. "Dr. Livermore must have been talking about somebody else's test. I took it months ago. It couldn't have taken that long for the results to come back."

"It didn't take that long. Dr. Livermore told the man the results had come back right away, but he'd been too busy to go over them, which is why he hadn't challenged them before. He said the situation has become dangerous — his words, not mine — and the person in question needed to be institutionalized for the benefit of mankind."

The confusion in my head was clearing like a buffalo herd after a rifle blast. "What did the man in New York tell the doctor?"

"He hung up on him, but not before Dr. Livermore

mentioned a name: Julianne Rose. Is that you?"

"That's what he calls me. It's my given name. He uses it just to irritate me, which it does. He'd just better not call me Bernice," I said.

"What's that?" Posey asked.

"It's from a story called 'Bernice Bobs Her Hair,' by F. Scott Fitzgerald. You've probably never heard of him."

"Indeed I have. I've read many of his works," Posey said. "I'd like to hear what you thought of that particular story, though."

Posey's asking price that day was nothing more than the few cookies left on the plate I'd brought. I thought her services were invaluable, and I saw a chance to prove that with Fanny Grundy's upcoming wedding.

Apparently Fanny's mother herself was married in a simple home ceremony. Convincing her to pay for much of anything associated with the wedding, let alone hair styling at The Golden Curl, required negotiations that rivaled the peace talks recently concluded in Europe. First she wouldn't go south of Boundary Street until Fanny agreed to wear Mrs. Grundy's 1890 wedding dress, which had an empire waistline and a fitted skirt. Then she wouldn't step inside a Negro-owned establishment until Fanny consented to wear the dress with only one alteration: a wavering hemline. When Mrs. Grundy heard that Pinky was going to drive us over in his automobile, she parlayed with Cora Mae to make Fanny's wedding cake for the cost of ingredients. She wasn't happy to be associated with me — the fallen woman — so I agreed to play for the wedding at half my normal cost just to get her to go to Posey's shop. For a woman who fainted so easily, she was a robust negotiator.

Cora Mae tried a different cake recipe every day for a week, and Mrs. Grundy and Fanny wanted to taste them all. Every day after lunch, I'd shoo Pinky, Hooch and the animals out the back door and clean the kitchen right up to the moment the mother and daughter arrived at the front door. They disagreed on every recipe until Cora Mae suggested a layer cake. Mrs. Grundy wanted white cake for her layers. Fanny chose devil's-food.

A few days before the ceremony, just after sunset, we arrived as scheduled at The Golden Curl. The window in the front door had been replaced, but like every other window at the shop, it was covered by a curtain. We went inside, and when the smell of beauty hit, Mrs. Grundy pulled a crumpled handkerchief from her bosom and held it to her nose.

Posey greeted us with tea and little heart-shaped cakes she'd made especially for the occasion. She brought out a box of hand-held fans, and Mrs. Grundy took two. I watched while the other women wandered around, admiring the furnishings, asking about Madam Walker's photo and smelling the contents of every jar and bottle. When they finished, Fanny announced her intentions: She wanted a permanent hairdo. She was bored with her hair.

I thought Fanny's hair was lovely. It was silky and blond and hung to her shoulders — a few inches longer than the last time she'd had it bobbed.

When Mrs. Grundy heard of Fanny's intentions, she collapsed into one of the chairs at the center of the room and waved her fans with both hands in front of her face.

"It'll be fine, Ma. A girl at college got a hair permanent. Her long, straight hair turned into spiraling curls that lasted for weeks."

Fanny looked in the mirror, pulled her hair away from her face and scrunched it up to make it look curly. "If Ma won't let me bob it, which is the preferred style of the Miss America contestants, I'll get a permanent."

That got everybody talking. We were all disgruntled that the second highly anticipated Miss America was only 15, when the rules specifically required a minimum age of 16.

Mrs. Grundy roused herself. "That contest lacked decorum. It was shameful to see those girls in their bathing suits, showing off their arms and legs. Thank heavens the winner was one of the few with natural hair, a regular Gibson Girl."

"Natural? Ma, she had a permanent just like what I want."

"I would discourage it myself," Posey said. "I've studied the procedure, and it's not 100 percent reliable. Besides, I don't own the electric heating device that's used after the mixture is applied."

"Your father is paying a small fortune for this wedding, Fanny. We're practically going belly up to pay for a photographer, the cake and music." Mrs. Grundy looked at Cora Mae and me. "Stop harping about the bobby cut, Fanny. The permanent is taking us out on limb — morally and financially. How much did you say it cost, Posey?"

Posey looked at me. "Two dollars? However, as I mentioned, I'm not equipped to do the procedure, which done properly takes three hours. I could do a shampoo and cut in an hour for just $1.50."

But Fanny wouldn't be talked out of it, even if the heating device was missing, and I offered to help so Posey wouldn't be held solely responsible. She wrapped Fanny's hair around brass rods, each of which weighed two pounds, and I applied the smelly potion that made it everlasting.

We had three hours to kill. Fanny spoke with her head frozen in place. "You know, Ma, lots of girls these days are wearing above-the-knee black velvet dresses to their weddings. Some of them are even getting married on flagpoles and underwater."

Mrs. Grundy ignored her, holding up a jar of white cream. "This label says it's scientifically proven to banish blemishes and clarify the skin so it looks like satin. In 40 minutes."

Posey applied the cream in even strokes then offered to shampoo Mrs. Grundy's hair for free. Mrs. Grundy agreed, and after a half hour of Posey massaging her scalp with Madam Walker's vegetable shampoo, she asked for a trim. "A little trim is all. Mr. Grundy likes it long."

"Doesn't a little trim cost the same as a big trim?" I asked.

Posey held her scissors and comb while she studied Mrs. Grundy's hair. "That's right: 25 cents for a little cut and 25 cents for a big cut."

Later, she washed my hair and set it with pin curls. She was finishing a trim for Cora Mae when we heard a car come to a stop outside. Posey lifted the curtain at the front door.

"It's Dr. Livermore's Locomobile," she whispered. "He's getting out."

None of us wanted to have a conversation with Dr.

Livermore. As he climbed the front steps, we ran out the back door. Fanny's head wobbled under 12 pounds of brass rollers. We stood below a bank of windows, laughing, until Mrs. Grundy shushed us, pointing upward, and we realized the windows were open.

We could hear as Posey and Dr. Livermore exchanged pleasantries. He apologized for coming so late, and from the way the chairs scooted across the floor, they must have sat down. He asked her where she'd come from and about her family, then about the shop — how long she'd been open, how business was faring, whose photograph was on the wall. Then he asked whether she would give him a haircut, and Cora Mae almost burst into laughter. But Posey agreed and directed him to sit in the chair near the water basin.

We heard jars rattle, lids open and water trickle. Posey snapped a cotton sheet in the air. When the shampoo began squeaking, we settled ourselves in the dirt and leaned against the building.

"Very nice, indeed. That smells heavenly," Dr. Livermore said.

"Thank you, sir. I'm glad you like it."

"Posey, I've been wanting to talk to you face to face about our shared telephone line. From the little I've overheard when emergencies have required that I clear the line, you seem like a virtuous woman."

Scissors snipped rhythmically. "A little shorter on the sides," the doctor said. "In any case, I happened to hear about your front window being broken, and although I agree with the Klan's stance on the immorality of our young people today,

I dislike their methodology. I don't like them usurping the proper authorities."

The sheet snapped, the chair squeaked over the floor, and then came a faint rattle. "Where did this come from?" the doctor asked.

My fingers rubbed across the bare skin of my collarbone. I'd taken off the locket with the baby's picture inside when Posey shampooed my hair. I remembered leaving it by the telephone.

Posey snapped the sheet again, moved the chair, started with the broom. "A customer left it here earlier today. I'll return it tomorrow."

"I see," he said, and I heard the rattle as he tossed the locket back across the table. He paid and left. When we ran inside again, Posey handed me the locket and started on Fanny's hair. It was too late, though. The brass curlers made the ends of her hair crackle like the electric lines strung across town. Once Posey trimmed them away, Fanny had her bob.

GLADYS WISENHEIMER'S
Garden of Tidbits

Isn't it interesting how today's weddings are so very different from the ones we once enjoyed? Remember when a bride would be thrilled to have her nuptials recited in the parlor of her father's home? Afterward, she would graciously join her guests at a simple meal prepared by her mother, followed by the traditional fruitcake.

Well, those solemn occasions have gone the way of the horse and buggy. Today's brides demand white, formal lace dresses, often of an irreverent length. Entire families, including cousins, are members of the wedding party. The guest lists are so long, the brides' parents are forced to rent a hall or church (not to mention pay for a photographer, wedding cake, music and disdainful hairstyles).

On a brighter note, Mr. and Mrs. Grundy's daughter, Fanny, will be married today at the Wayside Church of the Lord. Her fiance, Mr. John Lewis, Jr., is the son of the church's pastor. Mrs. Grundy says the nuptials will be tasteful, reverential and not the least bit saucy.

CHAPTER 28

The Wedding

Fanny's wedding would go down in Garden City history as the nuptials of collapsing vows. I'd remember it for another reason.

Cora Mae and I wanted to get an early start, to evade the worst of the summer's relentless heat. For weeks, I'd planned my outfit — my slightly worn, pink Mary Janes shoes and my navy dress with white pinstripes. Unfortunately, when I put the dress on early that Saturday morning, it didn't fully accommodate the extra curves I'd acquired. The only way I could fit into it was by dragging out my rubber maternity girdle.

Of course, Pinky and Hooch weren't on the wedding guest list, but they'd promised to drop us off on their way to see their ma.

I didn't recognize them when they drove up next to the dirt that was Cora Mae's front yard. The shimmering maroon Packard had been replaced by a solemn black Model T. It was a beautiful car — a sedan with an electric starter and removable roof — but it was a commoner's car. So many people in Garden City had black Model Ts, they tied flags on the exteriors to tell them apart. Besides, Pinky had sworn never to patronize the pacifist Henry Ford.

When I carried out a basket of food for the reception, I asked Pinky about the car, expecting he'd reply with one of his irrelevant Babe Ruth quotes. "It was on sale," he said. "But what about them shoes you're wearing?"

I followed his eyes to my feet. "They're called Mary Janes. They're all the fashion."

"They're baby shoes."

"Ladies everywhere are wearing them."

"Why do they make baby shoes in ladies' sizes?"

"I don't know. Why do men wear yellow shoes?"

Pinky shrugged. "Ask Babe Ruth. Let's get to going. Ma gets real mad if we don't show up on time."

Hooch carried out the wedding cake, which had been packed in ice so it wouldn't melt. Cora Mae had created another beauty — real sunflowers arranged on vanilla frosting over two layers each of Fanny's devil's-food and Mrs. Grundy's white cakes. I tucked my piano music into a satchel, and away we went.

We took the main road toward Rosebush. It was already so hot that despite Posey's efforts, my hair crested like a directionless desert. The girdle was suffocating, and my perspiration stiffened the cheap plastic. Even the sunflowers alongside the road were wilting, making me think about poor Mrs. Benedetto's dead baby, and then mine. I tried not to imagine what the flowers on Cora Mae's cake would look like by the time we arrived.

In the distance, the Wayside Church of the Lord spire rose like the landmark it had always been. As children, Art and I had competed to be the first to see it. Now, the sight cloaked me in loneliness. I felt for the locket tucked inside my dress and reached for Cora Mae's hand. She was pointing out the window, though, showing Pinky where to stop.

The one-room church had been built before I was born. My mother used to say it was an overnight job, evidenced by the gaps in the siding and around the windows. Winter services were drafty and cold. But in the summer, the church seemed to close in on itself, shooing away the slightest breezes and sealing in the flies and smells of candle wax, musty hymnals and shoes spiked with horse manure.

The cake arrived in better shape than I'd expected, and while Cora Mae added the finishing touches, I went to the piano. In front of it sat a stool that I'd spun on as a child until I was dizzy. I plunked the keys. It sounded as if it hadn't been tuned since my spinning days. I was warming up with "Secondhand Rose" when out of the corner of my eye I saw a woman holding a baby. She stood nearby, tapping her foot to the music.

"That was grand," she said. "I'm tone deaf — can't carry a tune in a bucket — but my baby loves music. As soon as he can reach the pedals, I'm putting him in piano lessons."

I spun around, and the dizzy feeling of my youth came right back at me. It was the dark-haired woman pictured in the locket — the photographer's wife, the woman who had allowed a spider to kill my baby girl. I checked my locket. It was exposed, poking through my dress buttons, and the woman's eyes had followed my hand.

Neither of us spoke, but the baby fretted. He looked about the same age as Baby Ruth would have been had she lived. He must have been her brother, but was he adopted or their own child? He wiggled in his mother's arms, reaching for the freedom of the floor. She gave me a puzzled look as she stroked his curly hair down over his forehead.

"Where did you get that baby?" I asked.

"He's mine," she said. "Where did you get that locket?"

Dr. Livermore stepped between us. "The bride is waiting, ladies. Take your seats."

He leaned toward me, and I could see a fleck of tobacco lodged between his front teeth. "Your behavior is threatening our community, Julianne Rose. I can promise you that your colored friend's hair salon will be closed up tight if you continue."

When I looked back, the woman with the baby was gone. I went up on tiptoes to scan the room and saw Fanny and Mr. Grundy waiting in the back, looking at me. I spun around and started on "I Love You Truly," the locket bouncing across the keys as I made one mistake after another.

At the altar, Fanny's fiance — a scrawny fellow with a bad complexion — picked at the skin on his forehead then wiped his hands on his suit pants. His father, the minister, was a lumbering man in a black robe. He mopped his face with his sleeve until somebody handed him a handkerchief.

The heat had blown every scrap of solemnity from the room. The pews wavered as folks fanned themselves with whatever they could find — handkerchiefs, napkins, hymnals, old bulletins. Children fussed, babies cried and parents quietly squabbled over who got to take them outside. Cora Mae stood in back holding the cake together.

On cue — three nods from Fanny — her two cousins from Nebraska came to stand by my piano. I counted off, and the three of us launched into the song Fanny had wanted above all others at her wedding, "Makin' Whoopee." The cousins' voices blended beautifully, rising above the badly tuned piano, and the room grew quiet as they sang about a bride and groom, rice and shoes, and making whoopee.

Just as they reached the first of the often-repeated "making whoopees" in the song, a crash came from the altar. I looked over just in time to see the minister tumble over in a dead faint, taking with him Fanny and her sweet pea bouquet. The congregation gasped in unison, except for Mrs. Grundy, who fainted. People surged out of the pews and out the door for fresh air. Fanny was untangling herself as the minister came to. Dr. Livermore jumped over them.

"You are man and wife," he said breathlessly. "I pronounce it."

The room was nearly empty as Dr. Livermore and a few other men tended to the collapsed bundle at the altar. I collected my music and was heading for the door when I saw the photographer walking toward me, his wife and baby trailing behind.

"You're the one who took my locket," he said. "My wife says yours is similar, and now that I get a good look at you, you look similar as well. That was the last photograph I had of my little girl, and you stole it."

Suddenly Dr. Livermore grabbed my arm and steered me outside.

"You've just earned your entry ticket to the Home for Hopeless Women," he said, squeezing my elbow. "Now, you have a choice. Get in my car peacefully, or the Negro's hair salon will be shuttered. Perhaps more than shuttered."

Still holding my elbow, Dr. Livermore walked me to the Locomobile and opened the back door. I slipped into the seat beside the gurney and put the locket in my pocket. Even though I knew the baby was dead, holding onto her photograph gave me the strength not to jump from the car as it rolled down the road.

I missed the wedding reception, which Cora Mae later told me was as ragamuffined as the wedding. Apparently the minister and Mrs. Grundy both recovered enough to each eat three pieces of cake. The Nebraska cousins brought moonshine, and Fanny got corked before upchucking all over her wedding dress. Pinky and Hooch missed most of the reception too. Even though they weren't invited to the wedding, Cora Mae had hoped Pinky might show up at the reception in time to turn a few dances with her. But for nearly three hours, he and Hooch were nowhere to be found. Cora Mae told me that when Pinky finally returned to drive her home, her hurt feelings were only pacified by the two new silk sweaters he gave her.

BABE RUTH ADMITS HE'S A PROUD PAPA

In a story that stunned the nation, Babe Ruth confirmed today that he is a father. The secret was revealed when Ruth's wife, Helen, showed up for a Giants game at the Polo Grounds carrying a 16-month-old girl.

Confronted by reporters, Mrs. Ruth said the child, Dorothy, had been hospitalized since birth and the delivery kept a secret because of the baby's life-threatening low birth weight. The baby was born on June 7, she said, at St. Vincent's Hospital in New York.

However, Mr. Ruth, when contacted in Cleveland, said the birth occurred Feb. 2 at Presbyterian Hospital in New York. Reporters are working to clarify details.

CHAPTER 29

The Home for Hopeless Women

The Home for Hopeless Women was like a True Story magazine snuggled inside a fairy tale. Despite his threats, Dr. Livermore had obviously never seen the place. He had to ask for directions twice once we reached Rosebush.

From the curb, the house was distinguishable only by a small address marker that was nearly concealed by flowers. Houses stood on either side of the stone building. None of them had been here when I was growing up.

We both stared in silence for a few moments. The house had ivy climbing to the second floor and a steeply pitched roof covered in green tiles that looked like thatch. Three chimneys stood over three turrets. The windows were made with lead glass, and I half expected to see fairies peering out.

We knocked at the doorway — it was an arch of rough-hewn timber — and the woman who answered could have been the Seven Dwarves' grandmother. Silver spectacles sat on the end of her nose, and she wore her gray hair bundled on her head. She was plump, with rosy cheeks and a white pinafore pulled over her dress. When she hugged me, I swear I smelled gingerbread.

She introduced herself as Miss Clarkson, the head matron, and she smiled when she took the papers Dr. Livermore handed her. "Has anyone ever told you that you look like The Sheik?" she asked. The doctor gave her a thumbnail smile then left without stepping inside, as if such a place might cast a spell of goodness over him.

The main room had a stone fireplace and a fully loaded built-in bookcase. Arched doorways led off the room. All of them were shut except one, which was where Miss Clarkson led me by the hand.

"Let's have a chat in my office then take a look around," she said.

Miss Clarkson's office, which apparently doubled as her bedroom, was a mess that rivaled Cora Mae's kitchen on her worst bad-recipe day. As soon as I crossed the threshold, the fairytale ended and the True Story began. Rumpled clothing and dirty dishes covered the floor. The door was propped open with stacks of magazines, newspapers, stationery and envelopes. Miss Clarkson tossed the binder from Dr. Livermore on top of a pile. She gave me another ginger-laden hug.

"Welcome home, darling. Please let's sit."

She sat on the unmade bed and plucked a vase of dead flowers off a chair so I could sit there. "Now, dear, I want to hear every little thing. Where you're from, who you were with, what you did, how it felt, why you were sent here and what's in your carrying case."

I told her I had nothing more than the clothes on my back and my satchel of music from Fanny's wedding. I didn't mention my maternity girdle, which she could probably smell, or the locket, which was painfully digging into my thigh. Miss Clarkson smiled again. "Don't fret, dear. The church ladies donate their old dresses for the little mothers and, in cases like yours, the little mothers who've already delivered. Your shoes are adorable, by the way. Where'd you get them?"

I started to say she could have my shoes if she would just let me out of there, but Miss Clarkson hadn't finished. She took my satchel of piano music. "You won't mind if we look for ourselves? Almost every little mother arrives with one of those confession magazines, and the girls pass them around like a communicable disease. I'm afraid it's my duty to confiscate them. The magazines, I mean, not the disease, for heaven's sake."

While Miss Clarkson examined my music, I looked out the window, where a half-dozen women in dresses were doing knee bends. A few were so pregnant they couldn't see their knees, but their leader, a vigorous redheaded woman, urged them on anyway.

"Nothing in here breaks a rule," Miss Clarkson sighed as

she returned my satchel. "Our home has seven rules, just like the seven dwarves. No confession magazines, no men, no profanity, no makeup, no smoking, no drinking and no names."

"You mean no name-calling?" I glanced out the window. Now the women were taking a break, talking in pairs or small groups. The leader had disappeared.

"I mean no real names. We believe it's vital that the little mothers not develop relationships that would encourage future deprivations. Everyone makes up a name, dear, so think about what you'll want to be called."

A commotion came from the floor above. Loud groans and screaming. Miss Clarkson looked toward the ceiling. "That must be Hazel. It's her time."

The women outside glanced toward the upstairs window, tightening their circles. One woman pulled a pack of cigarettes from her pocket and passed it around. A packet of matches went from hand to hand.

Miss Clarkson smiled. "Now tell me every little thing. Then we'll take a look-about."

I told her about meeting Jiggs and about how good-looking he was. I didn't mention that I'd been drunk in the wheat field when the fireworks exploded.

The screams grew louder during our look-about, so I tried to be like Mrs. Clarkson and ignore them. She let me look through the books on the built-in shelves. There were hymnals and Bibles but a few Zane Greys too. We visited the kitchen — where the little mothers took turns cooking meals — and the crapper —where the little mothers lost their meals. The second floor had an identical layout, but only a piano, easy chairs and a sofa occupied the main room.

Behind the closed doors on both floors were bedrooms. Each had three beds with identical covers pulled tight, which was quite an improvement over Miss Clarkson's bedroom. Nightstands stood between the beds, and Miss Clarkson rummaged through the drawer of one. She smiled triumphantly as she waved a True Tales magazine in the air.

"Unfortunately, this is a really old edition." She tucked it under her arm. "The little mothers get these on their outings. Once a week, they go downtown to see a motion picture. It's a shame they abuse the privilege. Well, I've got to go now, dear. The last bed from the door is yours, so make yourself comfortable. Tomorrow our nurse will do your examination."

A whistle blew. From behind the sheer window curtain, I watched the women line up single file at the door before clattering inside and up the stairs. I stuffed my girdle under the mattress of my bed and hurried to lie down, exhausted but feigning sleep. Two breathless, sweaty women filed into the room. One had a child's body, thin and undeveloped. She couldn't have been older than 15. Her bed was in the middle, where Miss Clarkson had found the magazine. The girl opened the drawer, shuffled through its contents then looked accusingly at me. I shrugged and she lay down, turning her back to me.

The other woman, obviously pregnant, grunted as she lowered herself onto a bed. "She's Alice, and I'm Lorelei. What do we call you?"

I started to say Bernice but caught myself. "Ruth, truth be

told. Like the candy bar."

Lorelei rolled her pillow into a ball then kissed it with so much passion, my birthmark grew warm. "My fiance loved Babe Ruth," she said. "How did you get knocked up?"

"Good Lord, why do you ask?" I said. "I don't know."

"Then you're either a complete ninny, or he used knock-out drugs. That's what happened to me. Larry called it headache powder, and I did have a headache."

Lorelei pulled the pillow in for another kiss. "He was Italian, very strong hands, determined to have his way with me. We would have married, but he had to go back to the farm when his pa died."

The girl from above screamed. "That's Hazel. It's her time. Did you struggle?" The child, Alice, turned toward me, propping her head on her hand.

"I really don't recall," I said.

"Then you didn't," Lorelei said. "Larry said I struggled, but not in a bad way."

"Lorelei was corked when it happened, so she doesn't remember much. Did you have a boy or girl?" asked Alice.

I hesitated, trying not to cry. "A girl. She was adopted, and she died from a spider bite."

Lorelei tossed her pillow to the floor. "Mine is definitely a boy. Right after my menses went off course, I started eating nothing but tomatoes, which they say is a sign of virility."

Alice laughed. "Did you try to get rid of yours? Most of the girls here did, but as you probably know, nothing works before, and nothing works after."

The whistle blew again, three shorts, and Alice jumped up

and ran down the stairs. Lorelei moved more slowly.

"That's our supper whistle," she said. "Just so you know, Alice's father knocked her up and sent her here. Don't tell her I told you, though."

Twenty-four girls were staying at the Home for Hopeless Women — so many that we had to eat in shifts. The whistle blew every half hour for two hours to signal the arrival time for a new group. Each group had a different whistle, reminding me of the party-line telephones back home.

As tired as I was, sleep was nearly impossible. The room was stifling, the mattress lumpy, and Hazel from above moaned and screamed until well after midnight. I heard her newborn baby cry, and that kept me in tears for a few hours. When I finally slept, I dreamed I was feeding poundcake to a stork. With every bite, its beak nicked my fingers.

A knock on the door pulled me from sleep. Alice and Lorelei were gone, their bedcovers seamlessly smoothed. The door opened, and a syrupy voice from the past called my name. "Julianne Rose?"

It was "Maudlin" Maude Murphy, Dr. Livermore's nurse. Her red hair was pulled back in the familiar bun, and her white nurse's pinafore was as clean and starched as ever. "Julianne Rose? Miss Clarkson told me you'd been committed."

I sat up, pulling the bedcovers to my neck. "Maude? What are you doing here?"

"I'm the head nurse here." She closed the door behind her then walked over and sat on Alice's bed. "I've been here since Topeka."

We talked for nearly an hour. I told her about the photographer's booth at the county fair and the locket with the photograph of my dead baby. She apologized again for how she'd treated me when I had Baby Ruth, and I told her I'd forgiven her, which I had, almost.

Maude told me about the lady in Topeka that Cora Mae had recommended. The place was filthy — no running water or electricity. She'd sat in a waiting room with a dozen other women for hours. The woman in charge had offered nothing more than a swig from an ancient whiskey bottle before the procedure, which from Cora Mae's description didn't sound too different from what Florence Heidlemyer had done to herself.

Finally Maude stood, straightening the covers behind her. "I took a job here to do what I can for other women who find themselves in the same situation that you and I faced. We should have some control over our own lives. We aren't criminals or morons, and we shouldn't allow ourselves to be labeled as hopeless.

"Miss Clarkson probably told you that every Friday the little mothers are allowed to go to the theater. This coming Friday they're seeing a Fatty Arbuckle film. You may not be among his fans, but I'm telling you that you must go to the theater with the other girls." She handed me two crumpled dollar bills. "Buy lots of refreshments."

I learned a lot over the next few days. Everybody at the Home for Hopeless Women had a story, and most of them wanted to share it. Hazel paraded her baby around for a couple of days before both of them vanished. Maude and I worked in the garden. She told me about Margaret Sanger and her sister, who'd opened a clinic in New York to provide women with birth control. Maude said she wanted to do the same in Kansas.

After lunch on Friday, we gathered in the main room before our departure to the theater. Miss Clarkson reminded us of the seven rules, emphasizing that all confession magazines would be confiscated. At the door, she and Maude handed each of us a cloth bundle tied with a ribbon.

As we walked, Lorelei explained that everyone's package contained a quarter for admission, a nickel for candy and a tin circle of a ring, which we were to wear on our left ring fingers to placate the good citizens of Rosebush. I pulled the ring from my bundle and tried to put it on. Obviously, my imaginary husband was a cheapskate who'd believed his wife to be a starving Cinderella. The ring was so small it wouldn't go over my knuckle, so I stuffed it, along with the entire bundle, into my dress pocket. The locket was around my neck.

A chill hung in the air, making me wish I'd worn a sweater. Maude's dollar bills rode along in my left Mary Jane. We didn't have far to walk, I knew, because we took the same route Pinky had in his Packard. Past the market would be the post office, and around the corner would be the bank where Pinky had hoped to see Jesse James' gun.

In fact, an unoccupied Model T was parked right where we'd waited for Pinky that day. It was black, like they all were, with the same bug-eyed headlights and shiny grill. As we walked closer to the car, though, one barely discernible feature whispered its exceptionality. A string of rabbits' feet was tied to the hood ornament, which was a silver-plated angel.

I followed the others across the street to the theater, where Miss Clarkson tried to count heads as we handed our quarters to a leering man in the ticket booth. Inside the lobby, any semblance of order vanished. Little mothers could be seen huddled around the concession stand, disappearing into the powder room and hurrying into the theater to secure their seats. The last time I saw Miss Clarkson, she had her hands full of popcorn, soda and candy.

The line at the concession booth was as slow as molasses. The movie had started by the time I got my Baby Ruth bar, so I stuffed it into my pocket. When I looked out the lobby's double doors, I saw Pinky sitting behind the wheel of his Model T, beckoning to me to get in.

"The Babe said it first, but I'll repeat it here," he said. "Watch my dust."

The rabbits' feet fluttered in the breeze we left behind.

I was certain my absence wouldn't be noticed until Fatty Arbuckle's last bow on the big screen. Just in case, Pinky said he'd take the back roads home, where Cora Mae was waiting. For most of the drive, I didn't know where we were, but I tried to relax by putting the window down and bumming a cigarette.

Hooch sat in the back seat, which made sense at first. There hadn't been time at the theater for me to crawl back there. Once we passed into the countryside, though, he turned down my offer to switch places, saying he had a better view from the rear. I didn't argue, although it was questionable that his vision had improved in the week I'd been gone. Nevertheless, I could sense him looking out the back window every few minutes, as if he suspected we were being followed.

Pinky told me that Maude had arranged for my departure from the Home for Hopeless Women. Fanny had kept Dr. Livermore preoccupied with a concocted newlywed ailment while Maude and Cora Mae schemed over the telephone lines. He and Hooch had carried out the plan.

I didn't have much to show my gratitude to the brothers, but when Hooch complained that he was hungry, I remembered the Baby Ruth bar in my pocket. I reached for it, and out came the bundle with my undersized wedding ring and a sheet of folded stationery that I hadn't noticed before. I gave each brother half of the candy bar, returned the ring to my pocket and unfolded the note. It was my official discharge notice from the Home for Hopeless Women, signed by Maude Murphy. Just below the signature she'd written: "Please forgive my dishonesty. I'm dedicating my life to make up for it."

My thoughts spiraled with uncertainty. What was she talking about? She'd apologized for being cruel when Baby Ruth was born. I'd told her I'd forgiven her, which I had, almost. What else could she mean? I stuffed the notice into my pocket.

Pinky distracted me by turning in his seat and speaking with nougat and caramel embedded between his teeth. He gave me a cluck and a wink. "Guess you didn't hear the news at the Hapless Women's Home, but Babe Ruth's got a baby girl."

"I hadn't heard. You must be thrilled."

"Thrilled is right. Not sure where she came from, though. That waitress wife of the Babe's got her story crisscrossed for the newspaper fellows. Babe says the baby was born at such and such a time, at such and such hospital. The wife twists it into another hospital at another time. It's a puzzlement why she got it wrong, that's a singular fact."

"Life is a puzzlement, and so is the route we're taking. Are you as lost as I am?"

"Not in the slightest. You lost, Hooch?"

"A little." The voice came from the back seat. "No wait, there's that house with the old boots along the fence and the devil dog that stole your Babe Ruth hat."

"Damn, you're right. I'm gonna see if they found my hat. Maybe shoot that dog too."

"No, Pinky!" I shouted so loudly that Hooch grabbed onto the back of the seat. "It was never really the Babe's hat, remember?"

"It's got sentimantic value. Cora Mae gave it to me." Pinky pulled into the driveway, and when the brown dog with the scarred nose rounded the corner, he honked the horn. "I'd run over that damned animal if it wouldn't leave its bloody fur on my tires for Cora Mae to find."

I waited for the front door to open and the photographer to come out with his shotgun. The dark-haired wife would follow with the little boy I'd seen at the wedding. There'd be an argument, maybe warning shots. Maybe Pinky would get us all shot.

But the only sign of life was the dogs, which Pinky chased in slow motion to the back of the house. The wagon stood where it had been, but somebody had pulled a tricycle alongside it. The clothesline strained under a load of freshly washed and starched sheets and towels, dresses, undershirts and diapers.

"See anything you want?" Pinky pulled beside it. "Seems to me they owe me, in exchange for my hat."

He pulled a diaper from the line, and the wire recoiled, the clothing bouncing to life. The scarred dog led the pack to Pinky's side of the car. Pinky waved the diaper out the window until the dog snatched it away. In the same instant, I took the locket from my neck and flung it over the clothesline. It bounced a few times but held.

BANDITS HIT A WALL IN BANK ROBBERY NEAR GARDEN CITY

A bank in Rosebush was broken into on Saturday, Aug. 12 by two or more bandits. The burglars dug a large hole through the brick wall, not knowing that the vault was lined with steel and protected by a burglar alarm. As soon as they struck the steel lining, the alarm sounded, arousing the citizens of Rosebush, who immediately spread the word on the telephone lines. A call for assistance has gone out to surrounding counties. The bandits have not been captured.

CHAPTER 30

Finding Baby Ruth

A week after I was rescued, a package arrived for me from the Home for Hopeless Women. I thought Maude was returning the piano music I'd left behind. I carried the envelope to the front porch, and with Tin Tin at my feet, I opened it.

Inside was the packet of papers Miss Clarkson had tossed onto a pile in her room. They were my admission papers, signed by Dr. Livermore. Looking at them gave me the heebie-jeebies.

The first few pages provided details about my background. In Dr. Livermore's angry slashes were my name, date of birth, hometown and parents' names. Next was a sheet with "reasons for commitment" listed in two rows that went all the way down the page. The reasons were arranged in alphabetical order and included brain fever, desertion by husband, fall from horse, hysteria, imaginary female problems, menstrual derangement, novel reading, political excitement, religious excitement, superstition and snuff eating for more than two years. Dr. Livermore had circled feebleness of intellect, immoral life and nymphomania.

At the bottom of the stack was a page titled "Propagation Probability." I scanned the typewritten sentences that led to Dr. Livermore's signature. "Patient unable to conceive. Fallopian tubes cut during childbirth. Sterilized."

Shock waves went through my head. How had he? How could he? I wouldn't believe it was possible, although in the back of my mind was a vague memory of him discussing such an operation with Maude the night Baby Ruth was born. Had Maude stood there and watched him? The feelings running through my head changed as abruptly as the scenes in a Fatty Arbuckle movie. One moment I was confused. The next, I was angry. And in the end, I was sad.

I'd wondered what the doctor had meant the day Pinky had picked me up from the hospital after I'd had Baby Ruth. I could see him leaning through the car window, shouting, "There will be no more babies, Julianne Rose." Now I knew what he'd meant. I stuffed the sheets back into the envelope and shoved it into the bottom drawer of my dresser. Maybe I didn't want to get married and have babies, but it seemed like I should have had a say in the matter.

Hooch had given me a few fright-filled lessons on driving Art's motorcycle. I filled it with gas and sputtered out of town. When I came within half a mile of the photographer's house

— close enough to see the boot-lined fence — I turned away, down a smaller dirt road. It was remote and melancholy, with fenced-in cemeteries every few sections. It suited my purposes, requiring just enough concentration to maneuver that I couldn't think too much about what I was destined to become — a barren old maid with no family.

When the occasional car or horse-drawn wagon came toward me, I'd turn down another road, until I was unquestionably, hopelessly lost. It seemed fitting but ridiculous in a place where I'd lived my whole life and where, if you climbed the right dirt pile, you could see for a hundred miles in every direction.

Less than half a mile ahead stood a one-room schoolhouse. The exterior was more gray than white, the paint flaking away like the tattered pages of a worn book. Thistle grew uninhibited around an empty swingset, and the bell tower gazed mutely from the roof. As the motorcycle sputtered closer, I saw two vehicles parked in front.

I turned off the road onto a well-worn furrow that led to the building. No dogs appeared, but a woman and child watched from the door. They returned my wave, so I kept driving until I'd nearly reached them. The motorcycle stammered to a stop without my telling it to. I let it drop to the ground when I saw the two vehicles parked in the yard.

One was a brown Studebaker and the other a two-wheeled trailer labeled "Madam Isabella Luna's Spiritual Consultations." I looked toward the woman and child — they'd come over for a closer look at me — and sure enough, there stood Sister Margery and the miniature Madam Isabella Luna.

"What and who are you?" A cigarette wagged between Madam Isabella Luna's lips. I'd forgotten about her high-pitched voice.

I pushed up my driving goggles. "You didn't know I was coming?"

"Ish kabibble," Madam Isabella Luna said, and she laughed in that low-slung tone. "How did you find us?"

For about 15 minutes, they tried to keep up appearances. Sister Margery mangled her verbs, and Madam Isabella Luna flounced like a flapper, but it was pointless. They were both dressed in the same jewel-toned silk robes that Cora Mae wore, and Sister Margery had pin curls in her hair.

"Don't ask me why I bother with my hair when I live in a schoolhouse that's just west of nowhere," she said.

They invited me into the schoolhouse. They'd fixed the place up, but it still smelled like peanut butter and damp wool, with just a hint of the musky incense they'd burned at the boardinghouse. On a peg in the cloakroom, I hung my sweater next to the boa with fluttering sea-green feathers, then looked around the classroom. They'd made beds out of benches and pushed four desks together for a table. The traditional presidential portraits of Lincoln and Washington hung next to one of Sir Arthur Conan Doyle smoking his pipe.

Along one wall — reaching almost to the bottom of the window ledges — were piles of newspapers from every small town within a 30-mile radius. I leafed through them, realizing that within each stack was enough gossip to keep two fortune-tellers in business for years. And if they needed embellishment, they could consult one of the dozens of True Story magazines heaped in the corner.

On the chalkboard spanning the front of the room, they'd drawn a map of southwest Kansas, and below each town was written a list of fortunes to be told. Beneath Garden City it said: Mrs. Grundy's dead father-in-law, Dr. Livermore's dead son, Pinky's automobile garages and Baby Ruth, underlined, which made the heebie-jeebies crawl right up my spine.

We sat at the table of desks and drank whiskey from a water ladle. I told them about Jiggs coming to town and Baby Ruth's birth, about my telephone conversation with Ruby and Art's suicide, about Posey and The Golden Curl, and finally, about my time at the Home for Hopeless Women. I admitted they'd gotten a lot right — but not everything.

"Fortune-telling isn't as easy as it looks," Madam Isabella Luna said. "There's spiritual communication taking place too."

"Truth be told?" I said with a laugh.

"You know it, bunny. I told you to houdinize, and you did. I didn't tell you it'd all be the cat's meow, did I? Life isn't like that, but it could be worse. You got a ciggy, by the way?"

"I gave it up. I only have candy." I pulled out a handful of Squirrel Nut Zippers, and we each took one. "The truth is, my situation is worse than before. My little girl is dead, and Dr. Livermore cut me so I'll never be able to have more children, even if I wanted them, which I don't think I do. Still, it seems like the decision was mine to make, not his."

Madam Isabella Luna chewed slowly, shaking her head. "That doctor will get what's coming to him. Don't let me forget that, Marge."

Sister Margery jumped up and went to the blackboard.

Underneath Garden City she wrote: Dr. Livermore trouble.

Madam Isabella Luna lit a cigarette and turned back to me. "You houdinized, though, bunny. You went places and did things you never would have done in your previous life of drudgery. You used a telephone, you rode not only a bicycle, but this bicycle with a motor." Her eyes went to the window where Art's motorcycle was parked. "You socialized with a colored woman and even let her cut your hair. You survived your brother's dreadful death. You're stronger than you were, so strong you could most likely survive about anything. And now that you know how to drive the bicycle with a motor, you can keep going."

"I might be stronger, but I only feel empty inside. My family is gone. Everybody is dead." I fought tears, running my hand over years of initials carved into the wooden top of the desk.

"Didn't I tell you to watch for the boy where the boots line the fence?" said Madam Isabella Luna.

"That's another thing you got wrong."

"You think so? You really believe Dr. Livermore told you the truth about having a girl? "

"I had a girl. Even Maude said so."

"Jesus H. Christ, Jules. The doctor lied. Maude lied. You had a boy. He's living happily ever after with the photographer and his wife. You saw him, didn't you say? At the wedding?"

"I had a boy? What about the little girl who died from the spider bite?"

"That was their first child, adopted before yours and unfortunately passed away."

"Are you saying that my baby is alive?" I couldn't hold back the floodgates.

I tried to remember the little boy the woman was holding at Fanny's wedding. He had brown eyes and curly blond hair that his mother had swept over his forehead. Had I missed seeing a scarlet birthmark etched there?

I thought about Maude's message on my dismissal papers asking me to forgive her dishonesty. Why hadn't she just told me to my face? She'd better be telling the truth about dedicating her life to make up for it, because I was definitely not in the forgiving mood.

Madam Isabella Luna wasn't finished, though. "So, bunny, you have family, but you also have friends who are crazy like family and a home overflowing with doughnuts and two kinds of potatoes. You have a baby who has your gift of music and your mark on his forehead. You won't have to listen to him practice the piano, but you can go to his recitals. That's a perfect way to houdinize, in my opinion."

"And how," Sister Margery said, picking candy from her teeth.

My birthmark grew warm as I listened, and I realized it hadn't done that in ages. The whiskey they'd served me made it glow. It also made the future easier to see. We stayed up late into the night, eating fresh oysters and green olives while the two women made one prediction after another in their typical foggy fashion. Fear the angry little man with the dark mustache, they warned. Watch for four boys who'll sing their way across the ocean on the back of a bug. Look away from the people diving desperately off tall buildings. Listen for telephones that will speak from your pocket. None of it made sense until it got personal.

"Listen, sweetie. It's time you start helping others to houdinize," Madam Isabella Luna said.

"Who could I help?" I asked.

"All the poor bunnies of the world," she said.

I thought about the women at the Home for Hopeless Women, including Miss Clarkson, with her unfortunate interest in everybody's everything. I fumed when I thought of "Maudlin" Maude Murphy, but I calmed a bit thinking about how she'd help me escape the home and about her hero, Margaret Sanger. I remembered the photograph of Mrs. Benedetto's dead baby. I even thought about Fatty Arbuckle's girlfriend and Babe Ruth's wife. I made up my mind when I thought about poor Florence Heidlemyer, bleeding to death on the floor with a crochet needle sticking out of her.

When the whiskey and oysters were gone, I wrapped myself in a blanket and slept on a bench in the schoolhouse. I dreamed that night about my baby boy swirling through the sky in the beak of a sea-green stork.

The next morning, the women had me follow them back to the main road. I was adjusting my goggles when Madam Isabella Luna stuck her head out the car window.

"See you around the Big Dipper," she said. "Don't forget, the bumps just make the rest of the road seem smoother."

As always, she was a little bit right.

FINDING BABY RUTH

GARDEN CITY TRIBUNE · SATURDAY, AUG. 26, 1922

FANFARE MARKS OPENING OF MUNICIPAL POOL TODAY

The swimming pool will formally open to the public today. Garden City is proud of her municipal pool, for Garden City made it herself, just as the mayor asked. The pool is larger than a football field and holds more than two-and-a-half million gallons of water. It ranges in depth from 6 inches to 6 feet. It is so large that with a moderate wind blowing, miniature waves chase themselves across the waters. The waves are not as large as those at Long Beach or Atlantic City, but they convey the sensation of ocean bathing.

CHAPTER 31

The Big Dipper

Hundreds of people came to Garden City that afternoon for the grand opening of the world's largest free, outdoor, municipal, concrete swimming pool, known locally as the Big Dipper.

The scene that day looked like Cora Mae's cake. Everybody spread picnics on colorful blankets, and the aqua water rippled across the surface like an ocean. Pinky and Hooch arrived in their original strawberry-colored Packard, with Cora Mae and Doc Trundle in the back seat. The Grundys brought their cousins all the way from Nebraska, and Mrs. Grundy wore a moral bathing suit that looked heavy enough to drown her. Even Old Man Willie was there, fresh out of jail.

Posey sat with her sister and brother-in-law near the Negro section of the pool, and she returned my wave. If the fortune-tellers were there, I didn't see them.

Dr. Livermore didn't come, but the few times I'd seen him around town, he was gray and wheezy, without a trace of The Sheik remaining. He paid Hooch to drive him around in the Locomobile for hours at a time, claiming it was the only way he could sleep. Hooch said the doctor was running out of breath.

Photographers seeking to memorialize the event came from every small town around, and a few times I thought I saw the three-fingered one or maybe his dark-haired wife holding my baby. Once I glimpsed a man who looked like Jiggs.

I got a little nervous when it was time for everyone to go into the water. Water scares me. While the Garden City band played, Mayor Trinkle perched on top of a ladder and had us join hands. He counted to three, and everybody stepped into the water together. Truth be told, I didn't actually step. I jumped in with both feet.

Author's Note

"Finding Baby Ruth" was born after a long and arduous labor. It began more than 20 years ago, when my father was

My father at 9 months, 1922. The cover photo is also of him. I still have the hat he wore in that photo (see back cover)

almost 70 and facing his own demise because of ill health. He'd always known he was adopted — he carried his birth mother's name on a slip of paper in his wallet — but he'd never really tried to find his biological family. He didn't want to offend the parents who raised him.

The search began in earnest on Memorial Day of 1994, when my parents made their annual round of Kansas cemeteries to put flowers at family members' graves. They were in Garden City, Kansas, where my father was born, and found his birth mother's grave at the local cemetery. Other clues about my father's past began to surface. As a journalist, I leapt in to help sort through mildewed court documents, old newspapers and tattered telephone books. We confirmed that my father's biological parents were long dead, but we had reunions with

*My biological grandmother
(Jules in the book)*

their siblings, cousins, nieces and nephews. The characters these people described were so intriguing, I couldn't let them disappear again. As I recreated their stories, I tried to follow the actual historical timeline.

The true story is that my biological grandmother gave birth to my father in the aftermath of a snowstorm on March 6, 1922, at a Garden City hospital. She was 27 and single, and immediately gave him up for adoption. She was an accomplished organist who slept on a sofa bed in the parlor of her parents' home. Her older brother, who also lived there, had rheumatoid arthritis and killed himself in a fashion similar to the one described in the book. (My father also suffered from rheumatoid arthritis.) Ten years after my father's birth, my grandmother married a local man. She had no more children and died at age 59 of abdominal cancer.

My biological grandfather, nicknamed Jiggs, was from a family of 10 boys and one girl. He was a ladies' man who worked with horses and automobiles. He lived in Garden City for a few years before and after my father was born then moved to California, where he was hired as a movie extra for "All Quiet on the Western Front." Family legend has it that during one smoke-filled scene, he was playing the part of a dead man when he got up and ran off the set to get a breath of

My biological grandfather (Jiggs), second from left in the back row, with eight of his 10 brothers and their automobiles.

fresh air. He died at age 50, never having married.

The couple that adopted my father lived on a farm about 100 miles from Garden City. After seven years of marriage, they had apparently given up on having children of their own. They gave my father a good life. His adoptive mother — Ruth — was tone-deaf but insisted that my father take years of piano lessons. For the rest of his life, he played the piano and organ beautifully.

My father was ashamed of being illegitimate. In the 1920s, birth control was primitive and unreliable, and abortion was illegal. An "unmarried mother" was a social disgrace, a "fallen woman" who was expected to stay behind closed doors until the baby was born, oftentimes at a maternity home or at the home of a relative. Afterward, she might have remained an outcast in her community. Meanwhile, as often happens, the "unmarried father" was free of responsibility and, as Jiggs did, able to skip town.

My father and his adoptive parents along with his sister, who was also adopted.

A year after my parents married, they began thinking of a starting a family. My father, worried about what traits he might pass along, wrote to his mother for advice. On June 17, 1945, she replied: "Now I will tell you a little about adopting a baby in case you should want to get your family this way. The Kansas Children's Service League, through which we applied, accepts only such children for adoption who have every prospect of living a normal life. They are given blood tests and their mental history is checked. If a child does not pass these high standards, they are placed in an institution. Perhaps you remember the man we used to call 'the stork.' He had to use a little salesmanship to persuade us to take a white-headed, blue-eyed boy when we had decided we wanted a brown-eyed, dark-haired girl. So he said, 'I'll tell you this much, his ancestors are far above the average mentally, with a lot of musical talent.' We said we are always looking for the best, and up to now, we have never regretted it."

My father did remember "the stork." He was a short, round, bespectacled man who would drop by during the first 10 years of my father's life and bring everyone to their knees for long, impassioned prayers. My father believed the

FINDING BABY RUTH

man was a go-between, sent by someone who hadn't forgotten the white-headed, blue-eyed boy. Secretly, my father hoped his biological mother also watched over him as he grew. "Finding Baby Ruth" merges fact with fiction to bring that dream to life.

Not long after my father reconnected with his biological family, he wrote: "I have determined to continue the search for the sake of my family.

My father at age 4.

I am aware there may be pitfalls and things I really don't want to know, but for future generations, I think the truth must be searched."

My search for Baby Ruth uncovered compelling parallels to current events in the United States. We still question women's abilities to make their own choices about birth control, pregnancy, marriage, even clothing. Minority groups — African-Americans, Mexicans and, during the years of "Finding Baby Ruth," the Irish and Germans — still struggle for equality. We continue to use patriotism, religion and standardized tests to justify intolerance. And not unlike today, people of the 1920s wanted a celebrity like Babe Ruth, the baseball player, to be president. The good news is that in one way or another we survived those challenging times, as I believe we always will.

Many thanks to those who helped me to write "Finding Baby Ruth," including members, past and present, of the Slow Sand writers group: Jeana Steele Burton, Jerry Eckert, Denise Fisher, Jean Hanson, Colleen Fulbright, Teresa R. Funke, Luana Heikes, Kathy Hayes, Leslie Patterson, Paul Miller, Kay Rios, Elisa Sherman, Melinda Swenson, Debby Thompson and, especially, Karla Oceanak, who helped shape the book into its final form. Thanks also to Launie Parry, who designed the cover and interior.

I'm also grateful for the support of my book club, The Tattered Covers, and for the encouragement of my dear friends Paula Hunter, Kit Garofalo and Julia Ambrosich, who cheerfully listened to me yammer about "Finding Baby Ruth" for many years.

I'd like to acknowledge my mother, Zellamae Hoffman, who died in 2014, and my sisters, Jan Swingle and Celia Seastone.

A million thanks to my husband, Randy Myers, for his endless encouragement, and to my daughters, Kelsey and Morgan Myers, who inherited their grandmother's courage to keep plowing through life no matter what comes.

My parents at their wedding,
June 7, 1944.

Historical Notes

CHAPTER 1 - MADAM ISABELLA LUNA

In the early 1920s, Garden City had two newspapers, the Herald and the Telegram. The articles preceding each chapter in "Finding Baby Ruth" are from both sources but have been rewritten and attributed to a fictional "Tribune." Gladys Wisenheimer's column and the town of Rosebush are completely fabricated.

Spiritualism gained popularity in the 1920s because of the death toll taken by World War I (also referred to as the Great War or simply, the world war). Séances, fortune-tellers, psychics, Sir Arthur Conan Doyle and Harry Houdini were popular. Doyle's belief in spiritualism created a rift with his friend Houdini, who set out in the early 1920s

The Great Harry Houdini

Mina "Margery" Crandon with Houdini

to debunk self-proclaimed psychics and mediums. One of the most famous mediums Houdini exposed was Mina Crandon, known as Margery. *(Brownstein)*

The Santa Fe Trail was initially an international trade route between the United States and Mexico. It was later used by pioneers crossing the United Sates. In 1921, Kansas spent $1 million to build a 16-foot-wide cement highway over it. *(Reeve)*

Kansas has a long history of prohibition. It outlawed alcohol in 1880, becoming the first state to do so, and it didn't lift the ban until 1948, longer than any other state and 15 years after the nationwide end to Prohibition. *(Kansas State Historical Society online)*

Machine-made cigarettes were introduced in 1881. Because of their addictive qualities, they were dubbed "little white slavers" by Henry Ford and others. In the 1890s, Kansas was among the first states to pass anti-cigarette laws. *(McCutcheon, Wikipedia)*

Life Savers came on the scene in 1913 as peppermint flavor. By 1919, six other flavors (Mint-O-Green, Cl-O-ve, Lic-O-Rice, Cinn-O-Mon, Vi-O-Let and Choc-O-Late) had been developed. These remained the standard flavors until the late 1920s. *(Life-Savers.com)*

Women in the United States won the right to vote in a presidential

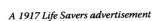

A 1917 Life Savers advertisement

FINDING BABY RUTH

election in 1920. Kansas, however, gave women the vote in school board elections the year it gained statehood — 1861 — and it would broaden that right to municipal elections in 1887. By 1899, Kansans had elected multiple women mayors. In 1912, eight years before national women's suffrage, Kansas gave women the same voting rights as men. *(Voices, The Kansas Collection Online Magazine)*

The vote freed women in other ways. Skirts and hair grew shorter, and corsets were shed, despite ominous warnings that doing so could lead to muscular, man-like bodies. The median age for women to marry was 21. *(The New York Times, Sept. 9, 1921)*

Clara Bow, "The It Girl"

To counteract the alarming social behavior that women were exhibiting, a movement was created to encourage women to be more passive and interested in the home and family. Advertising doubled in the 1920s, promising to ease the housewife's burden with appliances and cosmetics. *(Watson and Martin)*

The character of Dr. Livermore is loosely based on what I have learned about the doctor who signed my father's birth certificate. The man appeared to be so angry when he filled out the certificate that it's unclear whether my father had a sibling. In the space designated to indicate the number of previous children my biological grandmother had delivered, the doctor's mark was made with such hostility (according to a handwriting analyst) that it's unclear whether it's the number 2 or a checkmark.

Locomobiles were large, stately cars produced from 1899 to 1929. The first car in Garden City — purchased in 1901 — was a Locomobile. It was owned by a druggist and physician who wanted to better serve his rural patients. *(Henshaw, gardencity.net)*

Nearly 117,000 Americans died and 204,000 suffered injuries in World War I. In Finney County, Kansas, about 290 men served, 15 of whom died in action or from disease or accidental causes. To help with meat shortages during WWI, Finney County farmers shipped three train-car loads of jackrabbits to New York City. In the Civil War, which would have been fought by the parents of the characters in "Finding Baby Ruth," 620,000 Americans died, 476,000 were injured and 400,000 were captured or missing. *(Reeve, Wikipedia)*

CHAPTER 2 - EVERYBODY'S EVERYTHING

Actually, it's a myth that Thomas Crapper invented the flush toilet. Born in 1836, Crapper became a plumber who founded Thomas Crapper & Co., in London. He did help to increase the popularity of the toilet and developed important related inventions. Manhole covers with Crapper's company's name on them can be found in Westminster Abbey. *(Wikipedia)*

Garden City also had three railroads, a sugar factory, 11 groceries, eight hotels and rooming houses, a junior college, an opera house, two hospitals and "5,000 of the best people in the world." *(Garden City Herald, Feb. 2, 1921)*

The religious poll was actually taken in 1916. Of the 2,744 people interviewed in Garden City, 118 people indicated no church preference. Methodists numbered 813, which was nearly twice as high as the next largest category, Christians. African-Americans had their own Baptist and Methodist churches, each with about 50 members. Fewer than 10 people identified themselves as Spiritualists, Jews, Latter-day Saints or Lutherans. *(Reeve)*

By the early 1920s, Babe Ruth was a national hero who spent his abundant earnings on women, extravagant cars, liquor and lavish meals. He was not an orphan, but he lived from ages 7 to 19 at St. Mary's Industrial School for Orphans, Delinquent, Incorrigible and Wayward Boys. *(Montville)*

"Mrs. Grundy" was 1920s' slang for a priggish or tight-laced person. *(Potpourri: Slang of the 1920s)*

Babe Ruth on a 1914 baseball card

The first Studebakers were electric-powered and designed by Thomas Edison. The Studebaker model Sister Margery was driving would have been built between 1913 and 1920, and sold for about $1,000. *(Henshaw)*

Italian Rudolph Valentino was popular for his smoldering good looks and olive complexion, the antithesis of the typical Midwestern brother, husband or high school sweetheart. He was often cast as

Rudolph "The Sheik" Valentino

an "exotic" Arab sheik or Indian rajah, and starred in 14 films before dying at age 31 from complications of abdominal surgery. *(Leider)*

CHAPTER 3 – TWELVE TO 15 MILES PER HOUR

The moral gown was designed in 1921 by clergymen from 15 Philadelphia denominations. At a time when women's hemlines typically hovered 9 to 12 inches above the ground, the moral gown was ankle-length and covered all but 3 inches of the throat. More than a dozen states that year tried to pass laws standardizing the length of women's skirts and the amount of decolletage women could reveal. *(McCutcheon)*

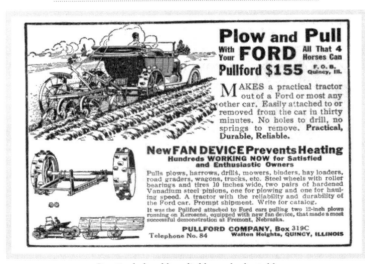

Practical, durable, reliable, and adaptable

The Ford Model T was the world's first mass-produced automobile. In 1921, more than half of the cars produced worldwide were Model Ts, which sold for about $500. The older generation feared automobiles would become "houses of prostitution" because of the privacy they provided young people. Farmers liked the Model T because its back wheels could be quickly replaced with adaptable tractor tires. The early models came with a top that could be raised or lowered. Options included self-starters, horns, side curtains and tire chains. The variety of options made every Ford unique and its owner identifiable. *(Reid, McCutcheon, Time Magazine Oct. 6, 2008)*

"Man's Strength and Woman's Beauty" was published in 1879. It was a compilation of writings by European doctors, edited by an American medical writer. A copy of the book was discovered, along with various gynecological instruments, in the summer home of a deceased physician.

CHAPTER 4 - A PLAGUE OF CHAMPAGNE

"Champagne is one of the most fascinating, but most desperately dangerous and deceptive drinks a young girl can imbibe, and should be shunned as the plague!" *("Man's Strength and Woman's Beauty")*

My oldest daughter Kelsey and I have faint scarlet birthmarks on our foreheads.

True Story magazine began publishing in 1919 and featured personalized accounts of how working-class Americans dealt with the controversial issues of petting, premarital sex, illegitimacy, adultery, drinking and partying. Jules references this cover in Chapter 14. The magazine's

A 1921 cover of True Story magazine

circulation reached nearly two million by 1929, rivaling the longer-established, better-behaved Ladies' Home Journal and Saturday Evening Post. *(bookrags.com)*

In 1855, emigrants from New York City established a vegetarian colony near a wandering stream in southeastern Kansas. The city was designed to be built in an octagonal shape, its eight sides each four square miles in length. An octagonal building to temporarily house residents was to stand in the center. Crude living conditions, disease and a lack of medicine and food led to the abandonment of the colony after about one year, although Vegetarian Creek remains.

(Allen County Historical Society online)

Carry A. Nation was in her mid-50s and living with her second husband in Medicine Lodge, Kansas, when she was divinely inspired to launch her "hatchetation" campaign to destroy saloons doing business despite the state's Prohibition laws. She eventually took her movement nationwide, paying for jail fines with proceeds from her lectures and sales of souvenir hatchets. *(answers.com)*

Carry A. Nation assembles her "hatchetation" campaign

CHAPTER 5 – ART'S MISFORTUNE

The French impressionist artist Pierre-Auguste Renoir painted thousands of works. He suffered his first attack of rheumatoid arthritis when he was in his 50s. He continued painting, although eventually the disease deformed and paralyzed his hands and arms. Four years before his death, in 1919, Renoir was confined to a wheelchair. *(about.com, Wikipedia)*

FINDING BABY RUTH

ZaSu Pitts was born Jan. 3, 1894, in Parsons, Kansas, and at age 9, moved to California with her family. She starred in silent films before finding success on screen in both comedies and dramas. Her film "Seeing it Through" showed in July 1921 at the Garden City Electric Theatre. One of Pitts' greatest disappointments was in 1930 when she was replaced in the classic war movie "All Quiet on the Western Front"

ZaSu Pitts stars in "Better Times," a 1919 silent film

because preview audiences found her performance too humorous. My grandfather (Jiggs) lived in California when "All Quiet" was filmed. He had several stand-in parts. *(Garden City Herald - July 1921, Wikipedia)*

CHAPTER 6 - THE OCEAN OF GARDEN CITY

For years, the pool in Garden City was advertised far and wide as the "The World's Largest, Free, Outdoor, Municipal, Concrete, Swimming Pool." The "free" was recently dropped because the city began charging admission to help pay for repairs. The pool, also known as "The Big Pool" and "The Big Dipper," has been used in the past for winter ice skating, waterskiing and as a bathtub for elephants from the nearby Lee Richardson Zoo. The pool's conception was inspired by Mayor H.O. Trinkle in 1921, and it became a hometown project, with citizens expected to donate whatever they could afford in labor, materials or money. The pool actually opened on

The World's Largest, Free, Outdoor, Municipal, Concrete Swimming Pool
(photo taken between 1920 and 1939)

July 18, 1922. It was 218 by 337 feet, larger than a football field, and contained more than 2 million gallons of water. *(Reeve, Kansas Sampler Foundation, Wikipedia, kshs.com)*

CHAPTER 7 – FATE'S PRANKS

At the outset of World War I, local governments in Kansas prohibited speaking German in public, teaching the German language and speaking German over the telephone. One Kansan, the daughter of Catholic Germans from Russia, recalled being in third grade when virtually overnight, she said, German textbooks disappeared and use of the language was prohibited among area residents, many of whom couldn't speak English. In southern Finney County, a German settler accused of "treasonable acts and utterances" was paraded through the streets naked except for a pair of overalls tied around his waist. *(Reeve)*

FINDING BABY RUTH

Rumors of a Mexican attack started after the British intercepted the Zimmerman Telegram in January 1917. The telegram proposed a military alliance between Germany and Mexico if the United States entered the World War. For its help, Mexico was promised the return of the territories it lost during the Spanish-American War of 1848. The telegram's contents were released to the public in March 1917 and are believed to have contributed to the U.S. entry into the war not long afterward. *(Wikipedia)*

Author Zane Grey

Zane Grey was born in 1872, in Zanesville, Ohio. He was a minor-league baseball player and dentist before beginning his writing career. He wrote more than 90 books, including "The Last of the Plainsmen," which was about Buffalo Jones, a founder of Garden City whom Zane had met. My grandfather (Jiggs) was an ironsmith who apparently worked with horses owned by Buffalo Jones. Grey often wrote thinly veiled sex scenes, although by the end of his career he took a more prudent tone. Here's a passage from "Wildfire," published in 1917: "She seemed strange, wild, passionate in her tenderness. She lifted her face and kissed him softly again and again and again, till the touch that had been exquisitely painful to his bruised lips became rapture. Then she leaned back in his arms, her hands

"Buffalo" Charles Jones (kansasmemory.org, Kansas State Historical Society)

on his shoulders, white-faced, dark-eyed, and laughed up in his face, lovingly, daringly, as if she defied the world to change what she had done." *(Reeve, Wikipedia, "Wildfire")*

"According to the statistical research of laborious writers … abundant proof is furnished that such diseases as insanity, epilepsy, hypochondriasis, mania, hysteria, and suicidal tendencies result from (not marrying)." *("Man's Strength and Woman's Beauty")*

CHAPTER 8 – THE MAN WITH THE YELLOW SHOES

President Warren G. Harding

Babe Ruth

The first time women across the United States were allowed to vote for president, Warren G. Harding was elected. He was a married man known for his good looks. His illegitimate daughter was the result of an affair publicly known after he and his mistress, Nan Britton, were nearly caught in the act. Britton wrote a book, "The President's Daughter," published in 1928, in which she claimed that she was the president's mistress throughout his term in office, and that their daughter was born in 1919. One passage told of their making love in a coat closet in the executive office at the White House. *(McCutcheon)*

Cabbage was a staple in 1920s' recipes. *(The Perry Home Cook Book)*

Babe Ruth had yellow shoes. His baseball contract for 1921 totaled $52,000. The average income in the United States that year was about $4,000. Ruth's contract had a special clause that he abstain from

FINDING BABY RUTH

liquor and go to bed before 1 a.m. during the playing season. *(Montville)*

Five-cent Baby Ruth bars

Hundreds of candy bars were introduced in the United States between WWI and the 1929 Depression. Brand names included Smile-a-While, That's Mine, Candy Dogs, Chicken Dinner and Prom Queen. A common ploy was to link a candy bar to a well-known person. There was a "Lindy" bar in tribute to Charles Lindbergh, and an "It" bar for actress Clara Bow. *(Almond)*

President Cleveland's daughter, Ruth

Baby Ruth, the candy bar, was introduced in 1921. The source of its name is disputed. Its creators, the Curtiss Candy Company, say it was named after President Cleveland's daughter, Ruth. Detractors point out that in 1921, Babe Ruth was a baseball player of unprecedented popularity, while Cleveland's daughter had been dead for 17 years. The company faced at least one legal challenge when a competitor (with the approval of Babe Ruth) tried to market the "Babe Ruth Home Run Bar." The Curtiss Candy Company successfully forced the competitor off the market because of the similarity in names. *(Urban Legends Reference Pages: Baby Ruth)*

In his book "A Secret Life: The Lies and Scandals of President Grover Cleveland," Charles Lachman wrote that President Grover Cleveland had an illegitimate son after sexually assaulting the child's mother,

Maria Halpin. The boy was born Sept. 14, 1874, in a hospital for unwed mothers. According to Lachman, the child was sent to an orphanage and the mother to a lunatic asylum. She was released, but when word about the child got out during his upcoming presidential campaign, Cleveland labeled her a harlot who had targeted him because he was the only bachelor among her "gentlemen callers." He won the election. *(The Daily Beast, May 23, 2011)*

The manufacturer of the Willys Knight Touring Car, John North Willys, would go on to produce the first civilian Jeep. *(Henshaw)*

CHAPTER 9 – THE YACK-YACK CLUB

Prohibition takes its toll.

Finney County sheriff's deputies had their hands full trying to put bootleggers out of business. One sheriff was nearly run over trying to stop bootleggers driving a Marmon roadster. When the car was later put up for public auction, the people of Garden City made sure the sheriff was the winning bidder. *(Reeve)*

FINDING BABY RUTH

"A whole generation had been infected by the eat-drink-and-be-merry-for-tomorrow-we-die spirit, which accompanied the departure of the soldiers to the training camps and the fighting front ... At least one could toss off a few drinks and get a kick out of physical passion and forget that the world was crumbling ... and so the saxophones wailed and the gin-flask went its rounds and the dancers made their treadmill circuit with half-closed eyes, and the outside world, so merciless and so insane, was shut away for a restless night." *(Allen)*

State and local officials often acted as chaperones or censors. State officials censoring movies in 1915 eliminated scenes with drinking, kissing, sudden deaths, wronged wives or husbands, fights and jail scenes. *(Reeve)*

Women who failed to cover their shoulders were considered likely candidates for goiter, an enlargement of the thyroid gland. *(McCutcheon)*

CHAPTER 10 – A CELEBRATION OF INDEPENDENCE

The federal Comstock Law of 1873 prohibited the mailing, transporting or importing of "obscene, lewd or lascivious articles." Thus, birth control became a home-based or cottage industry, using ingredients such as animal gut, rubber, metal and chemicals. Condoms, pessaries (vaginal suppositories), sponges, douches and crude IUDS were available. *(Reagan)*

Beecham's Pills "assist nature in her wondrous functions"

Rin Tin Tin,
the canine movie star

Rin Tin Tin, a German shepherd, was a popular film star of the mid-1920s. At the height of his fame, he earned $6,000 a month and had his own valet, chef, car and driver. He wore a diamond-studded collar, and an orchestra played mood music while he worked. *(Miller)*

First sold in 1875, Lydia E. Pinkham's Vegetable Compound was advertised as a blood purifier for women. It was rumored to prevent conception, but also to resolve infertility. *(Riddle)*

CHAPTER 11: THE IMPORTANCE OF A BOW

Electricity revolutionized housework in the 1920s. Sewing machines, refrigerators, irons, hot water heaters and vacuum cleaners were invented. Such innovations were expected to improve home management and became an offshoot of Frederick Taylor's scientific management theory that efficiency of motion led to greater production. Taylor's wife, Christine, wrote articles for the Ladies' Home Journal with tips on how to peel more potatoes and iron more shirts. *(Ehrenreich and English, Holt)*

An early electric suction
(vacuum) cleaner

FINDING BABY RUTH

CHAPTER 12: UNCLE SAM PROTECTS

"Don't Touch Me, You Beast!" was published in the fall 1921 *True Story* magazine.

Only a poor boob pays his money, loses his watch, gets the syph, and brags that he's had a good time.

A WWI flyer encouraging abstinence among soldiers

During World War I, the U.S. military distributed condoms to its members to try to combat venereal disease. Early in the war, about 380,000 U.S. soldiers were diagnosed with venereal disease. A 1924 study by a physician and birth control advocate found a 50 percent failure rate among couples using skin and rubber condoms. *(collectorsweekly.com)*

As more people bought automobiles, more roads were surfaced, and a proliferation of businesses opened to provide travelers with gasoline, refreshments and overnight accommodations. Tourist camps offered cabins or

A municipal tourist camp near Garden City
(kansasmemory.org, Kansas State Historical Society)

tents with cots, mattresses and central bathroom facilities. My father
believed he was turned over to his adoptive parents at a tourist camp
in Kansas. *(Reid)*

The influenza ward in 1918 at Camp Funston in Kansas
(kansasmemory.org, Kansas State Historical Society)

Influenza (later dubbed "the flu") routinely made its rounds in Kansas
and across the world. The pandemic of 1918-1919 was the most
deadly. In the winter months alone, more than 5,000 Kansans died
of the flu. Churches, schools and theaters were closed. Most of those
who died were between ages 21 and 30. The worldwide death toll is
an estimate because of unreliable vital-statistic keeping. Estimates
are that it killed more than 50 million worldwide — 675,000 in the
United States alone. Most deaths occurred in a 12-week period
during the fall of 1918. The pandemic may have originated just 30
miles south of Garden City, in Haskell County, where Dr. L.V. Miner
made the earliest published reference to the disease. Miner warned
national public health officials about a potentially fatal, severe
influenza outbreak he'd witnessed the first few months of 1918.

FINDING BABY RUTH

Miner and his son, Oliver, practiced in the Garden City area. The disease may have been spread by young men from Haskell County reporting for duty at Camp Funston, the Army training base on the other side of Kansas where Jiggs was stationed. Thousands of soldiers passed through Camp Funston and the nearby Fort Riley on their way to other bases in America and Europe. (Barry, Reeve, gardencity.net)

CHAPTER 13 – FATTY ARBUCKLE'S GIRLFRIEND

In 1921, Roscoe "Fatty" Arbuckle, a popular film comedian, was charged with homicide in connection with the death of an actress. The woman died, supposedly of internal injuries, after a party in a San Francisco hotel. Arbuckle was accused of raping her. He was acquitted after three trials, and the woman's death was attributed to a botched abortion. (Miller)

CHAPTER 14 – THE GIRL WHO LOVED NOT WISELY BUT TOO WELL

True Story magazine published "Mother or Murderess — Which?" in its fall 1921 edition.

Fatty Arbuckle is exonerated.

In the early 20th century, one out of every 30 women died in childbirth. More suffered from the after-effects. One Kansas woman wrote to birth-control advocate Margaret Sanger: "They tore me, and I didn't heal back right.

Walking through hundred(s) of miles of fire could not have been as bad as what I suffered for her (daughter). I am afraid now to give birth to another." *(Reagan, May)*

Abortion was usually referred to with euphemisms such as "being put straight" or "taking a rest" or "having it taken away." Abortions

MRS. BIRD, Female Physician, where can be obtained Dr. Vandenburgh's Female Renovating Pills, from Germany, an effectual remedy for suppression, irregularity, and all cases where nature has stopped from any cause whatever. Sold only at Mrs. Bird's, 83 Duane st, near Broadway. n24 3m*

TO THE LADIES—Madame Costello, Female Physician, still continues to treat, with astonishing success, all diseases peculiar to females. Suppression, irregularity, obstruction, &c., by whatever cause produced, can be removed by Madame C. in a very short time. Madame C's medical establishment having undergone thorough repairs and alterations for the better accommodation of her numerous patients, she is now prepared to receive ladies on the point of confinement, or those who wish to be treated for obstruction of their monthly periods. Madame C. can be consulted at her residence, 34 Lispenard st, at all times.— All communications and letters must be post paid.

An advertisement for two "female physicians," Mrs. Bird and Madame Costello

were illegal, but midwives, doctors and back-street workers provided them and were not usually prosecuted unless a woman died. A study of 10,000 women at Margaret Sanger's birth control clinic in the late 1920s found that 20 percent of all pregnancies were intentionally aborted. Surveys of educated, middle-class women showed 10 to 23 percent had abortions. Most women who had abortions at the turn of the century were married women who tried to self-abort by jumping off tables, moving or lifting heavy boxes or furniture, drinking nauseating concoctions or using sharp instruments such as knitting or crochet needles, scissors and hairpins. *(Reagan, Schneider, May)*

The wedding rings were advertised on the back cover of a True Story magazine in 1921.

As late as the 1960s, a single woman who got pregnant often chose not to tell anyone. One such woman told an interviewer that she gained 70 pounds, drank a bottle of castor oil to induce premature labor and threw herself down the stairs in hopes of a miscarriage. She eventually gave birth by herself in the bathroom of her family's home. *(Fessler)*

CHAPTER 15 –
A COBWEB AGAINST
DANGER

Logo of the Second International Eugenics Congress, in 1921

U.S. eugenicists recommended unwed mothers remain with their children, who were "hereditary lemons, destined to spread disease and feeblemindedness to future generations." As early as the 1920s, leading psychiatrists believed out-of-wedlock pregnancies were a sign of profound personality problems and neuroses.

"Feeblemindedness" was a common diagnostic label beginning in the 1910s. It was considered an inherited mental defect, a catchall category for people whose intelligence was rated subnormal, according to the newly designed scientific tests. Social workers found feeblemindedness everywhere in the prisons and reformatories, and linked it to most aberrant behaviors, including out-of-wedlock pregnancies. *(Kunzel)*

CHAPTER 16: HAPPENSTANCE

Newspapers of the time often gave heartbreaking accounts of the deaths of young children. In Harvey County, Kansas, a newspaper reported that one boy became ill in August 1906, on his third birthday, and died two weeks later. "All that medical skill could do, all that loving hands of relatives and trained nurses could accomplish, availed not, and the little sufferer, after a heroic battle for life, quietly passed to a better land." A story printed in 1907 reported that an infant who was almost four months old died of whooping cough. The baby's obituary said: "There is something unusually pathetic and touching about the death of a little child. The bud of promise has not fairly opened, the plans of loved ones are all so rudely shattered when a baby dies." *(Harvey County, Kansas, newspaper)*

"The Birth Control Review,"
edited by Margaret Sanger

CHAPTER 17 – BABE RUTH VISITS GARDEN CITY

Two psychologists from Columbia University tested Babe Ruth in a laboratory for three hours in the fall of 1921. He was given psychological tests, introduced during WWI, and physical tests that used a pneumatic tube, a chronoscope and an electric stylus. *(Montville)*

The Fondale brothers drove a green Essex similar to the one given to Babe Ruth in 1921 by a Louisiana car dealer. Later that year, Ruth drove another Fondale look-alike — a maroon 12-cylinder Packard, which "looked like a rocket ship and sounded like a fuel-burning calliope." Ruth broke speed limits, parked anywhere and hit things,

310   FINDING BABY RUTH

including pedestrians. He had at least one auto incident a year for awhile. *(Montville)*

"The Amazing Dunninger"
debunking fraudulent methods
of conjuring spirits

In the early 1920s, Babe Ruth attended a performance of the famed mind-reader Dunninger, who asked Ruth to write a question and his own answer to the question on a slip of paper. Without seeing the paper, Dunninger said the answer was 60. He was correct! Ruth had asked how many home runs he would hit in 1921, and like Dunninger, he'd also predicted 60. His actual number of home runs in 1921 was 59. *(Montville)*

A program from the
1921 World Series

President Harding attended one of the first games played at Yankee Stadium. Ruth hit a home run in the fifth inning, circled the bases and pinned a poppy on the president's coat. Four months later, after a cross-country tour that included Kansas, Harding died. *(Montville)*

Garden City's first telephone service, installed in 1900, consisted of three telephones. My maternal grandparents, who also lived in Kansas, had a party line. I remember being surprised during holiday meals when they would ignore the telephone if it wasn't their ring.

A 1917 wall telephone

CHAPTER 18 – THE GREAT ESCAPE

By the spring of 1922, radio broadcasting had become a craze. Radio broadcasts were as popular as mahjong would be the following year or crossword puzzles the year after. In 1922, the sales of radio sets, parts and accessories amounted to $60 million. It's uncertain whether the first radio broadcasts of the World Series would have reached as far as Garden City, Kansas. *(Allen)*

During the burial of Alexander Graham Bell, who died Aug. 2, 1922, every phone in North America was silenced in his honor.

A Rorschach inkblot

CHAPTER 19 – A TEST FOR MORONS

Intelligence tests were precursors to today's standardized tests. They were introduced in WWI to identify which soldiers were officer material and which were better suited to lesser ranks. Alpha tests were for men who could read; beta tests were for those who could not. The results were also used to foretell which soldiers might be susceptible to "shell shock" on the battlefield. The inkblot test was created in 1921 by Hermann Rorschach. *(Gould, Montville, Wikipedia)*

The U.S. eugenics movement saw segregation of "problem girls" as a solution to multiple social issues. Such women would no longer trouble their families or communities, nor would they be tempted to have sex and thus spread venereal disease or reproduce mentally deficient children. Isolation would ensure the growth of a superior, highly moral and intelligent race free from genetic deficiencies that led to crimes such as lying, thievery and sexual perversion. Indeed, the act of having sex outside of marriage was sufficient to label a woman deranged. *(Kline)*

In 1910, the term "moron" was coined by a psychologist to label people whose scores on intelligence tests indicated their mental development was that of an adolescent or child between the ages of 8 and 12. Women who scored in this category were considered more dangerous than the lower-scoring "imbeciles" or "idiots," who were deemed less likely to have sexual relationships. When officials realized that some unmarried mothers scored high on the intelligence tests, they created an alternate scale to measure "social intelligence." *(Kline)*

Charles Lindbergh

After failing several classes, Charles Lindbergh was dropped from the University of Wisconsin in February 1922. He was in his third semester. The next month he set out for Lincoln, Nebraska, where he'd been accepted into the Lincoln Standard Aircraft School. Lindbergh owned an Excelsior motorcycle. He could have passed through Kansas on his way to Nebraska. *(Berg)*

CHAPTER 20 – MAHJONG

The Tuskegee Institute, now a university, estimated 5,000 people were legally lynched in the United States between 1882 and 1959, when it discontinued its annual report. Lynching wasn't officially made illegal until the passage of the 1968 Civil Rights Act. *(Wilkerson)*

Created in China, mahjong grew in U.S. popularity in the 1920s. As many as 1.6 million sets were sold, ranging in price from less than a dollar to $100. The game tiles were also used for telling fortunes but weren't as popular as Ouija boards, which also came into use about that time. *(Miller, Allen)*

CHAPTER 21 – THE GOLDEN CURL

At the start of the 20th century, the United States had become home to millions of immigrants with much higher birthrates than those of white, native-born American Protestant women, who had the highest rate of childlessness on record. The falling birthrates among Protestants was called "race suicide" by President Teddy Roosevelt. In a speech on March 13, 1905, in Washington, he told the National Congress of Mothers: "No piled-up wealth ... will permanently avail ... unless the average woman is a good wife, a good mother, able and willing to perform the first and greatest duty of womanhood ... to bear (children) ... numerous enough so that the race shall increase and not decrease." When a Finney County man with 16 children sent a family photograph to Roosevelt, the former president sent a personalized note of congratulations. *(May)*

Madam C.J. Walker, or Sarah Breedlove, was born in 1867 near Delta, Louisiana. She was the last and only one of her parents' six children to be born outside of slavery. She was orphaned at age 7 and by age 10, was working as a domestic servant. She learned about the hair industry by working with her brothers, who were barbers in St. Louis. In 1906, after her third marriage, she developed her own line

FINDING BABY RUTH

Madame C.J. Walker with friends

of hair products, which she claimed were revealed to her in a dream. She was one of the first self-made female millionaires in the United States. *(Wikipedia)*

In the early 1920s, William Estabrook Chancellor wrote a biography about President Harding that implied the president's great-grandparent was African-American. *(New York Times, April 6, 2008)*

Ho for Kansas!

Brethren, Friends, & Fellow Citizens:
I feel thankful to inform you that the
REAL ESTATE
AND
Homestead   Association,
Will Leave Here the
15th of April, 1878,
In pursuit of Homes in the Southwestern
Lands of America, at Transportation
Rates, cheaper than ever
was known before.
For full information inquire of
Benj Singleton, better known as old Pap,
NO. 5 NORTH FRONT STREET.
Beware of Speculators and Adventurers, as it is a dangerous thing
to fall in their hands.
Nashville, Tenn., March 18, 1878.

A handbill encouraging ...can-American "Exodusters" to move to Kansas

In the decade after WWI, an estimated 550,000 African-Americans left the South for the North. They were free, but they still faced Jim Crow laws and other hostilities from white people. Nicodemus and similar towns were settled by freed African-Americans. Nicodemus was successful in its early years but is now unincorporated. *(Wilkerson, Wikipedia)*

CHAPTER 22 – BIRTH OF A BAD GENE

A doctor in Garden City, Kansas, (not Dr. Livermore)
operating on a patient in his home hospital

In the early 1920s, many women chose hospital births over home births because of the availability of anesthesia, such as ether and chloroform. The use of forceps, episiotomies and cesarean sections increased. Patients given ether were occasionally able to hear and see, but not move, under its influence. *(W. Tyler Smith, "A Lecture on the Utility and Safety of the Inhalation of Ether in Obstetric Practice," "Childbirthing in the 1920s," by Kaye Jones)*

A headline in the July 1922 Ladies' Home Journal: "Alarming Decrease in American Babies" *(May)*

CHAPTER 23 – DREAMING OF BENJAMIN BUTTON

F. Scott Fitzgerald was stationed with the Army at Fort Leavenworth, Kansas, when he began writing "This Side of Paradise," in 1917. He wrote the book during his spare time, partly as a way to be

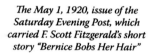

THE SATURDAY EVENING POST

The May 1, 1920, issue of the Saturday Evening Post, which carried F. Scott Fitzgerald's short story "Bernice Bobs Her Hair"

remembered after his death, which he fully expected to occur during World War I. "The Curious Case of Benjamin Button" was a short story written by Fitzgerald and published in 1921 by Collier's magazine. In 2008 the story was made into a movie of the same title, starring Brad Pitt and Cate Blanchett. *(Wikipedia)*

Infants often survived their first summer because they were fed breast milk. The second summer was riskier because by then they were typically given cow's milk, which was contaminated by flies, dust, lack of refrigeration and impure ice. A 1916 nationwide study found infant deaths in June totaled 3,250; July, 7092; August, 10,284; and September, 7,814. Maternity homes expected women, whether they were keeping or giving up their babies for adoption, to breastfeed for several months. *(Reagan, Reid, Holt)*

The demand for children to adopt exceeded the supply in the 1920s. Many adoptions took place without the supervision of official agencies. Social workers from the 1920s forward counseled parents to tell children they had been adopted. *(Melosh)*

Women often described giving up a child for adoption as the event that forever defined their identity. Unless they received guidance or counseling, such women could suffer from intense emotions, persistent guilt, damaged self-esteem and self-loathing. *(Fessler)*

CHAPTER 24 – THE VISIT

Diphtheria, scarlet fever, smallpox and typhoid were also threats to young children. Doctors treated illnesses with standby remedies involving castor oil, calomel, whiskey, turpentine, soda and salts. *(Reid)*

....

CHAPTER 25 – THE ROAD TO ROSEBUSH

Twenty-two of the 72 automobiles in Garden City in 1907
(kansasmemory.org, Kansas State Historical Society)

In his memoir, "Hurry Home Wednesday: Growing up in a Small Missouri Town, 1905-1921," Loren Reid remembers: "Every (automobile) trip was an adventure. Once we counted eight cars stopped alongside the road: one with a broken wheel, one with stripped gears, six with tire trouble … If you made a round trip without a flat, you boasted of it … We were entirely at the mercy of the weather. On the day of a trip, we anxiously scanned the heavens appraising each cloud, speculating whether we could get somewhere and back without encountering rain." A trip of 20 miles could take an hour and a half. A

15-mile-per-hour trip on dry roads could turn into a three or four-mile-per-hour trip on muddy roads. *(Reid)*

In 1919, there were 6.8 million passenger cars on the road. Ten years later, the total was 23 million. *(Allen)*

Gangs of bank robbers were common in Kansas during the 1920s and 1930s. They largely succeeded because they had faster vehicles and more powerful guns than law enforcement. Infamous gang leaders in the region included Ma Barker, Bonnie and Clyde, John Dillinger, Charles Arthur "Pretty Boy" Floyd and the Dalton brothers. *(Wikipedia)*

The infamous Fleagle Gang operated out of a "horseless horse ranch" about 25 miles north of Garden City. Law enforcement officials suspected that for 12 years, the gang scouted out banks, held them up during the day, then returned to the ranch under the cover of darkness. They hid their get-away cars in outbuildings with moveable walls. The gang robbed banks and trains in Kansas, Colorado, Oregon and California. Three gang members, including two Fleagle brothers, were executed in 1930 for murdering a doctor in connection with a bank robbery in Lamar, Colorado. A visitor described their farmhouse: "The faded green

Carl Banks' "Beagle Boys"

shades of the windows were all drawn tightly down, except one
... A woman was sitting in a rocking chair at that window, but we
only got a glimpse of her as she quickly jerked the shade down. The
house sits within a half-acre of ground enclosed by a fence, its posts
awry, the wire sagging. On this once were two box covers with this
warning scrawled in red chalk: Peddlers and solicitors keep out." My
grandmother (Jules) grew up with and attended the same church as
the Fleagle brothers, in the small town of Friend, north of Garden
City. Both families later moved to Garden City. The Beagle Brothers
comic strip, created by Carl Banks, was purported to have been
based on the gang. *(Reeve, Betz, Wikipedia)*

CHAPTER 26 – THE BETTER BABY CONTEST

A 25-cent pamphlet from the federal government in the 1900s
advised mothers to establish regular habits with their newborns. The
need for regularity "begins at birth, and applies to all the physical

A honey exhibit at the Finney County Fair
(kansasmemory.org, Kansas State Historical Society)

FINDING BABY RUTH

functions of the baby — eating, sleeping and bowel movements ... " (*Ehrenreich and English*)

Better Baby Contests were sponsored by the American Eugenics Society at state fairs around the country, starting at the 1920 Kansas Free Fair in Topeka. Winners were determined by medical exams, Wassermann tests, psychiatric assessments and family genetic history. The society also offered a $1,000 prize for the best essays on the causes of the decline of Nordic fertility. *(May, Kline)*

Increased production of appliances led to the call for better home management, resulting in lectures and demonstrations across the nation. In 1921, 235 women in Finney County gathered for classes on appliances, furnishings and the efficient feeding of the family. A local hardware store owner happily noted that sales of kitchen equipment increased after the class. (Holt)

Charles Lindbergh was part of a barnstorming team that flew over Kansas, Nebraska, Colorado and Wyoming in the summer of 1922. The first time he was in an airplane, on April 9, 1922, he was a passenger. *(Berg)*

Charles Lindbergh took his first flight in April 1922 as a passenger in a two-seat Lincoln Standard Tourabout.

A flying circus performed at a Garden City carnival in 1920. Advertised as "the world's reckless daredevils," the performance included 2-seater passenger planes and a plane-auto race. *(Reeve)*

In 1923, Otto Schnering, president of the Curtiss Candy Company, chartered a plane to drop thousands of Baby Ruths onto the city of Pittsburgh. Each candy bar was attached to its own tiny parachute. *(Almond)*

One single mother who gave her baby up for adoption received a photograph of the child, apparently mistakenly mailed by a company that had taken the photo in a hospital nursery. She kept the picture for 10 years "in a little brown frame in my drawer, hidden away. Every once in a while, I'd take it out. I always cried and cried." Eventually, she burned it. "I thought it would somehow get rid of the pain, but it didn't." *(Fessler)*

CHAPTER 27 – MISS AMERICA

In September 1920, Atlantic City businessmen staged a "Fall Frolic" to increase tourism beyond Labor Day. The next year, East Coast newspapers sponsored photographic popularity contests, with winners receiving all-expenses-paid trips to the Second Annual Fall Frolic. As part of the event, women competed in a beauty contest and vied for the Golden Mermaid trophy for being "The Most Beautiful Bathing Girl in America." Margaret Gorman swept both events and by September 1922 was known as "Miss America." She bore a striking

"Miss America," Margaret Gorman

resemblance to the popular screen star Mary Pickford, who was just achieving fame as "America's Sweetheart." The contest reinforced the changing view of American women from the fragile, delicate Victorian image to women who exercised, ate right and looked wholesome. Pageant rules required a minimum entry age of 16, but two titleholders later admitted they were only 15 when they won. The bathing review portion of the contest stirred immediate controversy when contestants were allowed to appear in one-piece bathing suits, which were technically banned from the city's beaches. *(Watson and Martin)*

By 1924, the Ku Klux Klan had an estimated 60,000 members in Kansas and nearly 4.5 million nationwide. The Klan most often targeted blacks but also opposed Jews and Catholics — especially those who immigrated from Ireland and Italy and might maintain allegiance to the pope rather than the president. The group's tenets

Nearly 30,000 Ku Klux Klan members from Chicago and northern Illinois attended this rally in 1920.

included Christianity, white supremacy, limited immigration, upholding of the U.S. Constitution and protection of "pure womanhood." *(Reeve, Allen)*

CHAPTER 28 – THE WEDDING

As a child growing up in Nebraska, I attended a similar country wedding one hot summer afternoon. Two men in the wedding party collapsed; one of them died.

CHAPTER 29 – THE HOME FOR HOPELESS WOMEN

To my knowledge, my biological grandmother was not sent to a maternity home. The Home for Hopeless Women is based on similar institutions of the time. A classmate at the University of Iowa's summer writing festival suggested the name, which he said was once a real institution.

Unmarried, pregnant white women seeking help in the early decades of the 20th century could have gone to an evangelical rescue mission or maternity home run by churches. The same women had the best chance of attaining a "normal" life, with marriage and future children, if they relinquished their babies. *(Solinger)*

Maternity home life generally included chores like washing dishes, helping in the kitchen or cleaning toilets. Girls were told to use an assumed first name when they arrived. Organized outings were arranged, and occasionally the girls were required to put on wedding bands when they left the building. *(Fessler)*

Unmarried mothers "almost universally came to the maternity home armed with a True Story magazine," a social worker said. Asked why they were attracted to the magazine, the women replied that its stories were just like theirs. From the time they entered a maternity home, unmarried mothers were frequently asked how they'd become pregnant. *(Kunzel)*

Maternity homes often operated under the guise of voluntary admissions, but if a woman escaped, she could be tracked down by law enforcement and charged with greater crimes (like abandoning her infant) which would lead to harsher incarcerations. Other homes were more forthright in their determination to institutionalize women. One home, which also took "juvenile delinquents," was surrounded by a 7-foot fence topped with barbed wire. Doors were locked day and night. A Midwest state used court orders to commit unmarried mothers to state institutions. *(Young, Kunzel)*

Margaret Sanger opened the United States' first birth control clinic on Oct. 16, 1916, in an immigrant section of Brooklyn. On opening

Margaret Sanger draws a crowd.

day, at least 150 women were waiting in line outside the door. After WWI, Sanger launched the American Birth Control League, and in 1927, she organized the World Population Conference in Geneva. Her reputation was tainted when she embraced the U.S. eugenics movement's focus on limiting the reproductive rights of the genetically "unfit." *(Miller)*

CHAPTER 30 – FINDING BABY RUTH

Babe Ruth's illegitimate child became public knowledge when his wife, Helen, appeared at a game with a 16-month-old girl in her arms. Ruth and Helen, questioned separately by reporters, told vastly different stories about the baby. Helen said the baby was born prematurely, on June 7, 1921, at St. Vincent's Hospital in New York, and kept in an incubator. Babe said the baby was born on Feb. 2 at Presbyterian Hospital in New York. "You know he's never good with names or dates," Helen said. More than 60 years later, Babe Ruth's daughter, Dorothy, would be told that she was Ruth's natural child, born to his mistress and taken from her to live with Helen and Ruth. Ruth and Helen separated in about 1925, reportedly due to his repeated infidelities. *(Montville)*

At the actual dedication of the "Big Dipper," on July 18, 1922, members of the public were told to bring their own swimming suits

A 1901 all-cornet band in Garden City
(kansasmemory.org, Kansas State Historical Society)

FINDING BABY RUTH

and towels. A band played as hundreds of people went into the water simultaneously to inaugurate Garden City's first summer swim season. *(Kansas Sampler Foundation online, Wikipedia, Reeve)*

Townsfolk gather around the edge of the Big Dipper
(photo courtesy of the Finney County Historical Society).

Selected Bibliography

Allen, Frederick Lewis. "Only Yesterday: An Informal History of the 1920s." New York: Harper & Row, Publishers, 1931.

Almond, Steve. "Candy Freak: A Journey Through the Chocolate Underbelly of America." A Harvest Book. Orlando: Harcourt, Inc., 2004.

Barry, John M. "The Great Influenza: The Epic Story of the Deadliest Plague in History." New York: Penguin Books, 2004

Berg, A. Scott. "Lindbergh." New York: Berkley Books, 1998.

Betz, N.T. "The Fleagle Gang: Betrayed by a Fingerprint." Bloomington, Ind.: Author House, 2005.

Brownstein, Gabriel. "The Man From Beyond." New York and London: W.W. Norton & Company, 2005.

Chevasse, P.H. "Man's Strength and Woman's Beauty: A Treatise on the Physical Life of Both Sexes, Embracing the Road to Life, Love, and Longevity." Detroit, Mich.: J.C. Hilton Publishing Company, 1879.

Cohen, Adam. "Imbeciles: The Supreme Court, American Eugenics, and the Sterilization of Carrie Buck." New York: Penguin Press, 2016.

Ehrenreich, Barbara, and Deirdre English. "For Her Own Good: Two Centuries of the Experts' Advice to Women." New York: Anchor Books, 1978 and 2005.

Fessler, Ann. "The Girls Who Went Away: The Hidden History of Women Who Surrendered Children for Adoption in the Decades Before Roe v. Wade." New York: The Penguin Press, 2006.

Gordon, Linda. "The Moral Property of Women: A History of Birth Control Politics in America." Urbana and Chicago, Ill.: University of Illinois Press, 2002.

Gould, Stephen Jay. "The Mismeasure of Man." Toronto, Canada: George J. McLeod Limited; New York and London: W.W. Norton & Company, 1981.

Grey, Zane. "The Lone Star Ranger." Originally published in New York by Harper & Row, Publishers, Inc., 1915; republished in New York by Pocket Books, 1969.

Grey, Zane. "Wildfire." Originally published in New York by Harper & Row, Publishers, Inc., 1917; republished in New York by Pocket Books, 1976.

Henshaw, Peter. "The Ultimate Encyclopedia of American Cars," Edison, N.J: Chartwell Books, Inc., 2007.

———. "History of Finney County, Kansas, 2." North Newton, Kansas: Mennonite Press, Inc., 1976.

Holt, Marilyn Irvin. "Linoleum, Better Babies, and the Modern Farm Woman, 1890-1930." Lincoln and London: University of Nebraska Press, 1995.

Kline, Wendy. "Building A Better Race: Gender, Sexuality, and Eugenics From the Turn of the Century to the Baby Boom." Berkeley, Calif., Los Angeles, London: University of Califor-nia Press, 2001.

Kunzel, Regina. "Fallen Women, Problem Girls: Unmarried Mothers and the Professionalization of Social Work, 1890-1945." New Haven, Conn., and London: Yale University Press, 1993.

Leider, Emily W. "Dark Lover: The Life and Death of Rudolph Valentino." New York: Faber and Faber, Inc., 2003.

McCutcheon, Marc. "The Writer's Guide to Everyday Life from Prohibition Through World War II." Cincinnati, Ohio: Writer's Digest Books, 1995.

May, Elaine Tyler. "Barren in the Promised Land: Childless Americans and the Pursuit of Happiness." New York: Basic Books, 1995.

Melosh, Barbara. "Strangers and Kin: The American Way of Adoption." Cambridge, Mass., and London: Harvard University Press, 2002.

Montville, Leigh. "The Big Bam: The Life and Times of Babe Ruth." New York: Broadway Books, 2006.

Miller, Nathan. "New World Coming: The 1920s and the Making of Modern America." Cambridge, Mass.: Da Capo Press, 2003.

———. "The Perry Home Cook Book." Oskaloosa, Kansas: The Independent Publishing Company, 1920.

Reagan, Leslie J. "When Abortion Was a Crime: Women, Medicine, and Law in the United States, 1867-1973." Berkeley, Calif.: University of California Press, 1997.

Reeve, Agnes. "Kansas: Constant Frontier, The Continuing History of Finney County, Kansas." Marceline, Mo.: Walsworth Publishing Company, 1996.

Reid, Loren. "Hurry Home Wednesday: Growing Up in a Small Missouri Town, 1905-1921." Columbia, Mo., and London: University of Missouri Press, 1978.

Riddle, John M. "Eve's Herbs: A History of Contraception and Abortion in the West." Cambridge, Mass., and London: Harvard University Press, 1997.

Roe, Sue. "The Private Lives of the Impressionists." New York: HarperCollins Publishers, 2006.

Schneider, Dorothy, and Carl J. Schneider. "American Women in the Progressive Era, 1900-1920." New York: Facts on File, 1993.

Solinger, Rickie. "Wake Up Little Susie: Single Pregnancy and Race Before Roe v. Wade." New York and London: Routledge, 1992.

Todd, Pamela. "The Impressionists at Leisure." New York: Thames & Hudson, Inc., 2007.

Tone, Andrea. "Devices and Desires: A History of Contraceptives in America." New York: Hill and Wang, 2001.

Watson, Elwood, and Darcy Martin, editors. "There She Is, Miss America: The Politics of Sex, Beauty and Race in America's Most Famous Pageant." Basingstoke, United Kingdom: Palgrave Macmillan, 2004.

Wilkerson, Isabel. "The Warmth of Other Suns: The Epic Story of America's Great Migration." New York: Random House, 2010.

Young, Leontine. "Out of Wedlock." New York: McGraw-Hill Book Company, Inc., 1954.

About the Author

Sara Hoffman is a former journalist and journalism teacher. She teaches writing in Fort Collins, Colorado.

Sara Hoffman, 2016

The author and her father, 1956

CPSIA information can be obtained
at www.ICGtesting.com
Printed in the USA
FSOW01n1238231116
27591FS